Tricked into Being

This is an IndieMosh book

brought to you by MoshPit Publishing
an imprint of Mosher's Business Support Pty Ltd

PO Box 4363
Penrith Plaza NSW 2750

indiemosh.com.au

Copyright © Maffy Vaz 2023

The moral right of the author has been asserted in accordance with the Copyright Amendment (Moral Rights) Act 2000.

All rights reserved. Except as permitted under the Australian Copyright Act 1968 (for example, fair dealing for the purposes of study, research, criticism or review) no part of this publication may be reproduced, stored in a retrieval system, or transmitted in any form or by any means, electronic, mechanical, photocopying, recording or otherwise, without the written permission of the publisher.

 A catalogue record for this work is available from the National Library of Australia

https://www.nla.gov.au/collections

Title:	Tricked into Being
Author:	Vaz, Maffy
ISBNs:	9781922912732 (paperback) 9781922912749 (ebook – epub) 9781922912756 (ebook – Kindle)
Subjects:	FICTION: Romance / General; Historical / 20th Century / Post-World War II; Women

This story is a work of fiction, including historical fiction. Real events, names, places, and dates may have occasionally been adapted to advance the narrative. No character in this story is taken from real life. Any resemblance to any person or persons living or dead is accidental and unintentional. The author, their agents and publishers cannot be held responsible for any claim otherwise and take no responsibility for any such coincidence.

Cover concept by Maffy Vaz
Cover design and layout by Ally Mosher at allymosher.com
Cover images used under licence from Envato Elements and Adobe Stock

Tricked into Being

Maffy Vaz

For

my husband and our two children ...
thank you for your support.

my grandmothers – Maria and Mary,
and my mother, Philomena.
Thank you for the precious stories you told me.

*'Earth's crammed with heaven,
And every common bush afire with God,
But only he who sees takes off his shoes;
The rest sit round and pluck blackberries.'*

— Elizabeth Barrett Browning

Contents

Part 1 3

Part 2 101

Part 3 175

Prologue

August 2016 – Brisbane, Australia

Just imagine, my best and worst moments of life had their beginnings in death-shrouded places! Dark and dreary; bright and brainy moments born under the shadows of tombstones and memorial gardens.

Imagine my bloodline of convicts, tricksters, thieves, rapists and murderers. Also, builders, peacemakers and nurturers.

Then, imagine I killed Ewa Bajek, my great nana on her 90th birthday.

Well, no, I didn't … but I had wanted her dead, for as long as I can remember.

Ewa had been a big, tall woman and walked upright, until the accident, when she struggled for two years with an injured spine but refused medical help. Instead, she borrowed painkillers from Nana or Mum. When she slipped on a slope outside our home and couldn't get herself up, Nana and Mum called an ambulance to take her to the hospital.

Her first and last hospitalisation.

There it was that I had been conniving chicanery concepts to hasten her death. These included removing her oxygen mask, overdosing her, stopping her painkillers — and leaving her in soiled clothes. Or hoping that a one-in-a-hundred-year earthquake would happen, causing instant death. Or a one-in-ten-year flooding would happen, the waters somehow rushing towards the tricky Cassowary Creek, which would carry her carcass away.

The dark side of my bloodline gave me such thoughts.

I didn't kill her. The good in me took over. I exercised my free will.

But she did die there at the hospital.

Now, I look up at the night sky to count the stars from the window of my own hospital bed. I see them twinkle — sometimes with slow spurts and sometimes with sharp, speedy ones. Or they stay static. So far away, yet so near. They wait to see the few last breaths of living beings about to die.

No, I'm not dying. I'm here for an age-old reason.

Imagine it's written in the stars that I search for my bloodline — a search that would take me on a heart-wrenching journey to expose a lie. I'd discover another maternal branch, and wonderingly, worryingly, confirm proven parallelisms between our lives and deaths — entwining a genealogical synchronicity. In some of us, the stars crossed, and in others, they aligned, creating a tempest or a tranquillity. Let's call it simply: fate.

Let's imagine and re-imagine my story with the famed '*I remember ...*' After all, aren't memories half-truths? Or untold truths? For we are all tricked into being. And trick others.

Part 1

November 2014 – June 2015

1.1

The night I dreamt Ewa died was the night she truly died.

That night, all who mattered were alive.

A beautiful, boneless, balmy feeling had my hand stretching towards my buzzing mobile phone. 4.45am. It was the call I had been waiting for.

'Daphne Brown? I'm so sorry,' said the night nurse at the hospital where Ewa was. 'Your great grandmother is no more. A massive heart attack. She couldn't be revived.'

'Oh, good,' I responded without thinking. 'I mean, that's okay. She ... she was ... sorry. Thank you.' I rubbed my eyes, my hand still holding the phone.

'Are you okay?' the nurse asked.

'Yes ... yes. Was asleep. Awake now. Thank you again. Yes ... yes. I'll let the family know.' I switched off the phone.

A slow smile sneaked across my face. It widened. And remained. My facial muscles ached. They hadn't been used in a long time. I sat cross-legged on my bed, my pink pyjama bottoms parting, and I ran a hand through my shoulder-length, wavy, dark-blonde hair and folded my arms. *Finally*, I thought. But I couldn't distinguish between my state of awareness and dreaminess. I rechecked my phone. Yes, I had answered a call from the hospital. I jumped out of bed and did a little jig, throwing my arms in the air and exclaiming, 'Yahoo!'

And then I began to remember ... many things ...

It must've been closer to my fourth birthday when I buried my first pet — a mouse.

'Daphne dear, he's dead. No life. You must give him a good burial,' said Dad. My wonderful, dearest dad, who always called me 'Daphne dear' and carried me over his shoulders so I could see everything above his head. He was tall, and from over his shoulders, I could also see over Ewa's head.

Until that day, I hadn't known what death meant or what death did to those who continued to live. And what was meant by burial. Instructed by Dad, I got my little pink plastic spade, dug up soft brown earth, wrapped the mouse in Dad's white handkerchief and placed him in the hole. Dad and I patted the earth mound. I felt the absence of life.

I refused to leave the little earth mound where my mouse lay. He had been with us for just four days. He had no name, and no one knew why he died.

'It's final. Death must happen to everyone because others must be born. If not, those being born will have no place to live. The Earth is not that big. But look up at the sky, Daphne dear. So big,' Dad said.

I looked up. Yes. The sky was big. So big that I couldn't see the whole of it.

'The last breath flies away into the sky, leaving the body behind.'

Despite my tears, I breathed in deep and breathed out, wondering if my breath would fly away into the sky to be the last. I took in another and threw out another. Death didn't come to me. Dad said death was not worth thinking too much about by children. He promised he'd get me a small kitten instead. He did, and I named her Kitty.

Kitty lived with us for about three years. When I found her lifeless a few metres behind our house one early morning, I cried. I buried her at the same spot where I found her. I picked some flowers and placed them on the earth mound, which was larger than the one I had for the mouse.

Late that night as we were at dinner, Ewa said Kitty died after consuming rat poison. It was a cat and mouse game, she said. People should learn how to care for their pets and not leave them to fend for themselves, she said. By then I had understood the finality called death.

Kevin, my twin, and my best friend, who was sitting next to me at the table, quietly squeezed my hand. He always took my side.

'Ewa killed Kitty,' I said loudly.

No one believed me. Nana and Mum, who were quiet most of the time, told me to hush. Ewa looked at me for a moment and began to peel her orange. Mum took my hand and led me away. Kevin followed. Nana continued to sit at the table, watching her own empty plate. Soon, she would collect all the dirty dishes and begin to wash them. Mum would join her at the sink, and Ewa would retire to her own bedroom.

These were my muffled memories. I had compelling ones too …

1.2

The day Ewa died, a storm had raged, powerlines had snapped, trees had fallen across the roads, and hailstones had broken windowpanes of houses in our township of Somerfield in Sunnyvale. The modest Cassowary Creek, which snaked half a mile behind our big house, had swelled with raging, muddy-brown waters, rushing with everything that came its way, all the way from mountains not too far away. Carcasses and new and old vegetation amid muddy swirls all raced towards an end.

Why it was called Cassowary Creek, no one knew. Those huge, flightless birds weren't seen anywhere near the valley. The female cassowary laid eggs, while the male cared for the chicks. Because of this, I often wondered why we said, 'mother nature' and not 'father nature'.

Yet, Cassowary Creek stayed doing its job of filling up, rising, carrying all that came its way and emptying itself before it returned to its calm, curvy course.

Somerfield's rainstorms were just like any other neighbourhood's rainstorms. Blinding lightning, deafening thunder, and rain sheets danced in the fierce whistling wind. The stately gums, the pines and the palms bent as much as they could, stealthily holding onto the soil, swaying dangerously, defying the dynamism of a formidable foe. Suddenly, hail would cover the grounds. It was a play between who was stronger — the life of the wind and skies, or the trees that had taken years to grow. Then, snap. A weak link would give way, and the tree would fall and lay across the road or on some unlucky family's housetop. Emergency services personnel wearing their high-vis jackets would swarm the area. TV news channels would display breaking news and high alerts.

That night, the house sat silent and stoic while the storm raged outside. It stood majestic, its whiteness gleaming, defying darkness as every streak of lightning seemed to add to its glow.

I looked through the glass windows outside just as a streak of lightning hit the darkened sky, flashing slim, sharp, steel wire roots painting silver into the room. I heard the roar of thunder with the whistling, whooshing wind as it beat upon the corrugated iron roof of the house. Like ghost-breaths blown by witches — one of whom was Ewa.

I smiled as I acknowledged that my dream had come true and reached for my mobile.

I could almost hear Ewa's loud voice commanding, 'Don't touch that! You silly girl! People should learn how to think on their feet! Don't you even take a moment to think?'

Like days when I got under her feet in the kitchen, when she'd stop what she'd been doing and focus all her attention on me. Her blue eyes would turn into big, bulging ones, and her big face would look uglier than it did every other day. She'd push her short, greying wavy hair behind her ears, her hands reaching behind to untie her apron strings. She'd shrug out of it, leave it on the kitchen bench, fling her kitchen gloves if she were wearing them and march out of the kitchen calling out to Nana. 'Juliana! Juliana! Take that child out of the kitchen! How often do I need to tell you that? People should learn how to look after their children. Or not have them.'

Ewa would call out to Nana, but Mum would hustle from wherever she was and tell Ewa to leave everything, then she'd apologise, calm Ewa, and only upon reassuring her, would she turn to me. She never asked what I'd done or what I'd not done. Her aim was always to get me out of Ewa's way. Her face set like a mask — no anger, no remorse. Head bent, she'd quietly do what she was asked to do.

Mum said she was the peacemaker. I wondered what things Mum used to make peace out of. She would shake her head and say it was time for me to read something or to finish my homework, or to have a shower or anything that didn't involve going into the kitchen, or nearer to where Ewa was.

I remember once, Dad returning home after many weeks from the Outback, having worked there. He was a builder. He built roads and bridges so people could drive on them and reach wherever they wanted to.

I was lucky to have parents who were makers of things — Mum made peace, and Dad made roads.

Whenever Dad came home to us, we'd be a family again and go out for picnics or to the beach. Just the four of us. Ewa and Nana left us alone when Dad was at home.

I can almost see Dad now, carrying his little brown bag, and wearing his old khaki uniform and a bush ranger's hat on his head, his light-brown eyes twinkling as soon as he'd see Mum. I'd run into his open arms while Kevin would follow, walking. Mum would look everywhere else and only go near him once she was satisfied no one else was watching. I believe he knew her dilemma, and therefore, his eyes held that twinkle. Nana said Mum was shy. Dad said it was a secret between him and Mum.

Dad always asked for a glass of cool water the moment he arrived. That day, I wanted to be the one to offer him that glass.

I had gingerly poured icy water from a jug in the refrigerator in a large glass and was looking for a tray to place it on, when Ewa noticed and screamed her commands, 'Don't lift that tray! You'll drop it!'

In that instant, the glass fell and shattered into a hundred pieces.

The shattering sound got Nana and Mum in the kitchen. Each of them looked at the scene, at me and at Ewa.

Nana went to Ewa, without touching her, because Ewa didn't like anyone to touch her, and whispered, 'Mel will clean the mess. It's time for your afternoon nap, Muh. Come.'

Nana called her mum 'Muh'.

My mum nodded and began to look for the dustpan, the broomstick and mop. I stood looking at the scene, with anger and frustration at Ewa. Dad took me away, saying he wasn't thirsty anymore. That moment, remembering the deaths of my mouse and Kitty, I had felt Ewa had to die. To be gone forever.

This had been our household for a long time — four generations living under one roof.

1.3

After the stormy rain came respite. Dead, wet and slippery brown moss could be seen on fences of some neglected Queensland timber homes. A few days later, bright-green shoots would break open the soft red-brown earth. Air reverberated with barks, mews, moos, bleats, grunts and chirps. And the two remarkable 'Ks' — the kangaroos and the koalas — came out, curious to know what all the fuss was about.

An occasional vehicle klaxon could be heard. A tang of wet soil assimilated with all these.

Some nostrils twitched, hurrying to confirm what the eyes were seeing. Dampness hung in the air like an unpegged diaphanous cloak ready to move away from the clothesline at the mere hint of sunlight rays and the lightest whisper of a breeze.

A few years ago, the local council had carved signs in concrete near stormwater drains, which said: *Protect our Waterways*. Clear rainwater gurgled through these on its journey to the river or the vast bay.

In springtime, the purple jacarandas bloomed, weaving a tapestry of blue skies, green grass and other greens, and the little pond, the driveway and walkways added to a perceived modesty of the dwellers inside. The rich pink bougainvillea climbed some gums forever, and the royal poincianas spread their canopies, adding to the vibrancy of (mother) nature.

During windy autumn days, when the leaves yellowed and fell, the house lay unrattled, taking in the views of the valley, including the Glass House Mountains, proudly unconcerned of who admired which part of its frame.

Nothing was different in Somerfield from the rest of the neighbourhood during stormy nights or sunny days.

The difference laid in the aftermath. In the dwellings. In the dwellers who dwelled in those dwellings.

Our house was a Queenslander — the big house that Nana inherited, including a special maintenance allowance. It was truly fortunate that she did because it allowed us to afford a modest lifestyle. Additionally, sometimes, we'd have boarders or nature walkers, as they called themselves, living with us for a few nights.

It was a low set, detached house, with a porch that covered the whole of the front and part of the two sides. It had six huge rooms and two living areas, and every room was accessible from every other room, including the kitchen. One door off every room led to the adjoining rooms — these doors were always locked to remove the anxiety of being caught unawares in pursuit of privacy. Yet, it was through these accidentally left opened doors that certain words left certain lips and entered certain ears, which they weren't meant for. These words caused issues.

The whole house, including the fence surrounding it and the corrugated roof, was painted white. It sat like a fat, white chook covering its chicks under its wings — a dwelling amid the green of all shades.

In the valley, it was the only house that had decorative, carved stumps to hold it aloft, with matching lattice work. The main entrance was accessed by a curved staircase in the centre.

I loved to run up and down the stairs. I imagined running up to catch Ewa and throwing her down, then running back down the stairs to avoid being caught by her. It never happened. Ewa never ran. She walked sure-footed like a mountain goat.

She was a goat. A big goat. The rest of us were sheep. Little sheep. It was written in small letters in the big book: *And He will set the sheep on His right hand, but the goats on the left.*

On the last day, those on the right hand — the sheep — would be saved. Those on the left hand — the goats — would be thrown into the everlasting fire.

Those were the thoughts of a seven-year-old. The thoughts continued, strengthened in greater resolve until the night of my dream in which Ewa died — and of which I learned in wakefulness — some twenty years later.

A wooden plaque with the word *Uralbah*, which must have hung at the entrance a long time ago, had been removed by Ewa and placed beneath the house.

'Why did you remove it?' I overheard Dad asking Ewa one day. A door to Ewa's room hadn't been locked, and Dad had walked in.

'I don't know the meaning.'

'It means a home between the hills. Which is where this house is,' he said.

'I don't like the name. Juliana too agreed it does not mean anything.'

'She'll agree to whatever you say. As will Mel. They are spellbound and dutybound only to you! But it stops there. My daughter will not be bound to you at all. I'll make sure of that!'

'She's her mother's child,' Ewa replied.

'And mine. Never forget it,' he said.

'I made her possible for you. You had better remember it!' Ewa almost whispered.

'Your role in everything, my dear woman, is etched in my brain. My heart is a victim, as you know well,' he said and laughed aloud. It sounded like a lied laugh.

To me, this exchange meant Dad didn't like Ewa either. I vowed to myself that once Ewa was no more, I'd hang the plaque back in place.

The house and the estate were my joy. Often, I'd run halfway towards the driveway, turn around and admire it.

1.4

I paused my memories and took a deep breath before leaving my bedroom to inform Nana and Mum about Ewa's passing. It was just before sunrise.

When I knocked on Nana's door, I knew it would be enough to wake Mum too. She came into Nana's room.

'She's gone,' I said straightaway.

Sober shadows sliced the outlines in corners of the room from lit candles. Nana looked older, her head bent, the increasing grey in her short, wavy hair, showing markedly as also the lines on her face while she sniffled and wiped her tears with a scented tissue. Both women were little, unlike me. All three of us had big foreheads though, and often Nana said women with big foreheads were intelligent. She raised her head now and looked at Mum first and then at me. I could read just one word there: responsibility. A worried responsibility.

Ewa had ruled her life and every other life in our home. She hadn't trained anyone else to take responsibility.

'I'll do it,' she used to say to any help that was offered. 'You go and look after your daughter.'

Nana looked after her daughter. Mum looked after me. I saw Ewa as the very source of evil in my otherwise simple life. I had such a deep dislike for her.

Some people in some families disliked some others for no reason. As Ewa and me.

'What will we do now?' asked Nana.

'Do?' I queried. 'We've got to arrange for the burial, of course.' I then added, 'I'll call Kevin later.'

Father Kevin Brown, my twin, now a Catholic priest, would manage it all.

'And we'll donate the 90th birthday cake I baked for Muh to the local charity,' suggested Nana.

A few hours later, our nearest neighbour, who lived five miles away, Mrs Watson drove to inform us that her daughter in Perth had given birth to a healthy baby boy. Such joy. Two women in my home were in mourning. Mrs Watson was basking in excitement but clearly felt sorry that we had lost a matriarch. It was so sad, she said as she hobbled to her small white car promising to bake something and bring it over to us, even though we said there was no need. But she hurried anyway, pleased to be the first to inform the community of Ewa's passing.

There was no stopping some people who loved to mirror their actions with pretended nobility.

At least from now on, I'd not hear the words I'd learned to despise: *People should learn how to ...*

1.5

It was the burial day. The rain had receded, but dampness filled the air.

We were in the local cemetery, where stood the weeping willow at the entrance. There were other trees too, heavy with rainwater. A huge fig tree, its roots creeping aggressively above ground, had broken some tombstones. The roots fed directly from the corpses. I shuddered, feeling cold, and I folded my arms as I continued to walk.

A dead leaf fluttered and rested on my shoulder. I didn't brush it off.

I remembered a story Mum had read once to Kevin and me as children, of a tender, beautiful new leaf on a tree. It laughed from the top when it saw the dying old brown leaf lying on the ground. The young leaf boasted to the old one, marvelling at her own new, tender beauty.

When old boots trampled the dying leaf, the old but wise leaf painfully whispered, 'You laugh at me today. The same fate awaits you tomorrow. Another new leaf will take your place and say the same thing. Just as I had.'

At that time, Mum had said, 'Life's cycle continues. It's all the same under the sun.'

She had then quoted from her Bible, from the Book of Sirach:

What has been will be again,
what has been done will be done again.
There is nothing new under the sun.

All I could think of at that time was that leaves don't speak.

Once again, I shivered as I felt Ewa's ghost hovering about. There were other ghosts hovering about as *there was nothing new under the sun.*

The branches of the gums swayed gently, shedding little drops of rainwater collected on them — like my heart swollen with profound, pent-up pain collected over the years, and shedding it but leaving an emptiness. All my yesterdays, which were, until now, bundled together and left hanging, now broke open like light from a multi-pronged chandelier spreading below. The darkness still hovered above, covering the ceiling.

When something goes out, a vacuum is created. I wondered what would now fill that vacuum.

The past was creeping into the present.

Ewa couldn't suddenly come back to life and demand she be declared alive again. No. That would be impossible, even for Ewa. I felt a giggle rising and quickly covered my mouth.

I wasn't shivering anymore. Some people came to us offering their condolences as we stopped by the gravesite. Some expressed that they were feeling sorry and pondering the loss of a strong, independent woman, while some expressed indifference, and some accepted a natural end of life.

I looked forward to my new life — wondering how it would unfurl without the ignoble presence of Ewa. Excitement was building within me, but I'd not show it to anyone. This was one trait I mastered because of Ewa. To hide my true feelings. To show a feeling that was exactly the opposite of truth — but only where Ewa was concerned.

Because whatever good Ewa saw, she cursed it into nothingness.
But Ewa was dead. And I need not act.

Father Kevin Brown and the parish priest led the burial ceremony.

Kevin adjusted his glasses over his nose nervously as he often glanced at the parish priest, clearly trying to confirm whether he was conforming with the needed rituals. I wanted to go to him to assure him it really didn't matter, but I restrained myself. Nobody cared.

The usual 'dust unto dust' part was over. Ewa was laid to rest six feet below, her casket sealed, and we could all move on with our lives — undisrupted like rainwater gushing downhill into Cassowary Creek.

That was what I believed.

Me today. You tomorrow, I read on a tombstone. Everyone was born to die. When I died, I'd clarify in my will that I am not buried but have my ashes thrown into Cassowary Creek. I wanted to go without a trace. No tombstone, no nothing.

Ewa had hired a lawyer, and there was a will, Nana had announced the previous day.

Who would have thought a woman like Ewa would do that? What had Ewa owned anyway?

Yet, I was grappling with feelings that I hadn't felt before. Death was final. But there was nothing final about Ewa; there never had been. Could she re-erupt, like a ghost out of nowhere? I'd somehow then have to kill her ghost, having not had the satisfaction of killing her body. That would be hard. I realised my fear hadn't left me, and the joy I felt earlier had a shallow foundation. *What would she have written in her will?*

While at the burial, the lawyer — a tall man in a black suit — informed us that we should all come to his offices in Brisbane at the earliest opportunity. I didn't want to go.

He said, 'Ewa had specifically asked that you be present. I understand most of it has to do with you.'

'Benny Barreto,' he introduced himself. He had a deep, authoritative voice, and I recoiled. If he was Ewa's friend, he was my enemy. But often, the very things you don't want, come to you with a full force and a life of their own.

I took his hand tentatively, but his grip was firm. I raised my head to look into his deep, almost black eyes and ridiculously long lashes. Eyes that seemed to peer right into me. His bushy black and thick eyebrows were raised questioningly. Black wavy hair was windswept and partly covered his broad forehead. His nose was longish, and he was clean shaven. His nostrils flared as he took a deep breath and cleared his throat. He had obviously noticed me noting him.

While I was 1.65 metres, he must have been 1.80 metres or more. His Adam's apple was bigger than I had ever seen.

Tall people made me nervous. One more legacy of Ewa.

'Mr Lawyer, I don't mourn Ewa's passing away. I don't want anything from her. Just bin her will. I don't care,' I blurted before feeling a nudge in my ribs from Mum.

'We'll all be there. Thank you,' said Nana.

It was like that in my family. We women were very conscious of not hurting our mums. I cared about my mum, she cared about hers and, in the end, it had all to do with Ewa queening herself. Even after her death.

Mr Lawyer looked at me, nodded, and then we began to walk away.

I turned to have a brief look at the earth mound where Ewa lay. It was bigger than the ones I had had for the mouse and Kitty.

1.6

We agreed to meet Mr Lawyer in his office the next day. I sometimes had to travel to Brisbane city by train for staff meetings. I worked as a government servant who no one noticed. Why would they? I was socially awkward — a plain girl who didn't wear makeup, didn't want to make friends, kept to herself, and was always lost in thought ... usually thinking about when Ewa would die, and after that, how I would change myself and my life. Waiting. Of course, no one knew my thoughts.

I worked at the customer service centre in the finance pool in Samford and drove myself in my little second-hand white car to the office. It was a small office with tired-looking walls and lit-up ceilings with browned and worn-out carpet floorings. Our city office was luxurious in comparison, on the thirteenth floor of the building. Any Friday on the thirteenth of a month didn't bother me, but I knew some who took the day off because they were superstitious.

I didn't climb the ladder and wasn't career conscious. I was content with my fortnightly salary, which hadn't increased much over the past eight years. I started there when I was nineteen and continued staying.

I did the same old job — with new people as they came and left, and others took their place. I was like a sign board carved on marble stone and cemented atop a heritage building. It read: *Daphne Brown. Est. 2007.*

Of course, I wanted to earn more and talked to Mum about it once, who then spoke to her mum, and I overheard Ewa saying, 'She should look out for another job. It's easy. Who doesn't want more? People should learn how to keep on looking for ways to earn more. Or give us a hand here.'

Since that time, I lost whatever little career ambition I had. The ordinary embraced me.

It distressed Kevin that I chose to remain so stagnant.

'You have so much to give, so much to do, Daphne,' he'd say often.

I'd smile and tease him, saying, 'You could've done so much too. Gotten married, given me a good sister-in-law who I'd love to bits, and we'd take sides against you. And given me some nieces and nephews, to spoil. Instead, the "Brown" line is forced to stop. All because you're taking all your talents to your grave.'

He'd merely shake his head. Sometimes, he'd say, 'And I'm looking to that day when I've a brother-in-law and nieces and nephews too. You better hurry up, Daphne, or there won't be any good blokes left.'

'Oh, never you mind, Kevin. I can always come to your seminary and steal one.'

But of course, we both knew I'd never do that. I didn't harbor any illusions that I was a ravishing beauty who could tempt any of those saintly men. My Kevin was a saint; I was awkward.

Nana and Mum didn't mind what career I chose or what I did, as long as I came back safely home each evening. Ewa continued with her grumbling, and I continued to ignore her and waited for her to die.

Later, I'd learned that at some point in our lives, we wanted that which was denied to us.

1.7

Three women were led by a priest into the legal offices in the Brisbane CBD.

Nana and Mum were dressed in sombre brown dresses, very ladylike, wore light makeup and carried their little ladylike handbags, holding scented tissues among other ladylike things. They wore low-heeled shoes.

Kevin was in his usual white shirt, with his priestly collar and black formal trousers. 'Don't look at the collar, Daphne. Look at the man behind the collar.' That's what he'd said soon after his ordination. What was he behind his collar? My twin. Soft spoken, a smiling face, calm, courteous and kind. Cultured and learned. I'd die for him. But he became a man taking an easier route to live his life on his community's terms. His personal possessions were his clothes, his missal, a wristwatch, mobile phone and a rickety car.

We were ushered into a brightly lit conference room — one of those that usually had a polished, solid oval wooden table with upholstered chairs around it. There was a white board on the wall, a telephone, a jug of water and a few glasses on the table. We all drifted towards the chairs without thinking who was to sit where.

Nana took the first chair to her right as we entered. Mum followed her. They sat quietly, their hands folded in their laps, ladylike in their chairs, their eyes taking in the décor and waiting for they knew not what. Kevin and I sat next to each other.

Mr Lawyer walked in with quick steps. His eyes were covered in black-rimmed glasses, through which he looked at me for a few moments and then nodded. He wore a black suit and tie — nothing extraordinary. Until I saw his hands. Long, slender fingers. A black ring on his ring finger, nails nicely trimmed and the half-moons in prominence. All black and gloomy. I looked away.

I felt conscious of my appearance. I'd worn a simple, baggy beige cotton top and loose blue cotton pants picked up from one of the shops in the local mall on the Boxing Day sale. My hair was tied in a ponytail, and I wore no makeup. A tote bag hung over my shoulders, and sneakers covered my feet. I felt sweaty, and the faint odour of my unshaved armpits reminded me of my school day basketball games.

I didn't belong in this neat and tidy corporate place. I wanted to get this farce over and done with.

After greeting and thanking us for coming, Mr Lawyer took a seat at the head of the table, removed his black attaché and placed it on the table. Opening it, he took out a brown travel case.

The moment I saw it, I said, 'Where did you get that from? Did you steal it from Ewa?'

A chorus of 'Daphne!' filled the room.

Mr Lawyer said, 'Ewa had given it to me with instructions to hand it to you. That's why I wanted you all to be here today.'

I laughed. 'Told you so. Evil Ewa speaks from the grave,' I said to Nana and Mum. Then turning to Mr Lawyer, I asked, 'How did she befriend you? She didn't trust another human being, let alone a lawyer!'

A chorus of 'Daphne!' rang out again.

Kevin said, 'I apologise. We don't know what the outcome of this meeting will be nor what it is about. We are all uneasy, and my sister is particularly more so.' His eyes were pleading with me to agree.

Very rarely, have I not done something that he's asked me to. This was one of those rare moments. I refused to apologise. Reaching for a glass of water, I took a few sips and waited.

Mr Lawyer said, 'Ewa engaged me to do a job. It's a bit complicated, but I will try to be as clear as I can. You are free to ask any questions later. And,' he said to no one in particular, 'this isn't about friendship. This is a business transaction.' He didn't hand over the travel case to me.

The complicated part, it appeared, was that there were letters in the case that Ewa had explicitly instructed were only meant for me. I couldn't read all of them in one go. That was the stipulation, and therefore, a complication.

'I understand there are some instructions for you,' said Mr Lawyer.

Four pairs of eyes looked at me with unasked questions.

'You "understand", do you? You should've got the travel case on the day of the funeral and buried it in her grave,' I said and heard a collective, 'Daphne!' again. 'I'm not taking any instructions from anyone.'

Mr Lawyer didn't respond to my outburst. He merely pursed his lips, raised his eyebrows, joined his hands on the table and said, 'You and Ewa must have had a unique relationship.' Then there was an immediate, 'Sorry. Not my business.'

The 'sorry' word coming out of his mouth pleased me.

'I agree. You, Mr Lawyer, shouldn't have assumed. What would you know?' I asked.

Kevin, Nana and Mum shifted in their chairs. I was being rude.

'You are to read this one before you open the case with the other letters,' said Mr Lawyer, handing over a brown envelope to me.

The brown envelope was sealed — glued and cello-taped over and over, marked 'personal' and addressed to me.

'If she wanted her ashes to be spread over on our property, it will be a big no. Why would we contaminate our property?' I asked angrily.

There was a silence. It stretched and stretched like chewing gum between a child's mouth and hand. Then, it snapped.

Mr Lawyer pushed his chair, got up, collected his mobile phone and rearranged the papers back in the case, saying he had another meeting, and if we needed anything, to ask one of the girls at reception. He shook hands with everyone except me.

Not his fault. I held onto my glass of water in one hand and the envelope in another and refused to let go of either. I didn't want to take his big hand in mine again. He looked at me, lowered his gaze and walked out of the room.

I wasn't fond of travel cases. Especially leather ones. They reminded me of animal hides. And they reminded me of Ewa's threat — 'I'll skin you alive', she'd say sometimes. 'Kevin, do you remember when I went into the attic and got out this leather case?' I asked Kevin.

He nodded.

'When Ewa had seen it in my hands, she had shrieked and made me put it back in the attic. Had I known what it held, I'd have brought it down again and burnt it.'

'Let's not talk about that now,' Kevin said.

'Okay. I've never owned a travel case. I've bad memories of them. Wonder what evil this one contains,' I said. I was then forced to read Ewa's secretive secretions. No one asked me whether I wanted to or not.

I placed my glass on the table and turned the envelope. It hadn't been pilfered with. I sniffed it, trying to find a musky, tangy kind of a smell. I don't know why I did that or why I associated a particular smell with Ewa. I felt uneasy. Anyway, there was no smell except the smell of old paper. I wanted to place it under my sweaty armpit, so it would become soggy and stinky so no one could open the envelope. But my armpits were not so sweaty now that the air conditioning had done its job. What a stupid thought!

1.8

I opened the envelope. Inside, there was another envelope.

I scoffed. Typical of Ewa. She took longer to reach a point when she thought it suited her purpose, and she was doing it again. I held up the envelope and showed it to the others in the room. I wanted them to reconfirm my own thoughts about Ewa's characteristics. Nana and Mum looked at the envelope and shifted in their chairs, their eyes looking every other way; Kevin urged me to open it.

I ripped open the envelope without using the scissors and found a neatly folded typed letter. It was dated 20 November 2013 — last year. I quickly read it and slumped in the chair. Then, I reread it. My head hurt, eyes rolled, and I was shocked into silence.

Kevin grabbed the letter from me and began to read. Then he too slumped back in his chair, muttering, 'Oh my God!'

Nana and Mum first looked at each other and then at Kevin, clearly worried.

'What is it, Kevin?' Nana asked.

'Nana, Mum … please promise me you'll remain calm. Drink some water first,' he said, pouring water into two glasses and pushing them towards Nana and Mum.

Dear Kevin. Always thinking of others.

Nana and Mum drank the water, while I simply sat stunned.

Kevin began to read the letter aloud, and I folded my arms to listen and to reconfirm what I had just read.

My Dear Daphne,

You will feel like you are reading a novel once you have read this letter. I believe such is the stuff that movies are made of. Or at least a story. They used to — in my times.

As you are now reading this, I must be cold in my grave. I do hope you were there to see me buried — as now I speak to you from my grave. I can see you smirking. In a way, I think you have been expecting something like this.

You and I share a bond. A bond of dislike. Also, of admiration. Laugh if you must. You are the only one who challenged me. You kept my life from continuing to be boring, although you entered my life quite late. That's it! Our age difference made all the difference. Which is why I will share a secret that I've been holding from the world.

I am not your great nana.

I brought up Juliana as my own child. Fate tricked me too, Daphne. Do not think for a moment that your nana and your mum are martyrs.

Now that that is out, to know more, you will need this young lawyer's help. I've left all instructions with him. He will give you another letter. And another. Only after you read them all in sequence will you know what this is all about. As you have finished reading this letter, the second letter awaits you.

You surely did not think I'd make it easy, did you? I am smiling even as I type this letter. I can imagine your reaction. How I wish you could see mine!

You think I was always this way — the way you knew me? Angry, shouting, controlling? I was a baby, a child, a teenager once too. Until I was forced to become a mother to a child who was not my own. But do tell Juliana that she was the reason I had to stay. Or she may have landed in an orphanage. It was not her fault; none of us ask to be born.

Sleep on what you have learned today. When you are ready, the next letter awaits you.

A great nana you loved to hate and who secretly admired you because you refused to bend.

Ewa Bajek
nein
Helga Hoffmann

The silence stretched. I could hear the soft whirring of the air conditioner. Nana and Mum were looking at Kevin, who had closed his eyes.
Is he praying?
'It's a mistake. Maybe that letter was meant for someone else, and maybe it isn't from … from …' Nana said before she passed out.
Mum turned to her, distressed, mumbled about feeling giddy, and closed her own eyes.
Typical Mum. Like an ostrich, she'd lie still and hope the problem would go away.
I got up and sprinkled water from my glass on Nana and on Mum. Nana's aged, light-green eyes opened. Mum, seeing Nana seated upright, took her hands in hers and did the same in her chair, and waited. Kevin and I looked at each other through our own bright-green eyes.
Kevin muttered, 'Thank God!'
'Thank Evil Ewa,' I whispered.

1.9

Ewa's letter enveloped us totally. When the shock stabilised, it elated me. My emotional state was like that of a lonely, old widow who had dreamt throughout her life of winning the lotto, found that she had at last, but now was confused about what she'd do with all that money.
Ewa had tricked us all into being who we were not.
Last Friday, I had to bear the occasional silence and the tears that followed. Nana and Mum were shaken, and I wasn't ready to

offer them any comfort. We couldn't watch out for the other. The inner battle was individually independent. Still, Nana reached out to Mum and hugged her — one seeking comfort and the other offering it.

Dazed, Nana said, 'Can it be true? She wasn't my muh? And who was my father?'

'Yes. She treated me well too. Except when ...,' said Mum.

Whatever it was, she left it unsaid.

Nana looked at her and then away.

After a while, they both turned to me with questioning eyes.

'We shouldn't have gone to Benny's office,' said Nana.

Mum nodded.

'What?' I asked, amazed at their naivety. 'I can't describe how happy I feel,' I said, my eyes dreamy as I flopped on the sofa, grabbing a grey cushion. I looked about the room. Everything was black, white and grey, except the polished brown wooden floor. Ewa hadn't liked colours indoors. *I'll change the look of this room*, I thought, *and everything else*, as I hugged the grey cushion.

'Daphne, it's not about you nor me. It's about what Nana feels,' said Mum, who hardly gave an opinion.

That didn't sound nice. I drifted like a soldier trained to muster courage out of thin air.

It must have been hard for Nana. Had Ewa adopted her? Stolen her when she was a baby? Like many others of her age, Ewa was a post-Second World War Polish migrant widow who came to Australia with a baby. That was all that we knew.

'I'll wake up from this dream and everything will be back to normal again,' Nana said.

'No! It's no dream. Call Mr Lawyer and ask him,' I said.

In that moment, my joy dissipated. A strange feeling crept in me like a parasitical mesh over a tree. Any attempt to remove the mesh would kill the tree. I stayed alone in my space. But now that space was being intruded upon.

Mr Lawyer would be more trustworthy in the eyes of Nana and Mum than me. *Why had Ewa entrusted all her deceptive discoveries to him, and how much did he know?* Nana and Mum, as a result, would also grow closer to him, a stranger.

I didn't join Nana and Mum at dinner that night, feigning tiredness and saying I had had a cheap burger earlier that day.

I did have a burger. And fries. And an iced cola.

My guts gnawed, griped silently. I felt sick in all ways.

Nana and Mum had been silent peace corps between Ewa and me. It was still Ewa and me.

Each of us now were lost in our own little capsules, floating in all kinds of powdered, bitter herbs. Luckily, a little particle of one or more would heal some part of the wound, I hoped.

I didn't sleep well that night and ignored Kevin's calls and texts. He must've known the turmoil going on within the three women who adored him. He had rushed to the presbytery instead of being with us.

He should have come home to peaceful Somerfield.

1.10

Somerfield's serenity was unique. When one entered the town, there was a sign that read: *The Town of Yesteryear*. The main street — Draper Street — was draped with charming, colourful cottages now transformed into cafés.

The golden wattle, our own Australian floral emblem — its bright ball-shaped yellow flowers and bright-green leaves, when in full bloom — added to the mystical beauty of Draper Street. There were stories here of people who'd lived mixed lives of the two world wars. Pain when death came and bursts of joy when they received their sons alive. A memorial site stood as witness to such fallen men, on the side of the street, which was partly covered with the golden wattle.

Ewa said the golden wattle was too bright.

Some trees on Draper Street were yarn-bombed last year. Colourfully clothed tree branches added a unique look to the street.

Nana and Mum had knitted the longest piece, and it still covered one of the tallest branches of the poinciana tree inside a roundabout. Mum had climbed a forklift to join the seams. They had laughed about it, but Ewa termed it a 'frivolous exercise'. Not wanting to displease Ewa, Nana and Mum wanted it removed, but the council refused.

The council did get some things right, sometimes. I bought more yarn and learned how to knit, but I found crocheting easier and quicker and crocheted a piece with big gaps, and then I climbed on a forklift and joined the seams on the same tree. I had a laminated note stuck to the tree. It said: *Lovingly made and donated by the Brown family.* I took a photo, framed it and placed it on the side table in the lounge area at home, next to a vase of bright sunflowers.

Nana, Mum and Ewa saw the photo. No one said a word, and no one removed it. *Good*, I thought. Loudly, I said, 'The Brown family has done something good for our community.'

I've always been baffled at the irony of driving through Draper Street, which also houses an information centre, a Catholic school, church and cemetery, and the ambulance service depot, the local police station, and the fire brigade offices. Further down is the local hospital.

This was the route taken by an unwell person. First, the ambulance was called for, then it went to the hospital. If dead, the body was taken from the hospital to the church, and at last, to the cemetery. This was the route taken by Ewa when she died.

Hearing urgent sirens of a motor chase or an ambulance rushing to save a life, sobered some people to accept the vagaries of both life and death and to make the most of their own life, or the death of another. Joy at birth; reflections at death.

One of the old streets heading towards the rail station had tall trees on both sides. The council cut them regularly. The arborists and the cutters shaped them. Overhead, there were exposed electric wires running simultaneously. Cutting and shaping the branches kept the wires from getting tangled in the branches. Therefore, the tree branches were cut off. Also, the local buses and vehicles used the road. The branches were sized and shaped into inverted 'L' shapes. Like L canopies. We called them the half-trees.

Just like our half-lives of pretended penances. We did wrong. We felt the guilt. We compromised or we confessed and made repentance. Only to do it all over again, as Kevin said. Humans, after all.

My grandfather died before my mother was born. He died at a construction site. Nana said he died because he couldn't balance himself on a pole and fell, hitting his head. He never recovered consciousness. Or he couldn't balance his life with Ewa's interference. Who knows?

With Mum, Nana had to come back and live with Ewa. That was hard, as Ewa had to feed another mouth. Mum felt the need of obligation all the time around her.

But after a few years, a government officer visited them and informed them that my grandfather had been the sole benefactor of a big parcel of land and a huge house in the interior of the valley. The big, white Queenslander that housed us. The only thing was that Ewa also moved in.

Kevin and I didn't know anything about our great grandfather; Ewa refused to mention him. Nana said he'd have been a soldier because in those days many young men went to war. There were no photos. People didn't talk much about their painful past lives.

As for my father, we were told he had disappeared into the bush; he was never heard of again. We assumed he was dead. My father loved me and Kevin. He was a good man. So, why had he disappeared? Mum said that such things happened.

But Ewa had whispered to me, 'People go into the bush because they don't wish to return home. They're tired of what their family want from them. That's why he left.'

'No! You're a liar,' I had said and run off.

My father's name, Bob Patrick Brown, was registered in an archive where they held names and details of those who disappeared in the bush. With him gone, Ewa took full reign over all of us.

Ewa told me that there was another register where the names of Dad and Grandfather's ancestors were written in, because they were petty thieves who were sent to Australia as convicts. Nana said Ewa was older and knew more about such things, and Mum agreed with Nana. Nothing more was ever discussed about any of the men. Not even their names. Past painful events could not be talked about.

Sometimes, I thought Mum was as insipid as a woman who had cleaned floors throughout her life and done nothing else. She appeared more dead than alive. At times, Mum's attitude towards everything annoyed me. Ewa had made her like that. After Dad disappeared and was presumed dead, Ewa also blamed Mum for his disappearance. She said Mum let go of a fine young man because Mum was weak. Of course, no one questioned Ewa's analysis.

My mind slipped back and forth with memories.

With her revelations, Ewa had put a brake on my plans for living a free life. *That's how she planned it*, I thought. *I must be fed piece by piece.* I was wary about her next letter.

1.11

Back in the same room in Mr Lawyer's office the next week, I was handed a familiar-looking cello-taped envelope. I opened it and began to read.

Daphne,

I've made you happy at last. You are excited, I can feel it now as I type this letter. Now that you know I am not your great nana, you are curious to know who your real great nana was.

I lived and grew up in Munich, Germany. I met a young, handsome officer named Henri Stein at our local club on my sixteenth birthday. I belonged to the German League of Girls, proudly helping in whichever way I could. Because war was good. War was virtuous. The Fatherland was beyond reproach.

That day, I was serving wine to the young men in uniform who had stopped by. Henri refused to get drunk, saying we needed to remain sober because we were at war. I thought that was very good. But he had been testing me.

He said war was not fair for the young people, that his parents needed his help to farm their land. Instead, he was forced to be a soldier. He was not interested, and never wanted to be near the frontline, and he wondered why young people were being forced. I was stunned and reported him. When I was called to meet the senior officers, he was there, and he applauded me. He said I'd passed the test and that I should be prepared to take on greater responsibilities. They called me a star! How it had thrilled me then. Henri and I exchanged addresses and began to write to each other.

So, Ewa was a German, not Polish, as we believed. My heart rate increased. What a liar!

This letter told me about Ewa and Henri. Ewa grew up to serve her country with pride. She was attracted to him and believed he was to her, too. But she was tricked, she said.

Now that you know, read my third and last letter to you next week. In that letter, I will write about your real great nana. The poor girl! I don't know where she is and if she lives now.

Her letter ended, giving nothing more. Eerily evil Ewa.

1.12

When I reached home later that evening, Nana and Mum were waiting to know more. I simply handed over the letter to them. *Let them make whatever they feel like making of it.* Ewa's cruelty had the power to hurt. She could have let out all the information in one letter. That was how she'd functioned though — she extended the torture for as long as she could.

But it was traumatic for Nana. She had a faraway look as she sat in the rocking chair and rocked herself. 'I didn't call her Mother or Mum,' she said, talking to herself. 'I called her "Muh", which meant Mum, of course. I wonder if that was because I was not hers. What a sacrifice!'

'Sacrifice? Ewa? Not a chance. There must be more to it,' I said.

'Daphne, let go of your anger,' said Nana, and Mum nodded.

I looked around. The power supply had been cut off again tonight. The lit candles cast eerie shadows — not just on the walls, but in our minds. Mindlessness. Mindfulness. Mindsets. A set of minds. Who cared at that moment? As if I wanted to hold onto anger! But then, had I known anything but anger with Ewa?

'And who was my father?' I heard Nana ask.

We all had been centred more on another unknown woman after reading Ewa's second letter. Dead men were never discussed. Now, Nana's question about fatherhood further upset us. We'd be on the lookout for not just one, but two sets of families.

The following Friday, I wondered what Ewa's next letter would reveal. Also, if Mr Lawyer would hand over the entire travel case to me. And if he did, would I refuse to take it?

I went to his office, and it was the same conference room I was led to. Mr Lawyer was not in his corporate uniform. He was dressed casually — a black T-shirt and blue jeans.

We greeted each other. I watched as his long fingers moved while removing the travel case. There was no ring. Maybe he removed it and forgot to put it back on.

Or he was deliberately hiding his wedding band.

Ewa was right in this at least when she used to say, 'Some men love to wear a wedding ring. And some hate to wear it.'

I had never seen a wedding band on Ewa's finger. No one asked about it. Where was Ewa's wedding band? I'd have to ask Nana if she had ever seen Ewa's ring.

'My instructions were to hand over this case to you, after you've read the last letter.' He removed the envelope and gave it to me, together with an envelope cutter. Just like the first two envelopes, this one was also marked to me. Typed in bold were the words: *Third and last letter from Helga to Daphne*. He then closed the case and pushed it towards me. 'Ask reception to call me once you're done,' he said and left.

My heartbeats growing by the second, I cut open the envelope and removed the letter. This one was long.

Dear Daphne,

By now you must be feeling relief. I will tell you as much, but not all.

In June 1948, I was asked to come to Bombay, India. Most of us were in hiding. The Nuremberg trials had changed the world. The hunters were now the hunted — all over the world. Henri had arranged for me to live with an American family there while he had moved from country to country during those years. Finally, we would be meeting. I imagined we would marry, and then we would both travel to America. But it was to be a special mission. For our Fatherland. He told me the war was not over for people like us. He needed my help to take a baby out of India. I knew it would be dangerous. He assured me he could trust no one but me. I was to leave India with the baby and travel to New Zealand, and he would meet us there.

He gave me very little information. He said that there was a camp flourishing in Balachadi, India, at the time, where many Polish children were being looked after by an Indian king. A few years later, they were moved to the Valivade camp. It was here that the baby had been born. Yes — I still remember the names of the places. How could I forget? These names messed my life forever.

The mission was top secret, and we were both doing things for the future of our country and our people, even though the war was over. I felt lucky, and I was in love.

The very day I landed in Bombay, he handed me my new documents in a brown leather travel case. I was to be Kasia Jasko, a Polish refugee, a displaced person, he had told me. I was to be silent, vacant most of the time, having no past memory; my husband was supposed to be dead, and the baby was all I had. I was supposed to know some English but have no memory of Poland.

The next day, I was on a ship, with a baby, sailing to New Zealand for a new life.

The baby — your nana — was Juliana. Henri told me it was dangerous for all of us to travel back to Germany together. It was important for us young people to care for our future children, but unfortunately, this baby was an orphan. However, he never confirmed if the baby's parents were dead, or if they were alive and just unable to look after the baby.

I did not think of asking for help. We had grown up in an environment that made us do as we were asked, and not to question anything.

I did what I was asked to do, but I struggled to look after the baby — your nana. Other young mothers helped. They felt sorry for me, as they believed I was a war widow. It annoyed me. I had to wear a false band on my ring finger. I wished Henri would have put it there. I'd have never removed it then.

He did not write to me for a long time, and I was too afraid to ask questions, as that would draw attention to Juliana and me.

One day, about a month after I arrived in New Zealand, I received a letter from him saying I should travel to Australia somehow. I took Juliana and came to Melbourne. I again waited for Henri. I kept the letter, old photos and paper clippings in the travel case. When I could, I secretly wrote to Henri — but as I did not have his address, the letters stayed in the case.

Henri did not return. Years passed by, and I finally received a letter from him. He said that circumstances did not allow him to get in touch with me, as it continued to be dangerous. The world was still hunting for anyone who had been sympathetic to Hitler's regime, guilty or not. This was also the reason I hid myself and Juliana. He said he had been imprisoned for crimes he had not committed but was now living in another country and would call me. In those days, I volunteered as a telephone operator, and somehow, he would know when to call me. It reassured me that he was well-informed about us at the time.

The first time he called, I wept. I was hearing his voice after many, many years. He said he had to keep the call very short, which disappointed me, but I had not forgotten my strict training during my youth. I kept my emotions in check. I came home and wrote another long letter to him and placed it in the case.

But his next call was brutal. It was in September 1958 that my life would take yet another turn. He said he'd married since then because he had to safeguard his identity. I understood that very well; the times were such. Secret missions, falsified documents and everything had to be done secretly and precisely. His wife, he said, could bear no children. I understood it to mean that he was missing me and did not have those relations as a husband would have with his wife.

But he said in coded words that he was Juliana's father! He called her Juliana Stein! It must have happened while they were living at Valivade camp. No wonder he had used me to keep his dark secret. I felt betrayed and angry.

He had tricked me, Daphne. All along, the man had fooled and trapped me. I was a prisoner in a free country, afraid I'd be discovered. And he thanked me for raising Juliana. He wanted to visit us in Melbourne some time! I was angry and hurt, but I was damned if I'd arrange for him to see Juliana.

A few days later, I packed up from Melbourne and moved to Brisbane with Juliana. No one knew where I had moved to. While on the ship to Brisbane, I dropped the ring I had been wearing. It lies at the bottom of the sea, somewhere. I changed my name to Mrs Ewa Bajek.

You must remember the day when I asked you to go back into the attic and place the case from where you had removed it. All the letters, photos, documents were in that case. And it frightened me that you would go back there again. I had brought the case down some weeks later, and one by one, I burnt everything it held — all my memories. But one page of a letter that I had written to Henri is still missing. It is the paper that had flown away. Jog your memory bank. At that time, you said you did not find any paper that had flown away, but I still think you did and hid it. If you happen to find it now, burn it.

Anyway, two years ago, remember that trip I took to Melbourne? Well, I went to the old neighbourhood and from there to the aged care facility nearby to meet an old neighbour. She said a man had visited and had been looking for me and Juliana. I know it was Henri. He also said to her, she told me, that he believed my twin sister came to Australia.

I do not have a twin. But I recollect that when he gave me Juliana to look after, he had said he would be looking out for Juliana's mum's twin sister, so Juliana could be reunited with her family.

It means, your great grand aunt could be somewhere here in Australia, if not dead.

All your life you have done exactly the opposite of what I've asked you to. Yes, I know. You are the pluckier one. Your mum is timid and easily mouldable. Juliana had no choice — she only had me to look up to.

I depend on you. Only you can do this.

I want you to find Henri. Hand him over as a war criminal. I know he is alive somewhere. He must be punished for his crimes — the crime he committed against me.

Yes, Henri is your great grandfather. But I am the one who looked after your nana and gave her a normal life as much as I could. Did he repay me? No. Instead, he wanted Juliana, minus me. Why didn't I go in search of him? Because I did not want him to take Juliana away. I wanted him to suffer.

I know you won't rest until you find everything about your great nana and Henri. And what exactly happened between them and why I was used by him.

Do it for your own sake if not for mine; for Juliana and your mum.

There is one more dirty little secret I wish to tell you. Your dear Kevin. Such a sweet and willing boy. It was I who steered him towards priesthood. Why? Because only I knew Henri hated Catholic priests! Something more for you to think about.

I will continue to watch you. And the lawyer — Benny Barreto will be able to tell you more. An interesting young man, wouldn't you agree?

Yours,
Helga. Kasia. Ewa. (What's in a name?)

Kevin? She influenced Kevin? *No! Ewa lied!*

Mr Lawyer had gained Ewa's trust. There was something in all of this for him. Lawyers weren't to be trusted.

I folded the letter, placed it in the envelope and back in the travel case, picked up all my belongings, including the case, and without informing either reception or Mr Lawyer, I walked out of his office.

My head hurt, and I tried to jog my memory bank about Ewa's missing, unposted letter to Henri. I could remember nothing except a musky, tangy whiff. I needed time to let Nana, Mum and Kevin know about Ewa's last letter.

Christmas celebrations were sombre that year. No tree or decorations, gift exchange, nor roast turkey nor barbeque for Kevin and his friends at home. The only thing that remained unchanged was the midnight service we all attended in the parish where Kevin was the main celebrant. Christmas night, he joined us for a light dinner.

The year 2014 marked a close in our lives.

The summer heat was on. Hot gusts of wind blew at intervals. Temperatures soared, and temperaments soon would too.

1.13

I'm coming home tonight. They know, Kevin texted.

I smiled. Kevin and I had begun to talk about Nana and Mum collectively as 'they' or 'them'.

His visits home had lessened since Ewa's death. In the earlier days, he visited often more for my sake than his own. He had checked on Ewa and me and acted the chief mediator. Strange how everyone had tried to keep peace and sensibility between Ewa and me.

Since Ewa died, Kevin clearly decided his intervention was no longer needed. We three women were all right on our own.

But how would I break the 'dirty secret' of Ewa to him?

All those years ago, I remember, Kevin had only told me about his intention to join the seminary.

We had been walking through the Queen Street Mall one morning. We had both turned eighteen that year and had decided to tour the Brisbane CBD on our own that day. The plan was for good food, carelessness in drinking late into the evening, and most importantly, away from the prying home eyes.

An airplane crossed the sky above. He looked up, looked across the street — everywhere — and then he smiled after a while and took my hand, continuing to walk. For some strange reason, and feeling uncomfortable, I asked him what had happened to him. He had prayed, he said, prayed for all those people in the airplane, their families, all those people on the street, inside the shops, offices, cafés, people in their cars, cab drivers, bus drivers and their families.

Through his glasses, those light-green-grey eyes of his had twinkled, and he said he'd explain later.

We walked into Lorna's Café, which had an open-seating plan, and we drifted to the farthest corner table. This was Kevin's favourite coffee house. A family-run business housed in the rail station building. It was a small place, had less than a dozen tiny round tables each covered with a gingham-chequered blue and white or red and white tablecloth. The table had the usual condiments — salt, pepper, sugars, serviettes — placed in a wooden holder.

'Ah. Times are changing,' he'd said as he touched the transparent plastic cover on the tablecloth.

'Last time I was here, there was no plastic shield. It feels less homily now.'

A young waitress came over to clear the table beside us.

Smiling as he touched the plastic shield, Kevin asked the waitress, 'Never seen this before.'

'Oh. There's no one to do the washing now,' she replied. 'Gran's in a nursing home, and there's no time to do the daily washing. This is easier.'

'Yes. Yes, of course,' Kevin replied with a thoughtful look.

We ordered our two cappuccinos and cupcakes, and Kevin, with a faraway look in his eyes, began to talk seriously.

'Daphne, I believe we are all connected. All the people of the world. There've been wars, chaos, death, starvation, displacements with people crossing continents to make new lives and simply wishing to live. It continues. Each one's pain affects another. Each one's pleasure affects another. No matter where on this Earth we are born, to whom, how and where we are placed — we all want the same thing. To live in peace. Feeling good about ourselves.'

'And lording over others,' I said.

We were both silent. Contemplative.

Kevin was drawing invisible patterns on the plastic shield. I was trying to figure out if I could see any pattern or a picture. I could make nothing of them.

'I believe my small prayer sent to the heavens will aid someone. Praying for another is gratitude for your own life,' he said.

'Hmmm … do you think if someone somewhere had whispered a prayer for us, Dad wouldn't have disappeared? Or Mum could've joined him?'

'Maybe somebody did. We didn't land in an orphanage, or even worse,' he replied.

'Oh! You're starting to sound like a priest,' I said, alarmed. Kevin had always been a good person, but this thought was about an entirely different planet.

That was the day, after our coffee and in that little café, he told me that he was about to enter the seminary.

And now, according to Ewa's letter, she had manipulated him into making that decision.

How will he take it all in? What will he say to me? Should I let Nana and Mum know about it too? I was troubled. I'd thought about it since the day I read the last letter. Tonight, Kevin would know what was in there.

1.14

I knew Nana and Mum would be outdoing each other to have a real dinner spread — all because Kevin was coming. Kevin always brought cheer, even though he was a simple priest. They thought the world of him, of course, and I did too.

Nearing home, I sniffed the air outside. The smells mingled — the sweetness of a chocolate cake, the steaks on the barbeque, the pasta with Italian herbs and the fresh bread just out of the oven.

Chopping onions was left for me. I loved chopping onions. That was the only time tears flowed freely, fearlessly. No one demanded to know why I was crying. That was the time I could truly weep without drawing any curiosity. And they would come — both the tears and the emotions with them. On demand.

I'd not chop onions tonight, however. There was nothing to cry about.

The salad too was left for me. Not because I made good salads, but because they didn't want me to feel left out from contributing to the spread. That was an open secret.

I liked a colourful salad — green spinach, red tomatoes, orange capsicum, purple cabbage, brown nuts, boiled, shredded chicken and white mayonnaise. I walked straight into the backyard, washed my hands, had a glass of water, knotted my blue-chequered apron and asked Mum to chop the onions, as we had to hurry. Without a word, Mum set onto the task and soon had them on the barbeque.

I spread all the ingredients on the side table and began to toss a salad.

Soon, I heard Kevin get out of his car and I ran towards the door; I forgot about the salad. 'Oh, Kevin!' I exclaimed as I hugged him tight. 'It's so good to see you, and you're early too!''

'Good to see you too, little sister,' he replied.

There was a joke between the two of us about who was older. Kevin was born first, and within five minutes, I came. But ever since Kevin had told me the biblical story about the lesser-known twins, Perez and Zerah, we agreed to disagree about who was the elder.

'I was to be born first, but you pushed your way. Just like Perez did,' I'd say.

'Because you are truly the stronger one. I am the boy of breach.'

'Yes, I know the story. You are Perez because you can't function without your God. Whereas I, I am the writer of my own destiny.'

He would merely laugh, his eyes twinkling. We both knew my words were just plain words.

Now when he greeted me as his little sister, I said, 'Yes. You pushed your way. And sadly, since then, you've never pushed again. You are just content. All the time.'

He looked quizzically at me.

'I miss you, Kevin. Come in. They've been waiting for you and been cooking since you told them you'd be visiting.'

Nana went on to hug him, and Mum followed. I busied myself with the salad preparation and laying the table, while Nana and Mum asked him about his priestly duties.

Soon, we all settled down at the table, and he led us by reciting Grace. Raising his wine glass, he said, 'To my three favourite girls — the best in the entire world!'

'Don't forget Australia's first saint, who was a woman too. Ewa would have said that,' I said. I don't know why I said that. It came out of nowhere. There was an awkward silence. Ewa would never have said that. She hadn't been religious. She merely tolerated religious identities, as she did everyone else around her. Yet, she raised Nana as a Catholic, and we all stayed as Catholics.

Oh my God! Now I remembered a scene at the dining table all those years ago in a similar setting when Kevin had announced his intention to serve the church. Among other reasons, he had said Saint Mary McKillop had been his inspiration to serve. Mary had said something along the lines of 'never see a need without doing something about it' apparently.

While Nana, Mum and I were thinking about it, Ewa had clapped her hands, appearing pleased — a definite rare action for her, and said, 'Absolutely! You see a need and you do something about it. You become a Catholic priest and you begin to serve. Kevin, you are special. Do something special.'

Kevin had blushed. Nana and Mum had nodded, smiling.

'There is a need to continue the Brown family name too,' I had said, glaring at Ewa.

'Huh! There are plenty of Browns in the world. There're not many servers. Go, Kevin, become a priest.' She had had a sinister gleam in her eyes, like she was self-congratulating another victory over my wishes. Because she wanted Kevin, like the rest of the men in the family, to leave some day. She didn't show any surprise when he announced his intention to join the seminary. She merely whispered in my ears alone, 'And the curse continues.'

There were no more discussions. Kevin had left for the seminary. Ewa had succeeded in separating my twin from me.

Yes, that was Ewa's dirty secret all along!

And now here he was, at dinner and calling us his favourite girls.

'May her soul rest in peace,' said Kevin, his eyes closed.

'Whose?' I asked, showing my annoyance.

'May our great nana … Ewa's … uh … Helga's soul rest in peace,' he concluded.

It was a delicious meal, but the awkwardness was ever present. Questions quietly floated across the table unvoiced. Kevin invited all of us to tell him what had been happening since our last meeting with him. Nana told him that Ewa was being missed, and Mum nodded without looking up while I shrugged my shoulders.

I wasn't missing the miss-matched Miss who lied and became a Mrs. Like an irritating flea, Ewa had been brushed aside and left to die, never to rise again.

As usual, Nana and Mum fussed over Kevin — he had lost a lot of weight; fasting was good for the soul, they agreed, but he needed a strong body to keep doing the Lord's work … and so on.

He smiled, obviously amused, and secretly thrilled, no doubt. 'I will continue to visit my three favourite girls,' he said, grinning just like an indulging priest.

'For heaven's sake, Kevin! We're not your girls. One's your nana, the other's your mum, and I'm your sister! Stop talking to us like a priest. We are your family first,' I said, wondering why Kevin remained placid about the upheaval Ewa had caused with her revelation.

'Yes, yes,' Nana said, touching his cheek. 'Kevin is family first and then a priest.'

Mum came forward and touched him too, nodding.

With some more placid words, Nana and Mum said good night and retired for the night.

A few minutes later, Nana came back.

Kevin rushed towards her, asking, 'Nana, are you okay? Did you want anything?'

'I forgot about the sausages I had parboiled earlier. Can you place them in the fridge? I will barbeque them tomorrow.' Nana walked back to her room as Kevin assured her that he'd put the sausage bowl in the fridge.

Soon, Kevin and I finished cleaning up.

We moved the wicker chairs closer to each other and sat ourselves.

'All right,' he said, 'let's talk about your favourite topic.'

1.15

I made a face. Favourite girls, favourite topic! I handed him the letter, saying, 'Just warning you … you'll not like what you read. She mentions you. And don't you dare ask me about some stupid letter that's also mentioned there. I can't remember anything about it.'

I waited for a long time until Kevin read the letter — twice. He was quiet. Removing his glasses, rubbing his eyes, he reached for a glass of water.

'Have you nothing to say, Kevin?' I asked.

'Looks like most other families; we have a family history too,' he said, seemingly with uncertainty, having folded the letter and placing it back in the envelope.

'A history based on lies. Who knows what lies ahead? But is it true? Did Ewa push you, as she claims?' This part had bothered me the most.

'I don't think so. Not entirely. Biblical stories had always fascinated me, as you know. Mum used to read to us. As we grew up, they continued to interest me, while you got more interested in knowing about cats and dogs and birds and gum trees. But Ewa always spoke to me about serving and encouraged me to spend more time with selfless men, such as the priests in our community. That's when I began to learn more about them.'

'So, she did push you towards it. How do you feel about it now? I mean, what will you do? And please don't tell me it's God's plan,' I finished, raising my hand, irritated.

Kevin laughed softly. 'I was about to say exactly that. I won't do anything, except continue doing what I've committed myself to do. I love it, Daphne,' he said.

Yes, Kevin was committed. He'd never leave his vocation.

It was a quiet night most of the time as we talked quietly, mindful of Nana and Mum sleeping in their bedrooms. The quietness was disrupted when a car passed by, or a toad croaked, or a gecko made its presence felt. Crickets cried too. There was a heaviness in the air and the gentlest breeze. In such stillness, sometimes sounds from Cassowary Creek could be heard — the water gurgling, hurrying, racing to empty itself.

'What shall we do?' I asked.

'Is it bothering you? This ... this development?' he asked.

Yes, it did. All I had wanted was Ewa to be away from my life, and now that had been achieved. But Nana and Mum were sad and confused. In turn, it saddened me.

Kevin said it would be interesting to find out more. He was curious. And that it would be interesting to visit India. It all had begun from there, according to Ewa.

'Do you know that Nana's documents don't say she was born in India?' I asked.

Kevin nodded. 'Documents must have been changed ... as Ewa says in her letter.'

'You mean, forged, don't you?'

Sweet, sweet Kevin. He was always the one to use passive words. Humility, docility, dutybound priestly characteristics. He abounded in them. *Jeez,* I thought, *my twin is so different to me. No wonder I was Daphne the Zerah. Did I want to be a part of this search for our family tree? No. Did I care what it all would mean to me? No. Was I devoid of feelings? Perhaps.*

Some feelings I had experienced. Some I didn't want. Some, I didn't even know existed. I stared into the darkness of the night. Or was I going through the 'dark night of the soul', as Kevin once said? We all went through it at some point in our lives — only, we didn't know it until it had passed over. It was all very mysterious, and people used it to explain things any which way it suited them and their circumstances at the time. Kevin soaked all things relating to the dark night of the soul.

The silence stretched. Kevin had closed his eyes, and I knew he was praying silently.

I was still staring silently at the night sky. The stars shone. The Southern Cross would be somewhere if I tried hard enough to look. But the future was already written in the stars. What had to happen would happen. Kevin — or maybe I too — would go to India. To search for our roots. It was a confusing thought.

Kevin opened his eyes. 'Daphne, I can tell you were lost in deep thought.'

'Well, I was thinking. How deeply, or otherwise, I don't know.'

'You bite your lower lip with your front four teeth and move your jaw from side to side. Then you do the same with your upper lip and your lower teeth. When I notice you doing that, I know you're in very, very deep thought.'

'Oh! Very clever! You know because we're twins. I know certain things about you too,' I said. *No, I didn't*. How could twins be so different, I often wondered. Kevin was all charity, clarity. I was the opposite of all things charitable. 'All right. Here. I've stopped biting my lips. But I'm still thinking.'

He laughed. 'What's truly bothering you, Daphne?'

'Sometimes, I scare myself.' I realised I'd spoken aloud.

'What with?'

'Fear. The fear of hating too much. Nana said I should let go of my anger. But I manage anger better than I manage fear.'

'It's necessary. To have some element of fear.'

'Ha. Would you rather not say the fear of loving too little — in biblical terms?'

'One can love and hate to various degrees.'

'I don't want you to go anywhere, Kevin! What's the need? Ewa is gone! Who cares?' I blurted.

He moved closer to sit beside me, and holding my hand, he

said gently, 'Sometimes, Daphne, I need to do things for myself. See … I'm no saint. Just human.'

It was getting late. He put Nana's sausage bowl in the fridge, said good night and left.

I looked up at the stars. What were they plotting now?

1.16

The next morning, having finished my morning ritual of washing, cleaning, changing my bed clothes, I walked towards the kitchen. My nose was twitching. I saw the platter with the now barbequed par-boiled sausages with herbs and sauces. I breathed in long and hard: a musky smell — tangy and familiar. And in that instant, I remembered.

Ewa had barbequed sausages for Dad during his last visit home many years ago. The musky, tangy smell had permeated the air from the smoke that had come out, and Dad had said, 'Yum … these are just like the ones a mate made for us once. Bratwurst — he'd parboil them first and then up they'd go on the barbeque. Germans cook them that way, he'd said. Did you make them the same way?' he'd asked Ewa.

Ewa had turned aside and nodded. 'I bought them at the Sunday markets. They're made locally.'

'Very good. I'll have to tell my mate that I had a retaste of them, made by my grand mother-in-law to perfection,' Dad had said as he winked at me, emphasising the word "grand". 'In fact, I'll bring him here someday, just to taste these. He'll love 'em.'

Late that afternoon, when the others had retired for an afternoon nap, as it was windy outside, I had seen Ewa tearing and placing papers in the ambers of the leftover coals and burning them. The brown travel case was on the floor beside her. Suddenly, some papers had flown away, and she had quickly collected them. But I had seen one paper that got stuck in the rosebush. It was folded and had wrapped itself on a branch but was neatly hidden. I almost went to retrieve it and hand it to Ewa, but at the last moment, I decided

Tricked into Being

not to. Instead, I came forward and asked her, 'Why are you burning papers?'

'Because you touched the case with your dirty little hands.'

'I didn't touch any papers.'

'Just go away,' she'd said and continued with her task.

I had gone to the rosebush, got the paper out and grazed my hands with the thorns. *It must be an important paper*, I thought, *as Ewa hasn't burnt it.* So, I ran inside to my room, emptied my pencil box and placed the paper in it. Then, I walked nearby to where Kitty had been buried, dug up another hole and neatly buried the box.

At dinner that night, Ewa asked everyone if they had seen any papers stuck anywhere, as she was missing one.

Everyone answered they hadn't.

'Did you see any paper, Daphne?' she asked me.

I shook my head.

However, as soon as Nana and Mum went to clean the dishes, and Dad and Kevin left the table, she had turned to me and said, 'If you lie, you will be punished.'

'No, I won't.'

'Well then, something bad might happen. If you find it, bring it back to me. Okay?'

I nodded.

Now, remembering that event after all these years, I ran to the place half hoping the box would still be there and hoping it might not, because I was afraid of what I might read in that paper. It didn't take me too long to dig it out with the steel spoon I grabbed from the kitchen on my way out. I just had to pull some vegetation that had grown over it. The spoon hit the tin box, making a scraping sound.

The box was rusty, and it took a while to click it open. The lid separated itself, and inside, I found a neatly folded, yellowed piece of paper. I closed the box and took it to my room.

Gingerly, I opened the folded paper, which tore in some places, and placed it on my table. On the furthest right-hand side were the words: *page 2*.

Oh no! My first reaction was that of being disappointed. The first page was missing, but I began to read what I had in front of me. It was handwritten on both sides of the paper. Some words were blurred, because of moisture.

How I hate you now! You said training helps. It does not. I feel abandoned. Here's a list of what I've done for you:

- *Believed you and remained faithful to you. Remember the camp where I had to choose a young man and have sex with him so I could fall pregnant and give a baby to the country? That was the only time I feigned illness and did not do as asked. And when it was your turn, you took your pick of girls, not just once but several times. It hurt so much, yet you said it was expected of you and that if you did it, I'd be left alone.*
- *I learned English because you asked me to.*
- *I served the American family because of you.*
- *When you called me to India, I came without asking any questions.*
- *I believed you when you dropped a baby in my arms and packed me off to another country — promising you would join me.*

You married, and because you did not have a child, you wanted Juliana. I will never give her to you — neither Juliana nor any children she has in future. You will never find us.

Quickly I called Kevin to tell him about my discovery. Shaken, he said, 'To think you correctly recollected everything — and all because of your sense of smell and those sausages! Amazing!'

I was amazed too. Not with my sense of smell, but at Kevin's reaction. 'Kevin, don't you understand? The letter she wrote to Henri and didn't post ... and she never meant Henri to find us. If he is alive, we must find him and our real great nana ... and her twin,' I said. *Were they alive?*

'Yes. I've always wanted to visit India, and I had briefly mentioned it to Benny too.'

This was news to me. We said our goodbyes shortly and I disconnected the line.

I had to talk with Benny.

I was shown to the same conference room — the room where my life-changing moments had enfolded.

'You and Kevin have been talking behind my back, haven't you?' I asked Benny without answering his, 'Good morning, how are you?'

In smart formal corporate clothes, he looked ready to go out for a meeting. 'Strictly speaking, no,' he said after a small pause and giving me just that one look over. 'Kevin wants to go to Kolkata, to Mother Theresa's original convent, and he sees this visit as his God-given opportunity — under the pretext of finding family stories,' Benny said.

Kevin was a do-gooder, a sacrificial lamb. But this "opportunity" had come too soon.

'I'll get on with it. Leave it with me,' Benny had told him.

Benny would make all his arrangements.

'Tell me about you and Ewa. How did you meet, why did she choose you for this ... this task?' I asked, trying to check my rising anger.

He was clearly startled with my abrupt question. I startled myself. I hadn't meant to ask him about Ewa.

'Some other time,' he replied. 'Ewa believed she was tricked throughout her life. We met accidentally.'

Ewa was tricked? She had made fools of us all, including you, I longed to say. Yet, I stayed quiet. I felt he wanted me to ask the obvious question, just as I expected him to tell me more without asking. We left it unsaid, unheard.

'Will he be safe there?' I had to ask.

'He will. Some people known to me will keep an eye out for him,' he said. 'Even if you don't trust a lawyer.' He curled his lips.

A few days later, Kevin came home with a brown leather suitcase to place his meagre belongings and carry it all the way to another continent — to find our roots ... or to find himself, which was the part I didn't wish to know. What did people mean when they said they first needed to know themselves or find themselves before they moved on? Crazy!

'Brother Justin lent it to me,' he said, smiling down at the suitcase. 'Why buy a new one when I can make do with this one?'

'Well ... I hope it's strong. It looks old and worn,' I said.

The suitcase did look like it had seen many a travel. The corner brass caps were hollowed in places, and the scratch lines were easily viewable. 'Do the locks work?' I asked as I touched the case feeling its coarseness. I did not want the locks to work. He should have a new suitcase.

'Yes,' Kevin replied, still smiling, caressing it gently. 'It has travelled most continents except the one I'm taking it now to. Brother Justin insisted I take it, so the suitcase story completes itself. That of having travelled all around the world. It was used during war times.'

I'd lost my argument. War memories were as sacrosanct as folded hands in prayer.

The most important content of Kevin's suitcase was the other small old brown travel case with photocopies of Ewa's letters. Those letters that had uprooted our roots here in Brisbane. And the reason that Kevin was flying to the Indian subcontinent to Mumbai, previously known as Bombay — from where he would go to serve and experience first-hand a life of servitude in Mother Theresa's convent in Kolkata.

That was what he had meant that night when he'd said he needed to do something for himself.

1.17

We went to see Kevin off at the Brisbane Airport. Nana wept, begging him to look after himself, instructing that he drink boiled water and milk and not to eat spicy food and to call each night.

Mum merely repeated all that Nana said. Mum didn't know any other way.

I hugged Kevin when it was my turn. 'Take care,' I whispered. 'Once you're done at Kolkata, I'll come over and meet up with you, and we can look for our missing family links.'

'Why are you whispering?'

'Shush. Nana and Mum don't know that I'm thinking of going to India too, and it's not worth telling them yet.'

'All right. Please stay in touch with Benny.'

'Benny? Why?'

'I've asked him to keep in touch with my three favourite girls. No. Seriously. He is to be your Kevin for the time I'm away.'

'Not funny, Kevin. No one can take your place.'

'Agree. Absolutely.'

I turned, as I recognised the voice of the man himself. *What is he doing here?*

I let go of Kevin, and he in turn moved forward to greet Benny. 'Hey, Ben,' he said.

Ben?

'All set, I see,' said Benny.

Nana came forward and took both his hands in both of hers, saying, 'Thank you, Benny. These have been challenging times for us. Muh entrusted you with our family secret. I can now see why. We are grateful, and we will try our best not to vex you, but I am relieved to know you have our backs.'

'Any time,' he said. 'I won't replace Kevin,' he whispered to me. 'I don't see myself as your brother.'

'Ewa must have paid all his fees in advance,' I muttered and at once was greeted by three voices exclaiming, 'Daphne!'

The force of that three-voice shriek soberly silenced my mutinous thoughts. Mum turned towards me, her eyes pleading. So, I stopped, only to please her. 'Sorry,' I said, but I couldn't resist whispering to Benny, 'Not.'

Nothing more was said. But I saw his smile before he turned away.

The enormity of Kevin leaving us for the next few months hit me, and I again gathered him in for a tighter hug. No tears were shed, but I felt alone — and I was angered by everything, of course.

Kevin walked to the departure gates, and we waved until we could see him no more. The three of us — and even Benny — were lost in our own private thoughts as we began to walk out of the airport. Nana was sniffling. Mum did the same.

I forced myself not to cry. I succeeded.

Benny invited us all to join him at the closest tavern for wine and dinner, which endeared him more towards the two women. I tried to get out of it, saying I'd drive myself and pick them later, but Nana intervened, and Benny said the invite was for all three of us. So, I found myself joining them at the tavern.

I thought Nana and Mum would ask Benny questions — about Ewa, his own life and family. They didn't. I hoped Benny would volunteer. He didn't.

Red wine for the two, a tall glass of beer for himself, and a Moscato for me, some fries on the table. He made small talk with the other two women and ignored me completely. Not that I wanted to engage with him. He turned to the wall TV, which was playing a past rugby match, and was soon engrossed. There was an awkward silence at our table. It was as if we were all waiting for some divine intervention that would enable us to break the silence and talk as we were meant to.

I pushed aside my glass, walked to the counter, and got myself a vodka. I sat back at the table, and the Moscato remained untouched. Three pairs of eyes turned on me. I sipped some vodka and followed with a crispy fry. I offered the bowl of fries to Nana and Mum, placed it back on the table and continued to sip.

The silence continued. I saw Nana discreetly wipe a tear.

Pasta and pizza were ordered and eaten partially. I was on my third vodka. Finally, reaching for the Moscato, I gulped that down too. 'Shame to waste it,' I muttered. I also chomped on the remaining fries, which were cold and no longer crispy, but the bowl was left clean of them.

We left the tavern, and just before I could step into Benny's car, I threw up. I didn't apologise. Waiting and daring for anyone to say anything, I took the tissues Benny handed to me, cleaned myself as much as I could and sat in the car.

Benny walked back to the tavern and came out with a cleaner to clear the mess where his car was parked.

The ride back home was uneventful.

1.18

It was a beautiful, bright Friday afternoon as I walked in the Brisbane Botanic Gardens. I loved walking in the gardens each time I came to the city, and I made time to come here during my lunch break.

It was mid-March, and the colourful beds of tenderly and — yes — wisely planted flowers that had sprung all throughout spring were now no more. The pathways had crunchy dead leaves strewn about. Some of them browned and went mushy as they floated in the water spaces. Autumn's subtle warm air could be felt off and on. The cheery gardeners in their hi-vis vests were busy with their tools and readying the beds for the next season. They proudly spoke of their demanding work, if anyone seemed interested, and why they did what and how.

How simple life would be if we knew exactly when, where, and how to tweak nature so it could yield just what it delights in giving after receiving from us. I smiled and waved at the gardeners as I walked on the cobbled pathways, carefully avoiding spots where bird droppings were obvious. I was rewarded by a low whistle and beaming smiles from the group. It felt good.

I stopped midway to watch two kookaburras hanging on a slim rope-like branch of a tree. Below was a small pond. Each one was flying down, one at a time, swooping on the water surface and flying back to the hanging branch. They would flutter their wings, swinging, swooping on the water with such joyous abandon. When

I came closer, they flew higher up the tree, laughing raucously. Some toddlers were laughing close by too. And I laughed aloud, hoping my laughter would not be questioned by anyone as it mingled with theirs.

I felt happy. It was thanks to the sun and shine that was in our sunshine state of Queensland. Beautiful one day, perfect the next, as per the slogan.

Further on the pathway, spider silk swung gently in the breeze, and a stray yellow leaf floated, swaying to the ground, obstructed occasionally only by the shrubbery below. Above, a lone white cloud glided graciously across the blue skies, humming the continuity of a blessed day. It was written all over the skies … and on the ground, which pushed to sprout yet another blade of new grass.

My thoughts led me back to Ewa and Benny. I battled internally to see what it was that I couldn't figure out.

Ewa had been a bitter woman. Never, ever had I done as she had asked me to. But now that I didn't have to look into her eyes — those glassy blue eyes — I felt free but also confused.

Why had she singled me to find Henri? I had only wanted her dead, and all her stories to be dead with her. But what if she had lied about Henri? What if there was more — more about Nana that would impact the rest of us?

And that other letter from her to Henri? What a revelation that second page had been!

I knew Benny knew more. Why had Ewa chosen him to deal with all of this — with me?

Because Ewa had entrusted him with our family secrets, I didn't trust nor like him. And now, Kevin was in his grip too, because of his connection to the other country.

I left the kookaburras, spiders, the flower beds behind and continued walking in the gardens, no longer interested in the beauty outside but battling the beast inside, when I bumped into Benny.

He looked as startled as I was.

Annoyance must have shown in my eyes, as he raised his brows to question me.

Tricked into Being

I stepped aside to let him pass, but he suggested we walk together.

'Mr Lawyer, I don't like you,' I started, looking up at him, my arms folded. I had shocked him and myself too.

'I know you don't,' he answered. 'Ask away.'

'Ask what?'

'You want to know what I can tell you about Ewa.'

There was no denying it.

'Why did she come to you? How did you meet her first?'

'Let's sit on that bench there …' He pointed to one that was shaded with the thick branches of the banyan tree — one of the few wooden benches left in the gardens. The old wooden benches were now being replaced by iron, metallic ones. Painted green, of course, to blend in, but they were hard to sit on for longer periods, and the palings felt hard and gave a rustic smell to the fingers when rubbed. They were cold. They had never known life.

Reluctantly, as I followed him, I noted his black business suit. He looked tall and formidable. I peered at my black pants and beige top with a light, black jumper that I tightly covered myself in. The only common thing between us at that moment was the colour of our clothing: black.

He removed his pristine white handkerchief, dusted off a few twigs and dried leaves from the bench and then motioned me to sit down. He neatly folded the handkerchief and placed it beside him. Like a lawyer, I thought, he was covering every base.

'Tell me about Kevin, and I'll tell you about Ewa,' he said.

That was easy. I loved to talk about Kevin, and I told him so. How much I cared about him, how close we were, how good and noble he was, so completely self-sacrificing and always smiling at whatever life threw at him. However, it wasn't as if Kevin was a saint. Everyone loved him, I said, and he had this habit of turning every conversation, every feeling around with just his smile.

There had been four women who had thought the world of him, including Ewa in her own weird way.

'Kevin grew up without a male presence. Maybe that's why a part of his heart is more feminine, more appealing to all. He understands and feels pain,' I said to Benny. 'Although, he's always said to me that I act more like a man than a woman. Maybe that's why Ewa resented me, and I resented her more than anyone else,' I continued.

Benny listened to me without interrupting. It felt good.

'After Dad disappeared — presumed dead — Mum was on her own. I think she grew tired as the years went by. Afterwards, she only did what her mum … my nana asked her to do. And Nana, of course, wanted to please Ewa. And so, the cycle continued.'

I stared into nothingness, silently wondering how Mum would have coped with two young children. 'Kevin, of course, did everything to help all three of them in their chores. He took on the role of a handyman as well as a driver, who took them shopping. For me, he occasionally became a tutor. "Don't waste your time with her," I had overheard Ewa say once to him as he'd mentioned he would be sitting with me and helping me with my homework. "She's not interested in studying. She'll join the arts and take the angry actress roles in some theatre."' I grinned at the thought and continued, 'Kevin had smiled and hugged her — something that Ewa allowed only Kevin to do. We three women could never hug her.'

When I lapsed into silence, thinking of those times, Benny accepted those silent moments, like as if he was imagining the scenes.

I talked again. '"Nadee," Kevin said, "she's my little sis. She'll be okay." Nadee was the word that Kevin used for her. Mum had asked him to call Ewa 'GG' — great grandmother — and the word he came up with was Nadee. Ewa loved being called Nadee and not GG. I was asked to call her Nadee too, but my word for her was "Ayeya". I didn't speak much with anyone except with Kevin. I felt safe with him, and somehow, I also wanted to protect him. I noticed other girls wanting to be with me because of him. I didn't want to share Kevin with anyone else. It was I who told them, without thinking at the time, "Kevin is to become a priest." I did this only so they would leave him alone. But Kevin thought my words were prophetic. He truly was thinking on those lines. "You can't be serious," I had told him. "You expect me alone to put up with three older women? I'm leaving home too!" I never did, of course. And Kevin embraced his vocation.' Now, I was breathless, realising that it had been so easy to tell Benny about Kevin.

'So, you're both very close to each other,' Benny said.

I nodded. 'We're twins. Of course, we're very, very close,' I agreed. 'Now, tell me about your relationship with Ewa.'

1.19

'I met Ewa in unusual circumstances. Three years ago,' he began. 'I was on my way to an open house but was running late. Ewa was at the pedestrian crossing after buying the newspaper from your local newsagent. It had been raining, and I was distracted, knocked her, and braked. She fell on her hip but insisted on getting up.'

She should have died that day, I thought at once. Benny wouldn't have been in our lives, and Ewa would have gone three years earlier. She wasn't your dear old lady crossing the street. But he assured me that she was one that day. He'd stopped, helped her, and offered to take her to the hospital. She'd refused.

Ewa had never visited a doctor her entire life. We knew that she preferred to heal herself. She didn't trust them, she often said. Of course, none of us knew then what we knew now. She had been in hiding all throughout her life. She was paranoid of being found out because of her bloodline. And ours.

So, Benny had given her his business card, assuring her she could call him any time.

'I heard back from her within the month. She came to my office just once. On all other occasions, we would meet inside a library or at a local park. The library would be during those times when there was a need for paperwork to be done.'

He was looking at the two water dragons engaged in a territorial fight, their torsos red and their tails lashing. It lasted for a while until they hissed their way into the nearby bushes. He had remained silent while observing them, and so had I. When they disappeared, he leant forward and turned towards me. 'If she wanted to talk with me, it would be the local park. Or here in these gardens. This bench,' he said softly while looking intensely at me.

I stood up trembling with anger, finding the bench suddenly sullied. 'You both have sat on this very bench?' I asked, my voice shaky.

He stood up too. 'It isn't a private park nor a private bench,' he said.

'It's been my best spot to read, each time I've come here,' I almost shouted. 'You both have tainted it from now on.'

'It was her favourite spot too. After our talks. To continue reading.'

'Ha. Ewa didn't read anything except the weekend newspaper.'

'She did. She read books on the two wars. She was well informed about Germany, the United States and India too.'

'India? And none of us knew she'd been reading!'

'You both didn't want the other to know about your passion for reading.'

I glared at him. 'I don't read fiction,' I said, not knowing why I had to say that. I did read fiction sometimes. But I didn't want him to place me and Ewa on the same platform.

'Neither did Ewa. She read history — about post-Second World War. You read more about the glen and the glade. And everything in between. The gums, the koalas, and the rainforests. Correct?'

He knew everything, of course.

'And some fictional stories too,' he whispered.

Sighing loudly, I sat on the bench again.

Seeing me seated, he sat down too.

Yes, I was a typical recluse, deeply buried in my books. And my dislike of Ewa.

Siting there beside him, I remembered a day at school when I took a surprise dictation test and got all my spellings correct. Proudly, I had shown it to Mum, who told me that the more I read, the more I'd get better at my spellings. At that time, I wasn't a huge fan of books, and I had said I didn't like to read.

Ewa had overheard and said that Mum was wasting precious time in encouraging me to read. As usual, Mum didn't say anything.

I had walked into the school library the following day, picked up several books, and there was no stopping after that.

I always hid my books from Ewa. I placed them in my shoeboxes and covered them with my footwear. I believed she wouldn't check my shoeboxes, which were just white polystyrene foam boxes we got from our local grocer and that lay beneath my bed.

It was strange that I remembered little incidents like these at such times. Yet, the bigger ones continued to elude me.

We continued sitting quietly on the bench, until a bush turkey came close by, followed by a white ibis, and I came back to the present. Both were disinterested in us as we were in them. They moved away. A few moments later, a tired-looking water dragon moved triumphantly and stood still soaking the sun. A winner of the fight earlier.

'Many secrets lie open,' Benny said after a while. 'And there is always a winner in a fight. Even if he's self-declared.'

The deep melancholy ended as we both heard the plop of a bird dropping and saw the gluey grey and white mush dribble in the gap of the wooden palings of the bench in the space between us. I was surprised to see Benny pull his neatly folded handkerchief and wipe away the gooey stuff, carefully wiping the inner sides of the palings too. He balled it, walked to the nearest rubbish bin and binned it.

We sat down again, avoiding the middle of the bench, which was still wet.

'You don't have a handkerchief anymore,' I said, which somehow sounded silly, even to me.

'I've a few more in my car,' he said. 'Just as I've an extra set of clothing.'

'Of course,' I said. He was a lawyer. Always prepared.

He was circling his black ring, looking thoughtful. 'This ring is a good luck charm,' he advised, and nothing more was said.

Just then, a butterfly whizzed past, followed by a bee, and I raised my hand to brush it off. It disappeared. The butterfly joined the others. The vibrant colours brought a smile to my lips. When I turned, I found Benny's eyes on me.

'I was as serious as that swallowtail butterfly,' he said.

'That wasn't a swallowtail. It was a brown butterfly. Didn't you see its wings … the …' I stopped midway. He had baited me, and I fell for it. His deep brown eyes twinkled. I heard a soft laugh. I turned away, annoyed. He was as evasive as I expected.

'I'm a lawyer. My job is to help my clients find the best possible solution. I'm doing what Ewa engaged me to do.'

'Really? I think you lie. You know very well she expected you to tell me everything.'

'Not really. Ewa only asked me to help with things, and I was—'

'She mentioned you in the last letter. "Benny will tell you more",' I quoted. His face lost some colour, and I felt a 'gotcha' moment. I almost placed my hands on my hips, gloating. 'Caught between your own lies?' I asked, laughing a little.

He looked at me very strangely. We were strangers. *What am I doing here, with this man?*

He was a rich, successful lawyer. I was a public servant with no real ambition. I was just a liver of a life that continued to roll in its zig zag pattern. Like our Brisbane River turning and, in unexpected places, snaking through, occasionally flooding during heavy rains, creating fear, panic and discussions leading to political disharmony. Who was to be blamed? Water will always make its own way and life will go on.

But why do I assess us? This was a totally different terrain for me. Now I understood what it meant to be socially awkward. I groaned inward, wanting to disappear.

'All right,' he said. 'Let's talk.'

Surprised, there — on that wooden bench in the garden, where bird droppings had run off through the gap, which was wiped clean with his handkerchief — I heard a strange story from a stranger about Ewa and why she had entrusted Benny with her secrets.

'This ring,' he said, 'I wear it to remind myself that I've to be cautious and alert all the time.' He smiled as he removed the ring and placed it in my hand.

I felt the deadness of the metal, but it was warm in my hands. Well, it had to be because he had been wearing it until he handed it over to me. Observing it closely, I realised it was a brass ring. I imagined it lying in my hands right from its origin from the rock, melted, soldered, and processed; sized, sold and on to Benny's finger.

'It was Ewa's idea.'

'What!' I exclaimed, hating Ewa, Benny, the ring and its processors too.

'Yes. Strange.'

There was that word again. 'Strange' — a string of shapeless strangles.

'The accident. I was doing 70 in a 60-speed zone and had to brake quickly at the pedestrian crossing. I almost got her,' he said, shoulders shaking as if in fear. 'She knew that I was a lawyer, and that I had been rushing. A speeding fine would damage my professional image. So, to make a long story short, she let me go only after I gave her my business card and promised to meet with her later. Simple.'

'She was always manipulative. But surely this story is not so simple? Speeding, seriously?' I asked.

'It's true,' he said. 'Big things in life usually begin with small, simple things. It was the first time for me — to meet a woman who'd caught me speeding and be wary about her.'

'Why wary?' I asked.

'Because she could easily report me.'

I had walked into that one. I felt silly. 'Somehow, you manage to make me feel silly,' I muttered.

He smiled. 'I hope not.'

There is more. This is not just about a speeding fine.

But Ewa was shrewd, I told him. Surely, before she entrusted him with her secrets, she'd learned about his?

'Yes, but nothing dramatic. I know where I come from,' he said as his lips twitched.

'Let me guess. South European?'

'Not entirely. I landed here as a student. From India.'

India? My green eyes clashed with his deep brown ones, and his mouth twitched again.

'Fourteen years ago. Since then, I've not been back there.'

'Why not? Your family … folks must be missing you?' I asked.

'No. None that matter anyway. I travelled on a Portuguese passport at the time.'

'So, you are European.' I stated.

'Part Portuguese ancestry. I was born and raised in India. But before I tell you more, I've a small request,' he said.

'Yes?'

'Will you please stop calling me Mr Lawyer?'

I laughed. Soon, I covered my mouth, knowing I shouldn't have laughed. But there was a thrilly thread of knowing I had rattled him. 'But you are a lawyer,' I argued, just because I wanted to.

'Benny would be preferable. Thank you. Unless I start calling you Miss Miffed? We'd be even then.'

'Don't you dare,' I said, quite offended. 'All right. Agreed. Atoned, milord.' I couldn't resist adding the last bit. Inside, I loved the feeling of pure mischief.

Benny said he didn't have a big story about his past — only that his parents had died when he was young. He had an uncle and aunt who were forced to bring him up as part of the family, as that's how it was done. His aunt disliked Benny because she didn't want him to share in the family's wealth. He was raised with three cousin brothers, and the dislike was mutual.

He told me that he always dreamt of leaving his ancestral home and living in another continent. So, as soon as he finished his school years, he bargained with them to part with some money, signed some documents that he wouldn't have any claim to the family fortune and left that country to come to a faraway land. He didn't know what he'd be studying, but as he had signed those documents, he decided to study law.

'Simple. Uncomplicated story, as I said. They didn't want me. I left. Now that I've built a life here, I don't miss the one I left behind.'

There was an uncomfortable silence, mainly because I didn't know what to say. I could understand dislike, hatred for one person, but I couldn't imagine a child living in a household where not a single person liked him. No one to hug. No one to care for. No one to confide in. Was he still searching for himself — asking the all-important 'why' question of life?

Law was a perfect profession for Benny. He was focused on what mattered.

Ewa must have noted that too.

'Was it the India connection that she singled you out for?' I asked.

'Maybe.'

He wouldn't tell me anything more. I think he was remembering parts of his life he'd left behind, and maybe there were painful memories as bookmarks in the pages of a bulky, burdensome book for him. Who knew?

We all had burdens to bear. It wasn't the right time for me to ask Benny what his burdens were. I stuck to our subject matter. 'What's in it for you? I mean … I'm wondering about that invoice we'll receive in the mail from you.'

'You need not worry about that. I—'

'Why? Are we a charity case?'

'It's been taken care of.'

'By Ewa?'

He was silent. This was getting a bit mysterious, and I told him so.

He got up abruptly, which I thought was rude. 'I must go. I've an important meeting soon,' he said.

I got up too.

He came closer and placed both his hands on my shoulders. I felt a little squeeze. 'Listen, Daphne,' he said, his deep brown eyes forcing mine to look up at him. 'I know you dislike me. But believe me ... I won't act in any way that will hurt you or your family.' He turned and walked away while I was left with more confusing, contradictory, contemplations. He didn't reveal how his fees would be paid, which made me feel nervous. Funny thing was, I believed it for the first time — that he wouldn't hurt any of us. Why would he? We were all strangers.

It was also the first time he'd touched me. The tiny squeeze I felt startled me. It felt different to the squeezes Kevin gave me.

It bothered me — all this secrecy.

Ewa had held a big one and given it away only after she died. Benny had his own secrets. Kevin was secretive in his own way. I still struggled to understand why he chose priesthood. Who was the human element in his life who pushed him towards it? Ewa? Because Henri hated Catholic priests? But why?

Kevin wouldn't discuss the institution — the Catholic Church. He spoke about the Bible and religion. But I wasn't as strong a believer as he was.

Nana and Mum believed their lives were open and everyone knew everything about them. Yet, they too shut up when I asked questions about the men in their lives. Except for their wedding photos, none other existed — with the men in them.

My grandfather, who went to work one day and returned as a body. My father, who went bush walking and never returned. And these were the men they had married. They never spoke about their extended families. Did we have any cousins? Kevin and I didn't think we did. It was as if everyone wanted to live in the moment and simply live. No questions to be asked and none to be answered. As the years went by, I had stopped wondering.

But the secrets lay lurking loosely in some memories, as some often do. I believed it was called 'the subconscious mind'.

Did I have any secrets? I didn't think so. Then why was I the way I was? Distrustful of everyone. I supposed I could have gone to a counsellor who'd put me to sleep and make me talk and record it all. *I wonder if that could happen to me?* I was smiling as this thought came to my mind, but I knew I wouldn't go to a counsellor. I didn't want my life to be an open book for anyone who knew how to read, to read it. Although hardly anyone would be interested to know what lay in there. I was ordinary; the world was strewn with ordinary girls like me.

Big things in life usually begin with small, simple things. Benny's words echoed. I wondered how long the small things would continue until the big ones hit me.

With these uneasy thoughts, I returned to my workplace.

1.20

Benny frequently visited us. He kept his promise to Kevin, Nana said, of keeping an eye on us. Nana and Mum fussed over him as they would over Kevin each time he'd join us for lunch or dinner.

'They're treating you as they'd treat Kevin,' I told him, feeling indulgent myself.

'I don't mind,' he said, 'as long as you don't treat me like Kevin too.' His eyes were serious as he looked at me. I felt a strange flutter in my heart.

At the table, his hands — or rather, his fingers — irritated me. The strange slim ring that was there sometimes and sometimes wasn't. His nails that were always perfectly trimmed. Somehow, I always thought of those fingers holding a pen to sign something. Strangely, I never saw those fingers holding a pen. He typed everything into his phone.

His firm's website gave little information about his career, his area of specialisation, the awards he'd won. There were images of him at a few social functions.

I wondered how he functioned as a professional in his office or in the courts. Formidable. He was self-made and aloof. Friendless?

And so, I was surprised when unexpectedly, he asked me for a favour. 'Really? From me?' I asked, teasing.

'Juliana, I'm taking Daphne for a short drive,' he said to Nana with his eyes on me.

'Really? How about asking me first?' I queried.

'Will you refuse?'

I pretended to consider.

'Take her off our hands, Benny. It's time I had some time-off,' said Nana as she winked.

'Nana!' I rolled my eyes, and picking up my bag, I walked towards the door. 'Come on. Let's go for a drive,' I said to Benny, who got up at once, waived Nana and Mum goodbye and joined me outside walking towards his car.

Once seated and belted, he started driving. After a while, I looked at him. His face was set, keenly concentrating on the road and the bends in the road ahead. Speckled sunbeams spirited through the windscreen as we drove through our leafy suburb. He was quiet, like the quietness of those who silently battled inside first before the words were let out. His hands were steady on the wheel, and he drove straight ahead.

'So, what is it?' I asked.

'I'd like you to come with me tonight … for an office do.'

'What!' I almost jumped.

That was the moment he turned to look at me for a moment and turned his attention back to the road. He stopped at the lights.

'Why?' I asked him. And I answered my own question. 'Because Kevin asked you to.' I sighed and turned my head away, looking outside. He was clearly feeling sorry for me. Desolate, desperate Daphne. No fun in life. Burdened by boredom. Oh no! I was beginning to feel sorry for myself now. 'Do you feel sorry for me?' I asked.

'No, certainly not.' He expressed surprise. 'But if that's what you choose to believe, I can't change your mind. Seriously, I'd like you to come with me.'

He wasn't a mind-reader. And I refused to let him look into mine.

'All right. I will.' I surprised myself. But the joy I felt seeing him surprised with my answer would always remain with me.

'Can we go now and sort a gift first? And some flowers too?'

There's to be a gift and flowers? For a girlfriend? I didn't ask.

He switched on the radio. I assumed he didn't wish to talk anymore. I began to panic. Daphne's doldrum drive: impulsive first and regretful later.

I was not a shopper, and retail therapy was not something that I ever indulged in. Because of Ewa.

According to Ewa, I'd grow up to be a typical girl — a money-waster only interested in my own looks and life. Defiantly, I had begun to save every dollar. As a result, I didn't know much about serious shopping expeditions. I shopped for the basics and out of necessity.

'She'll be a party girl. I tell you now, she will have a boyfriend soon, run away and become an unwed mum.' Ordinary thinking in ordinary families, but Ewa had made it sound like a curse.

How would I explain all this to Benny?

Why, oh why does Ewa continue to invade my thoughts?

We picked up two gifts from a jewellery store: a pair of cufflinks and a gold bracelet. He asked me if they were okay. The price tags had my head wheeling. I simply nodded.

We stopped for a takeaway coffee.

Before starting the engine, he turned around and said, 'Now, I hope you take this in the right spirit … but would you like to pick a party dress or something for this evening?' He eyed my jeans and T-shirt.

I looked blankly first and then shook my head. I hadn't thought about that at all. I didn't own a party dress except some 'Sunday best'. I didn't tell him that, though. Instead, I said it was all good.

He drove me back home.

Nana and Mum were delighted when I told them about Benny's invite. High time I partied, said Nana.

Mum got me a few of her own dresses to choose from, and there was some excitement. Nana said Cinderella was going to the ball. It was all very embarrassing. Nana said I should forget about my ill feelings for Benny and be supportive. And live in the moment and enjoy life. And learn, so I could begin a social life.

Evening came and I was ready. My shoulder-length, wavy hair had been brushed and was shining. I'd curled a little tendril at the side of my face — all on my own. I'd also put on some makeup — mascara, the works — Mum helped, of course. She gave me a delicate pearl necklace with matching earrings and a bracelet.

'They belong to you now,' she said. 'My engagement gift from your dad.'

'And the only one she received from him,' said Nana.

'What? Why?' I asked.

Mum fumbled to answer, but Nana said, 'Because you and Kevin came before their first wedding anniversary, and he suddenly had three mouths to feed.'

My dress was midnight blue in soft sateen. A simple straight cut just reaching my knees. The dress hugged me. I wore Mum's black pumps.

I looked at the stranger in the mirror. I felt self-conscious. I felt beautiful. Like Cinderella.

It was good. No, it was nice. That's what Benny said when I sat in his car. Just 'nice'.

'So, I will do?' I asked.

'Fishing?'

I smiled; a little cheeky.

'Care to share?'

'Just wondering if I hadn't tried to dress up. Supposing I had just worn jeans and a T-shirt, what would you have done?' I saw his lips twitch.

'But you're dressed up. Thank you for that.'

Why did he make me feel so gauche?

1.21

Benny introduced me as a friend. I was nervous initially, but soon, my nervousness left me. It happened instantly because the girl who I met at his office once, recognised me and said, 'Daphne? You look so beautiful. I wouldn't have recognised you, if not for your eyes!'

I fitted in. It was easy from there on. Benny stayed by my side. When I got a chance, I whispered, 'Keeping an eye on me? You afraid I'll mess up your chance of a partnership?'

'Keeping an eye on you — yes. But not for the reason you seem to think so,' he answered.

He'd been offered a partnership, and a senior partner announced Benny's acceptance.

I also realised there had been no reason for him to take me along with him. There were so many beautiful young women working in his office and known to him. So why had he? Because he wanted to? No, he certainly felt sorry for me, I concluded. Somehow, all excitement ebbed out of me, but I moved with the party flavour, until it was time to leave.

It was nearing midnight. Back in the car driving on the Bruce Highway, I began to feel sleepy. Benny was whistling softly.

I must have dozed because when I drowsily opened my eyes, Benny had stopped the car and was trying to wake me.

'I'm delivering Cinderella back home.'

'Oh,' I muttered clumsily.

'Thank you for coming out with me tonight, Daphne.'

'Uh ... thank you for taking me out.' I was fully awake.

'And to answer your earlier question about what I'd have done had you not party-dressed,' he said, as he reached behind and removed a shopping bag. He handed it to me, saying, 'I'd have asked you to change into this. Your nana and mum would have agreed.' He winked.

Speechless, I took the bag.

'For you.' He got out of the car and came around, opening my door. 'Thank you again. We'll catch-up later.'

I nodded.

'Sleep well,' he said, smiling as he placed his hands on my shoulders and gave a gentle squeeze.

'Nice,' I muttered and walked slowly to the door. When I turned around, his car was moving towards the main road.

1.22

Transforming. I loved this word. It spoke to me like as if it belonged with me and I belonged to it.

Professionally, I signed up for learning sessions and enrolled for courses in elementary accountancy. I had a thing for numbers, I put in more hours; I even ran coffee errands at my workplace. At morning teas, I brought something more than chocolate cookies that I used to earlier. My arms were no longer folded in front of me, and my eyes were no longer looking down at the worn carpet. I smiled more. I was the first one to come in and the last to leave.

Earlier, I'd been content being a wallflower. Our unit encouraged mediocrity; new ideas were shunned, which suited me at that time.

These days, I wanted to be engaged and understanding of everything that went around.

Outwardly, I'd changed my wardrobe and bought new clothes for myself. I wore brighter colours, learned to use makeup subtly — experimented even — and was interested in my appearance. Simple changes.

On Friday nights, I joined the team for drinks and nibbles.

I wanted to share these exhilarating moments of happy hours at the pub with Kevin, and one Friday night, I accidentally dialled Benny.

I apologised, but he said that since I had already called him, I had better tell him the reason for my call. When I did — with not so much excitement — there was silence.

I was about to end the call when he said, 'Don't take the train tonight. I'll pick you up when you're ready to leave.'

'It's okay, Benny. Bob, a colleague, will be dropping me off at the train station.'

Silence. Then, 'I'll pick you up. Let me know when you're ready.'

'But, Benny, I don't want you to go out of your way, and Bob is—'

'I'll get on with it. Leave it with me.' He disconnected.

Oh well! How rude.

I was riding on a high now, never knowing before how it felt to be noticed, to be complimented. I had a couple of wines and texted Benny. I was ready to be picked up.

I was happily tipsy, but Bob's hand was around my waist as we walked from the pub. I liked the feeling. Of being held. I let him.

That's how Benny saw us. He gave a short, sharp honk, and I quickly let go of Bob to jump in the car.

Because I felt chatty and wanted to impress Benny, I told him about my free drinks and the compliments I received. I knew that later I'd feel silly about everything that I'd told him; maybe a little gauche and embarrassed. But at that moment, I felt like a teenager who was heady with her own success. It was the wine.

He remained quiet and concentrated on his driving.

I continued to be chatty. Every Friday night, I told him, I got invited to join the team for drinks. 'I'm feeling more self-confident,' I said to him. 'I'm transforming myself. And do you know, I've printed the word TRANSFORMING in bold capitals on single sheets and pasted it on the walls of my room and in my bathroom. I look at the word often and let it sink deep inside of me.'

He was still quiet, so I added, 'I know it sounds silly, but I don't care. Ewa is no longer around to tear those sheets off the walls. She has no power to belittle me.' He nodded.

After that, I shared what I remembered about how Ewa affected my self-confidence, and I shared some stories, even though I wondered about the promise I made to myself that I'd stop thinking of her. And I concluded by saying that Ewa refused to let go of me even after her death.

'Maybe you're refusing to let go of her,' he replied.

After that, I kept quiet.

Silently, the drive continued until he dropped me home and saw me at the door.

In my tipsy state, I tiptoed towards Nana's room. I found her weeping, seeking some solace in the arms of Mum. They were both in the room, sitting on Nana's bed.

'I never, ever expected this. It must have been very hard for her to bring me up and keep me safe. No wonder she never spoke about my father. But (more tears and sniffles), she did give me a good life. She kept me safe, and she did all the right things by me. She took on the role of a mother and a father, for my sake. She could have easily decided to give me up or dump me somewhere. Who was my birth mother? Where is she? Oh my God! Who—'

It was at that moment that I got involved.

Moments. Moments that have affected my life. Moments that have made me make quick decisions, and momentarily have I regretted them. Life's cruel moments; life's decisive, disciplinary, derelict moments too.

I stood in the doorway, unsteady, my eyes fiery. 'I'll find out, Nana. I'll find out who your mum and dad were. I'll go to India,' I announced.

They both looked at me.

'You're drunk,' Mum said softly, coming to me.

'Leave her. It's good to see her drunk,' said Nana, despite her tears as she held onto Mum's hand and stopped her.

I moved unsteadily around the bed and sat down on the other side. When I looked at Nana, I blinked, rubbed my eyes, and stared into hers again. She was looking as though she were assessing me.

She wiped her tears and said, 'Then go now and find out. I may not live long enough to know about my family. Muh — Ewa — must have a reason to ask you to do it. As it is, we've not been too lucky with our menfolk in our lives,' she said, clearly alluding to my grandfather and my father, and her own father as well. Kevin, too. Same as Ewa had done.

I held her hand. She looked at Mum. But Mum was looking at one of the curved rockers on Nana's rocking chair. I turned to look at the spot where her eyes lay transfixed. I rubbed my eyes. A common spider was halfway through weaving a web. I got up and took the few steps towards the rocking chair. Placing my foot closest to the corner of the rocker, I tugged at the web, and with my foot, I crushed the spider. Grabbing a tissue off the table, I cleared all evidence and binned it. I took my place back on Nana's bed. By this time, I had become more focused, my tipsiness disappearing steadily. Mum's trance broke.

Mum, who had not shown interest in anything over all these years, was reluctant for me to get involved or go anywhere. Surprising. 'She's too young. She's never left Brisbane,' she said.

'Muh was younger ... she travelled across continents. And with a baby that wasn't her own.'

'She won't know what to do. She speaks only one language.'

'She's smarter than we all think her to be. She's brave. She's battled with Muh all her life. Both of us know that. And we did nothing to help her.'

'But, Mum, we don't know anyone there. Daphne may not be safe.'

'She'll find a way. Her instincts are strong. Her head is in the right space. Or is it yourself you are worried about?' asked Nana, her gaze piercing at Mum.

Yes, Mum was worried about herself. It would be only Nana and Mum once I left. What would Mum do to keep herself busy?

As they continued talking, a fearsome, fearless momentary madness began to take root in me. Excitement and dread. Nana believed more in me. Nana was less fearful. I'd not let her down.

'Just promise me this: that you'll talk with Kevin first,' said Mum.

'And with Benny,' said Nana.

I nodded, said goodnight, and left the room.

1.23

I called Kevin early the next morning. 'I'm not going to wait any longer. I'm coming to India and find Nana's family links,' I told him.

'So soon? Wait awhile,' was his response.

I could wait, but only for a few more days, I told him. Nana and Mum would get anxious more with uncertainty rather than my travelling, I said.

He also wanted to talk to Benny, which I expected, but it annoyed me. Why, I asked him, did we have to bring Benny into everything that we did?

Kevin said I needed to be careful. That I had replaced my hatred for Ewa with my dislike for Benny.

I told him to manage his own life and leave me to live my own.

Benny took his responsibilities very seriously. He kept in touch regularly with Nana and Mum, and sometimes with me — depending on his mood.

Next Friday morning, he called me saying he had tickets for Sunday's footy that week and would I join him. I wasn't a huge fan of the game, and I hadn't been to a match at Suncorp Stadium since I left high school. I didn't want to say no, but I didn't want to appear too eager either.

'Nana and Mum … they might want to—'

'I'll call you back. Leave it with me.'

Leave what with him?

Five minutes later, he called. 'All settled. I've got four tickets in all.'

'Benny, I'll have to ask them first.'

'I just did. They're joining us. Be ready by 2pm.' He disconnected the call.

Mighty Crickey!

I reached home to find a super excited Nana. Mum was too, in her own way. They were sorting their clothes — what to wear, which hat to put on, sunglasses, should they wear walking shoes?

When Benny showed up on Sunday to pick us up, the excitement was uncontrollable.

'Did you get both the flags?' Nana asked Benny as soon as she got in the car.

'Yes. Red and black.' He grinned.

'What do you need flags for, Nana?' I asked.

'Silly. To wave, what else? I'm not going to take any sides. When the red team scores, I'll wave the red flag. When the black team does, I'll wave the black flag. Queenslander! Queenslander! Queenslander!' she yelled.

'There's a red and a black team?'

'No. They are my names for each team. Like a pack of cards. Red and black. Easy to remember.'

'Very clever, Nana!' I beamed at her. 'It's been years since I went there,' I said. 'And you, Mum? When did you last visit?'

Nana jumped in, saying, 'Oh. She had a chance. She didn't take it. Years ago.'

'Mum!' said my mum to hers, clearly distressed.

'Why didn't you go, Mum?' I asked.

'Because Muh stopped her. And I didn't help her either. Anyway, let's forget all that. Benny, I want two beers and hot fries.'

I was seeing a different side to Nana.

When we arrived at the stadium, I was amazed at the big crowd, the arena, the seats, the big TV screens — everything. It was as if several thousands were breathing in and out at the same time. The air was heavy with eager onlookers of every age. It was easy to be one with the crowd.

Nana trudged along with her two flags. Mum followed quietly behind her, and I walked by myself, taking in everything. Benny led us to our seats, and we seated ourselves — Benny, Nana, Mum and me.

Each time there was a try or a score, there were loud shouts and claps and people raising their fists in the air. At times, the whole stadium erupted with 'booooooo'. And Nana pulled out one of her flags and waved.

The greatest surprise for me was watching Benny's reactions. He'd stand up, raise his fist and shout at the top of his voice. Excited. A different man. At times, I was sure he didn't know we were there too, although he looked at Nana and helped her with her flags.

And of course, there were bleeding noses, broken arms and frenzied falling over of the players from both sides.

Nana and Mum had enjoyed the day. Benny was now a clear favourite; he was also a footy fan. He said he'd been his school's football team captain.

Had I misjudged him? Had I transferred my hatred for Ewa onto him? Was he to be trusted, after all? Yet another puzzle remained to be solved.

And each day afterwards, I realised I had missed so much in life. Small, everyday things. I was blinded to everything good, due to everything ugly because of Ewa's evilness.

1.24

It was a Saturday morning, and I lay curled in bed, my mind wandering as I thought again about the reel of my life as it was playing now. Ewa had died and a new man had entered our lives. We now had several reasons to live unbored lives. We wanted to know our blood family; we had to prepare ourselves for more relatives; we also had to accept that we might not find anything and get back to our lives with all questions unanswered. But we had to try. And I'd be at the forefront of this new search.

I got out of bed and looked out of the window to see grey skies. It would rain again. Brushing my teeth, washing my face, I changed into a black T-shirt and yellow shorts and went towards the kitchen to make some tea. The house was silent.

I held my cup of tea tightly in both my hands, as I liked to feel the warmth of that hot cup seeping through my palms. Outside the window, I could see the lawn. Brooding silence greeted me. No new grass shoots had sprung up jostling for space. There were patches of yellow instead.

Further down, the majestic gums were trying to reach the skies. Autumn leaves were falling and baring the trees. The peeling paperbark, refusing to be rushed to fall, continued to hang on threads of hope. Why couldn't it fall gracefully and accept that its time was over, that it had to make way for the other, newer, younger covering? I sighed.

I had many questions. No answers. Was I weird?

Kevin had left Kolkata and was on his way to Balachadi. He called and said that while his experiences in Kolkata had been life-changing, he'd decided it wasn't the place for him.

'Why?' I asked him.

'Well, there are plenty of helpers who come and go. But I've realised, I'm no nursemaid. Being in a hospital continuously is overwhelming … now that I've seen what it is.' What had he seen?

He sent a video to show us — the nuns at work or prayer; the ever-increasing long queues of people waiting to be fed; the diseased bodies. It was depressing. I pretended to notice and placed my *oohs* and *ahhs* appropriately in my responses to him. No, this wasn't what he'd like to do. I agreed with him, secretly hoping he would now get on with the important task. Once he'd start that, I could quickly join him.

Benny and Kevin were in touch with each other. Benny chatted with Mum and Nana too. Not with me as much, which was fine, truly. How could anyone force someone's attention?

But because I needed to be needed, I volunteered to read to my colleague's grandmother in her hospital bed at the Redcliffe Hospital — one Friday night. Nana and Mum were pleased.

Funny Friday nights when many hurried to catch the happy hour that came with Friday night drinks.

And as the night progressed, a random ambulance could be heard squealing, followed by fire and emergency service staff. Poor paramedics were cautious with a wounded fool who had had too much of a drink and was fool enough to get punched. He wasn't the problem, of course. It was the Friday night, when siren sounds sometimes sounded suspicious.

I was in the waiting area in the hospital, wondering when my 'patient' would wake, so I could go up the room and start reading to her, when I saw the glass doors opening and yet another distraught, dishevelled, drab woman walking past and queuing up, clearly wondering whether to jump the queue and plead the urgency of her case or join as a walk in. Noticing all eyes on her, she decided to join the queue.

'Another case. Must be the daughter,' whispered the woman sitting next to me.

'Shush' I said. 'She's in tears.'

'Yes. The ones you see hanging and about to fall. A thousand more never come out. The tears, I mean,' she said.

I turned to look at her then — the woman sitting next to me. I had seen her somewhere before. I remembered, not because of her face nor her eyes nor the numerous rings her fingers held, nor the royal-blue dress she wore. I had noticed her hair. Her long, silvery hair, which she had tied with a black hair tie and brought forward, the collective strands now partly resting between her breasts and reaching right below the helm of her dress.

Of course, I remembered excitedly. There were three of them — the great nana, nana, and mum. They had been sitting in the front pew at Mass one afternoon in Saint Stephens Cathedral. Each of them had very long hair. I had been fascinated to see such long hair, deciding it must be a genetic thing.

'I think I've seen you before …' I began.

'You look familiar, but I don't think we've met,' she added.

We began to sum up each other.

Her forehead was large. She had pulled the end of her ponytail and started twisting it between her heavily ringed fingers. Her nails were neatly manicured, polished with a shimmering oyster-pink shade. There were aging lines on her skin. 'The hair. It runs in our family. All women have long hair. But we grey earlier, too,' she said. 'I'm Rosetta.' She left her ponytail end and extended her hand.

'Daphne,' I said, taking her hand in mine.

We smiled.

'There are three roses in this hospital right now. We could always check at reception, but I think, she'll throw us out.'

'Three roses?' I asked.

'Three of us. Ella Rose is my mum. I'm Rosetta, and Rosebud is my daughter. The fourth rose is my beautiful rose, my granddaughter, Rosalyn. We live in Roseville ... uh, in the Glass House Mountains,' she said. She told me four generations lived under the same roof, although Rosalyn lived in Melbourne but visited them sometimes. 'Ask me what's the fascination with roses,' she said.

I smiled and asked the question.

'We are all named as roses. And our house is called Rose Haven. It's on Rose Lane. No one can miss it. There are rose plants everywhere.' She laughed.

No. She's having a go at me. Rose? Rose Haven? Rose Lane? Roseville? Ella Rose, Rosetta, Rosebud, Rosalyn? She was making it all up. The Glass House Mountains was not renamed Rosy Glass House Mountains, or was it? I dared not ask her that.

'I need to smoke. I'll be back in a jiffy,' she said suddenly as she hurried away to the glass doors, which flung open as soon as she reached the invisible sensors, and then she disappeared into the cold, calculative Friday night outside as another siren sounded.

How strange, I thought. Four women and all called by the same name — a variation of a name, but even so. How could anyone remember which woman matched with which 'rose' name?

I felt I could do with a coffee, until I heard another siren and changed my mind. My ears were attuned to the sounds both inside the waiting room and outside, and deep inside of me, my heart continued to beat — a rhythmic, ritual reverberation that continued in the background as if it didn't matter.

We took heartbeats for granted, until the time when each one mattered ... when life was slowly ebbing away, and the monitor drew crazy lines on the screen in a hospital room. Then the heartbeats were no longer in the background. When the last one beat and flew towards the night sky among the stars, the heart stopped. As if it had never beat. As if it never was. As if it had been tricked into being in the first place.

A star shot past. Little did I know how this one chance meeting with Rosetta would impact our lives.

I opened my eyes and rubbed them. I didn't know at what point I had shut them.

1.25

Rosetta walked through the open glass doors. She had a takeaway coffee cup in her hand. She held it to me, saying, 'I got a cappuccino for you.'

'Thanks. But I—'

She didn't wait for me to finish. She was as quick on her feet as she was with her tongue. 'It's okay. You need it. Just as I needed a smoke.' She smiled, pushing the coffee towards me.

I took the cup. It felt nice and warm. 'Thank you,' I muttered.

Rosetta settled herself in her chair. She smelled of smoke. I imagined her throwing smoke rings in the air and watching them, her head tilted slightly, her long ponytail appearing longer still.

'Do you often give free coffees to strangers?' I asked her, still clutching the coffee cup.

'This is the first. I didn't know which one you'd prefer. So, I asked the young girl at the counter, "what coffee would a very worried, sad-looking young woman like to have on a cold, Friday night", and she said I couldn't go wrong with a cappuccino. So there ...'

Worried ... sad looking ...? Lordy, did I look like that? Tired, maybe, but worried and sad ...? Nah. Perhaps it was the hospital environment that did it to me. I was doing a colleague a favour, and happily so. I wasn't worried nor sad or broken anymore. I was whole, wholesome, and worthy. And I cared — carefully, categorically.

Rosetta nodded. Maybe I had voiced my inner questions.

'I've another two hours to kill. Tell me what you're doing here, when a young, beautiful woman like you should be out on a Friday night? The girl at the counter recognised you when I described who the coffee was meant for. She said she saw you come in tonight.'

I turned to Rosetta, feeling a little embarrassed. 'Yes. I came tonight in the hope that I might be able to give someone some ... hope,' I said, pleased with myself for how those words came out of my mouth. Smooth.

I didn't want to tell her much. Yet, sometimes, I felt safe talking to strangers. I didn't think Rosetta and I'd meet again. That felt good. However, there was something about her that made me feel uneasy.

'I'm just curious,' Rosetta continued. 'Feel free to tell me to shut up, and I will.'

I smiled. 'It's not a big secret. But I don't know where to begin.'

'Begin from the beginning. Let's find a corner. That way, it'll be less distracting to others.'

We got up and moved to a corner of the waiting room. The second-last row was empty, and the last row had just two chairs. *Perfect*, I thought.

'Perfect,' said Rosetta as she sat down.

I did the same. The cushioned seat compressed gently, voicelessly, taking all my weight upon itself. I felt a part of me being freed. Again.

'This is an ideal place. The waiting rooms. You wait here for things to happen,' I said to Rosetta.

She nodded. I think she partly agreed and partly questioned. She was seemingly trying to understand but didn't believe in her own ability to get my drift. I liked that. Why should my life be an open book for anyone to read? I'd make them read only those pages that I chose to. Life — with all its mysteries — was good. Not everything needed to be unravelled. Some things, sometimes, somehow needed to be cocooned. It was conniving, empowering to think of those things that way.

She thought I was sad when I wasn't anymore. Good.

I wasn't willing to share my story. I simply gave her the basics — about Kevin, and I informed her about Ewa's death, but not of our blood ties.

A hospital volunteer came to me asking if I would follow her as my patient was awake and asking for me. I thanked Rosetta for the coffee and followed the volunteer.

Rosetta could wait. In the waiting rooms.

My phone buzzed. It was Benny.

'What are you doing at the hospital on a Friday night?' he asked.

'Visiting someone,' I said.

'Okay. When are you planning to leave?'

'Another forty-five minutes or so.'

'Uh … I'm in the area. I'll see you soon,'

That's it — short, curt and dismissive. Even after a long gap of not calling or meeting me.

Fifty minutes later, he spotted me right away, parked and walked towards me. I was standing near the pickup and drop-off area. He didn't look at me. He never looked at me — just a first glance and then he talked as if to the wind.

Rosetta too, had left the main exit and came towards us. She was in a hurry, and I was glad about that.

Casually, I introduced them — Benny as a friend and Rosetta as the lady in the waiting room who I'd just met that night.

'Good talking with you. Ma wants to read something. Got to give her the book that I left in the car. Maybe we'll meet again.' She waved, acknowledged Benny, and walked briskly towards her car.

'Maybe,' I said and added, 'good night.'

Benny stood transfixed, staring, his eyes wide, the lines of his forehead creased. He shook his head just once and kept starring until Rosetta disappeared in the parking lot towards her car.

I followed his gaze, confused. 'You look like you're seeing a ghost,' I said, trying to smile.

'Who's she?'

'I told you I just met her tonight. They live in Roseville. On Rose Lane, and they have the word "Rose" as part of their names. So strange. Did you notice her hair? That's what I did. They all have long hair. Very, very long hair,' I babbled.

'Hair? Is that all you saw?' he asked.

'And her rings and—'

'Was that all?' he continued, and I noted his annoyance.

Confused and chaffed, I gave up trying to understand him. 'Oh … come on. Say it,' I said.

'Say what?'

'That I don't have your common sense, calculative instinct nor your bountiful intellect to see more than what meets the eye?'

'Ah. The eyes. I noticed her eyes. And—'

I laughed. 'How could you see her eyes in such a brief time?' I asked. 'Besides, it's dark.'

'Let's go to the tavern. We'll come back to pick up your car,' he suggested.

And that was that. He didn't look at me while I shifted uneasily in his car, feeling small.

Silence was truly golden. Like the golden-brown leaves in autumn. Some of them — they turned red, orange, gold, yellow, brown before they fall to the ground. Then, you could hear the crunch as your feet crushed them. The noise began then. And it did for me now.

1.26

I rushed to the restrooms as soon as we entered the tavern. Why was it that I moved like a pendulum between the times where I began to warm towards him, and those times when I wanted to be as far away as I could? It was confusing — not knowing. Not knowing if it was me. Or him.

In the toilet, at the far end of the wall mirror, was a little sticker, and I went closer to read it. It said: *You are more than what you see in this mirror.*

I looked at myself and critically assessed my face — yes, a big forehead, and wavy hair. I pushed some of it behind my left ear and a part of my fringe covered my right cheek while the rest was tied in a loose ponytail. The high cheekbones, long nose, and my shapely eyebrows that made my face oval — I decided. A bow-shaped upper lip, and my lower lip wasn't too thick. My collar bones stood out, and so did my long, slender neck. *Ah! I'm not too bad to look at. I'm fashionably slim.* This new me was quietly confident.

It was Benny's problem that he refused to look at me as I appeared to myself.

Of course, I didn't understand everything and might not understand everything. But it had given me hope that now that the major obstacle was removed — Evil Ewa was no more — I could live my life as it was meant to be lived. Life that concealed confusion carefully. I could walk away any time without feeling the burden of guilt.

But Nana and Mum were also an integral part of me. I cared for Mum, who cared for hers. If those two were sad and confused, how could I be free? I just had to try harder.

I hoped Kevin would find out something soon about our family. I was getting impatient to leave for India myself. If nothing was found, at least I could reassure myself that all was done in an accepted manner and there weren't long-lost relatives to be found. We could all move on with our lives, happy in the belief that at least we weren't related to Ewa. With that thought calming me, I walked out of the restrooms.

I headed straight for the bar and ordered a stiff vodka for myself. Carrying my glass, I made my way towards our table.

Benny had ordered a light beer for himself and sparkling water for me. He merely raised his eyebrows when he looked at my glass. I assured him I wouldn't be sick this time.

'Cheers,' he said.

We didn't talk. He was absorbed in the rugby game being shown on the screen and occasionally joined the crowd in either mourning a missed opportunity or saying a loud 'Yay' when the favoured players stuck gold. At times, I noticed him looking at me, like as if he was memorising my face.

A light dinner and we were on our way. He dropped me home. My car waited in the hospital car park.

I read a long email from Kevin the next morning.

He'd made enquiries about Balachadi but did not say anything about the purpose but instead, gave me a history lesson in that email.

Daphne, during the Second World War, an Indian king — called by many as the good Maharaja of Navanagar — had looked after hundreds of Polish children without any help from the British Empire. The entire Indian continent was ruled by the British. The world was a chaotic place at the time.

(I smiled, reading that — the world had always been a chaotic place.)

The war ended in 1945, and India gained independence from the British in August 1947. Anyway, those children were moved to another camp in Valivade, and from there, almost all left the Indian shores after some time.

Ewa hadn't lied in her letters. The places she mentioned existed. Kevin would be going to Valivade he wrote, but first he would be visiting villages in other states. In any case, with only a few letters and Ewa's surnames, it was proving difficult to find any trace in his search.

Kevin would return empty-handed in that respect — but richer in his own soul-searching journey. I knew what visiting villages meant to him. He had always wanted to see things for himself — how charity organisations like Caritas worked, and what more could be done to lessen administrative costs to ensure hard-earned donations went to the needy. This personal journey would help him understand his mission. Nothing could replace first-hand experience.

Well. Dear Kevin. Surrounded by females, he hadn't understood what each of us wanted, waited for, and wished for him to give us.

We all wanted a part of him. Ewa had wanted him because of her own muddled mind of vengefulness towards Henri. Nana, so she could say that there was one male in her world of females, and Mum, just because. I wanted to be near Kevin because he was the only one I was closest to. That was all. But he had left us all and joined the priesthood.

Leave the Church alone — the institution that was called the Mother Church but was controlled by the Fathers of the Church. Best to leave him be.

I wrote back to him:

Kevin,

Thank you for that information about the Balachadi and Valivade camps. You could have just added a website link with the information.

I do know you're more interested in your own exploration of that country. You saw this trip as an opportunity for that purpose. And that's fine. But you've been over there for a long time now, and we don't know anything about our 'unknown family'. Maybe I should come there quickly — for Nana's sake (and Ewa had wanted me to find out anyway); you should return.

Benny took us to the Suncorp Stadium for a Sunday night footy and we enjoyed ourselves, Nana particularly. But I don't think he is too keen to continue entertaining us forever. He's keeping to his promise he made to you when you left — that he'd keep an eye out for us. It's best that you return soon and let him get back to his own life. And you to yours.

To quote your favourite biblical quote: 'For I know the plans I've for you. Plans to prosper you and not to harm you; plans to give you hope and a future.'

Your future is here. Not where you are now. I'll book your return ticket from here. Let me know the date. Or maybe, once I get there, both of us could return here together?

Love aplenty,
D

There was no response. Had he read my email and decided to ignore it? What was happening?

1.27

Benny texted me one morning asking that we all be ready for a drive. He had a surprise waiting for us. Nana got excited as soon as I told her.

'I love the word "surprise". It delights me as well as makes me little anxious. But it means something is about to happen,' she said.

'It had better be a good one then,' I said to her, but I also felt a fear. If Benny did anything to upset Nana and Mum, I'd not know what I'd do.

Mum obviously pretended to be thrilled for her mum's sake. 'Let's go, Mum. What would you like to wear?' she asked.

An outing with Benny meant a lot to them. Whereas I thought of many ways I could get out of it.

We won't go if you don't come, he texted me.

Mr Lawyer! Was he somehow able to read my mind? The trip would be cancelled, and the two women would demand to know why. Best to go.

Benny drove us in his new flashy car; Nana could not decide whether to admire Benny or his car.

Roseville, a beautiful, leafy suburb, was dotted sparingly with one-level houses, painted white picket fences, and long driveways. There were acres of green pastureland that could be seen as the tall grass danced with the touch of a gentle breeze. I often drove there by myself sometimes.

People lined atop at the lookout spot looking down in the valley as the first sunlight rays appeared. The cows mooed each morning; a dog bark or a rooster's crow signalled the break of a new morn, and some residents hurried to reach their workplaces in the city some 70 kilometres away. Benny stopped the car at this lookout point, and we all got out.

It was a glorious mid-morning; the sun was out, and a few families were at the lookout point. He pointed us to the valley below and particularly to a house, white-fenced and covered with dots of every colour: flowers.

'We are visiting a family there,' he said, sounding mysterious.

'Benny,' I said, 'we don't know anyone there. I don't think Nana and Mum would like to meet strangers—'

'I'd not call them strangers, exactly,' he said, leading us all to a picnic table and bench.

Nana sat first, and he sat beside her, while Mum and I sat on the opposite side.

Benny then turned around and said to Nana, 'I don't want you all to get too excited … and I could be wrong … but I'm positive I've found a family who could be related directly to you.'

After the first silence, Nana's lips trembled, her hands were shaking, and her eyes became teary. Mum was afraid for her. She reached for her water bottle.

I was annoyed. If this was some joke, Benny would get a mouthful from me. 'If you could be wrong, why bring us here? Let's go for a drive instead,' I said.

'Had I been fifty years younger, you would be an eternally married man,' Nana said, squeezing Benny's hand.

I made a little noise and shook my head. 'Nana!' I screamed. Something that I'd hardly done before.

Mum blushed.

The man laughed, winking at me.

He was confident because he was teasing. I, however, was sceptical. He had made this appointment. He had better not be wrong. He said it was worth meeting this family, if just for friendship's sake.

Nana said she agreed with him. That it was high time we mingled and came out of our self-imposed seclusion. 'We should just go and meet them. I trust Benny,' she smiled at him.

Looking at me, Benny said, 'We must all thank Daphne for this,' he started.

Three pairs of eyes rested on me; mine popped out. If this was the surprise, I hated it. *What have I done now?*

'Some days ago, Daphne and I met a lady called Rosetta. And that meeting triggered my curiosity,' he said.

'What? Why?' I asked bewildered.

'Remember, I asked what you noticed about Rosetta that night?' Rosetta? What was he talking about? 'I had seen physical similarities between your nana, mum, and you too, in Rosetta.' Quickly, he explained to Nana and Mum about that night at the hospital. 'I made some enquiries,' he said.

'Did you hire a private investigator or become one yourself?' I couldn't help asking.

He ignored my question and continued to talk. 'I spoke with Rosetta and learned that Ella Rose, Rosetta's mum, had lived in India during and after the Second World War and had migrated to Australia on a ship from Bombay ... well, Mumbai. That's where I believe is the connection. I asked her if we could all meet. Ella Rose is more of a recluse, but Rosetta convinced her and ... here we are ... ready to meet them, an all-women family.'

While Nana and Mum were listening, I asked, 'Have you told Rosetta about Ewa?'

'No. Not my place. That's up to you. I gave the barest information ... just to start off this meeting.'

I looked away. Cars were wheezing past on the main road, and we were about to be 'surprised' in a big way. *What if Rosetta's family and ours are related? Are we about to find our real great nana? How will we know for sure? And what will we do, or what will that other family do?* I was overthinking.

'Daphne, I'd not do anything that I'm not meant to do.' Benny's voice sounded harsh in my ear.

'If I could believe the honesty of lawyers … but I'll make an exception in your case,' I said, smiling a little and was rewarded with a surprised look.

Back in the car, everyone else seemed as nervous as I was. Benny drove past the main street and turned into Rose Lane.

As soon as I got down from the car, I breathed in deeply. The scent of roses was heavenly. And heavenly was the scene before us. We were at Rose Haven.

The sun was smiling, the sky was blue, and the house was a quaint Queenslander. But one could hardly see much of the house. At first sight, it looked like everything was covered in rose plants, bushes, or creepers. Or rose petals on the ground. The stone pathway, the few steps leading to the small porch — it was fairyland. We stepped inside.

Benny introduced a woman seated in a wheelchair — Mrs Ella Rose Kowalski — first to Nana and Mum and then to me.

I walked towards her, forcing a smile, my hand extended.

Then the unexpected happened.

Ella Rose shrieked and turned her face away the moment she saw me. Mum pulled me behind her; Benny moved towards Ella Rose, and so did Rosetta, who had wheeled her in. Nana turned her face away. Someone placed a glass of water in Ella Rose's trembling hands.

Ella Rose was Ewa all over again. For me. Ewa used to shriek at me. Mum would pull me behind her. I'd make a face or say a nasty word or two and move away from both, leaving Mum to deal with her. It had been a familiar scene in my life.

1.28

Benny had given all of us fake hope. This all-women family was weirder than mine. But I couldn't leave. In the commotion, I had to have this drama played in full.

When some order returned, Ella Rose's deep-set green eyes looked in mine, and she said, 'You wait for me.' Just like a schoolteacher. She then moved her wheelchair towards an inner room.

Rosetta asked us to be seated and apologised but rolled her eyes, indicating that she had no idea what Ella Rose was up to. Crushed rose air whiffed everywhere with a lingering uncertainty.

Benny was talking softly with Rosetta. I could feel everyone's eyes on me. Rosetta was staring at me non-stop, her facial expressions changing every moment. It was as if she would peel one layer and gasp at what she discovered. Then she'd pull another and again gasp at a newer discovery. Had the moment not been as serious, it would've been funny.

Surely, I didn't appear as unrefined as a village girl, nor as grotesque as a witch? Where was the broomstick? I'd strike them all and fly away triumphantly. Such silly thoughts! But such silly thoughts guarded my sanity.

Ella Rose re-entered the lounge room, her wheelchair moving noiselessly, stopping near Benny. I quickly saw her aged, painted face, red lipstick and her greying hair tied in a bun with a red rose pinned to it. She was wearing a colourful flower-printed dress. In her lap was a little yellow sateen drawstring pouch. She began opening it.

All eyes were now on that little pouch.

The pouch held many old photos. Her gnarled fingers, with red painted fingernails, began to go through them, until she removed the photo she was looking for. She held it, looked at it and passed it to Benny, asking, 'Does she remind you of someone? Look closely.'

Benny took the old photo in his hands, looked at it and whispered, 'Oh my God!' His eyes moved from the photo to Ella Rose, to me, back to the photo and to Ella Rose. And then he stared at me again.

There was silence, and suddenly everyone wanted to see the photo.

Although curious, I folded my arms and looked at the scene playing in front of me. It had something to do with me, that much I understood. I wondered what I'd be blamed for this time.

The photo was passed on, and there were low noises of 'Oh my God!' from all. Everyone was looking at me. I stood mutely, like a mannequin in an Op shop.

Ella Rose got the photo back in her hands and said to me, her eyes tearful. 'I am so, so sorry, my dear. I should not have shrieked.' Her voice sounded pleasanter than her shriek. 'But look at this,' she said, pushing the questionable photo towards me.

At last, I took the objectionable, old sepia photo in my hands. And I stared. It wasn't grainy. The subject in it was … me. I shook my head, puzzled. 'She looks like me. But it's not me. I don't have that dress …' Slowly, comprehension dawned.

Ella Rose took my hand and said, 'My Anna Rose.' She turned to Nana and held her hand.

Nana came closer and slowly placed her hand in Ella Rose's hand.

Ella Rose said to Nana, 'You are my *siostra* — my twin sister Anna Rose's daughter. I am your *ciotka* — aunt.'

Those words turned our world. Our lives would never be the same again.

Rosetta and Nana looked at each other in alarm, their eyes popping out. Nana looked away, but Rosetta continued to stare as though she were assessing Nana, trying to see if there was any resemblance between them. Soon, tears started flowing freely from all eyes. Slowly, there were four women hugging each other. All crying.

That left me alone to join the four women. I went near them and took part in the collective hug. I felt a lovely warmth in me — a strange sense of belonging; it was as if I had come home. I let myself be hugged. I liked the feeling.

Here was history being made. I was part of it. I was it.

Rose Haven. The women who lived there lived in their own world, isolated but insulated in each other, with each other, for each other. Each was enveloped within themselves, each different, but the one bond holding them together — the roses.

'Come,' said Ella Rose to me, after the turmoil had subsided a bit. 'See my roses,' and she beckoned for Nana and Mum to join too. The crying had subsided.

There were plenty. Roses. White, red, orange, pink, lavender. All colours. Plenty of questions too — what, when, where and how.

Rosetta pushed Ella Rose's wheelchair along the narrow cobble way, as she did every morning, I was told. Like Ella Rose, Rosetta loved their roses and loved to watch them grow. And she watched everyone watching them.

The statue of the Virgin Mary, which had a place of honour in the Rose Haven house, didn't get a garland of roses or rose petals. The statue carried a rosary in the joined palms and had plenty of painted roses at its feet.

The roses were cut only for pinning in the hair of the women, or when pruning.

Ella Rose — the 87-year-old matriarch, her silver hair neatly combed and coiffured in an oval bun, and with a rose held in place by a single diamante pin — was still bright and interested in all that happened around her.

She had seven of those pins, she said, neatly arranged in a wooden box that had been gifted to her by her long-gone husband. Arthur had been killed by a single shot while training in the barracks. Before he left, he had plucked a beautiful red rosebud and presented it to her on that Valentine's Day, together with the little wooden box holding the seven pins. With those, he'd extracted a promise out of her. That she would never, ever cut her long hair. Just like her papa too had instructed.

Benny, whom we had all forgotten about, coughed, excused himself and left, saying he'd be back to collect us when we were ready. He was sure we had much to talk about, he said.

Nana invited me to tell everyone about Ewa's letters, which I did, not missing out anything, including Ewa's so-called love for Henri. *A love so strange that she wanted me to find and punish him.*

'Muh ... she ... she wasn't my birth mum,' Nana said painfully. 'And my papa would have been Henri Stein.'

There was silence. Ella Rose was examining her gnarled hands minutely.

'Do you ... did you know him?' Nana asked.

'Dear God! Both of us?' I heard Ella Rose say softly to herself. 'Yes. I knew him. Very briefly,' she said aloud, and then she was silent, staring blankly, her hands folded in her lap.

'It appears, we women are a cursed lot who can't keep our men.' Rosetta broke the silence.

Oh no! Ewa had said the same thing.

Our stories were exchanged briefly. Nana told her what happened to my granddad and Dad, adding she hadn't known anything about her own father, as Muh had refused to talk about him.

Rosetta's husband also had died within the first year of their marriage.

'He was driving in bushland and stopped to pee. A brown snake bit him. His mates found his body the next day,' she said. 'Stupid way to die. Since then, I've been living a carefree life,' she whispered to me alone. 'These rings you see ... they are all from my past and current lovers.' She winked, showing her hands. 'No one man has everything in him. So, I've different ones with different ... ah, talents. That's the best way for a woman, especially at my age. What do you think?'

I looked away — my red, puffed face would've become redder still, not because of painful tears this time, but because of a flustered secret. I hadn't been exposed to such talk.

She looked directly at me.

I knew she knew about my discomfort.

'Do you know I was born in a brothel? Ask my mum,' she said aloud.

'Oh, stop it!' Ella Rose commanded, but a smile twitched her lips. 'Yes, Rosetta was born in India, the year after India became independent from the British Empire,' she said.

'It was the year Gandhi was assassinated. My husband and I lived in a convent north, in a place called De ... yes, Dehradun. The convent was the safest place, as riots could break any time for any reason, and I was pregnant. It so happened that from there we went with the midwife to help a prostitute deliver her baby in the brothel. I too went into very quick premature labour myself and ended up delivering Rosetta there. That's the real story, but Rosetta loves to shock people by saying she was born in a brothel in India.'

Rosetta clearly loved to stun people. She winked at me, saying, 'It's true. I was born in a brothel.'

Rosetta's daughter, Rosebud, was at church, she told us. Rosebud preferred to do charitable works. While Rosalyn — Rosebud's daughter, the young doctor in training in Melbourne, who was my age — was missed as well.

Rosalyn and I first needed to meet face to face instead of messaging or talking on the phone. This was dictated by Ella Rose. It was important for young people to bond first, she said. No one disagreed with her.

Nana said, if that was the case, it would also apply to our Kevin.

Rosetta jumped up and joined hands with Nana. Yes, they both exclaimed. Kevin and Rosalyn would have to meet all the rest of us face to face. It was a fun-filled, exciting moment, and I revelled in it.

Benny picked us up late afternoon. Nana and Ella Rose couldn't stop thanking him. He was basking in glory. We were excited, exhausted, and empty too. There was so much to take in and so much to let go. Who would've thought that one chance meeting with Rosetta at the hospital, would've led us to this — because of Benny's eagle eyes?

As Benny drove us home, I looked sideways at him. He looked as happy as a man does when he's won a trophy.

Catching me looking at him, he asked, 'I don't have a Mr Lawyer face now, do I?'

'Who's fishing now?' I asked, adding, 'Thank you.'

1.29

I emailed Kevin, elated to give him our big news …

Dear Kevin

Hope you're doing well. We've not heard from you since my last email — by the way, did you receive it or not? I do understand that some areas where you are don't have internet or telephone connectivity. I'm hoping you receive this email as soon as possible and at least call me.

Ewa hadn't lied in her letters. Our great nana had a twin! Yes, we have found our cousins! Right here in Brisbane — Roseville! Remember that little Queenslander with the roof covered in creepers, and a high white fence around the house called Rose Haven? The one we can see when we're just about to go down from the main road? Remember, as you pass it, your senses are blasted with sweet-smelling roses, because that family only grows roses?

Well, we all visited that family today! The elderly woman in the wheelchair — who doesn't encourage any visitors, but somehow, through Benny — agreed to meet with us all. Yeah — Benny the saviour! Four generations live in that house — all women. Her name is Ella Rose, her daughter is Rosetta, whom I met at the hospital accidentally — now don't panic, I was visiting the hospital as a favour to a friend, and Rosetta's daughter is Rosebud. And her daughter, the beautiful Rosalyn, is our age. Both Rosebud and Rosalyn weren't home, but I saw some photos.

Yes — the obsession with roses! They live in Roseville, their street is called Rose Lane, and their house is named Rose Haven, and they all have 'rose' variations in their names! How weird is that!

And it so happens our great nana was named Anna Rose!

Anna Rose and Ella Rose were called the Gorski twins. So now we have a surname too. Apparently, I look like Anna Rose when she was young! Well, Ella Rose said I am a replica of Anna Rose.

To think it all started with me — and Benny, of all the people, was the one who saw similarities between Rosetta and Nana.

The sad part is we don't know if Anna Rose lives, and where she could be. The last part Ella Rose remembers was that Anna Rose had disappeared from the Valivade camp, and Ella Rose was forced to leave for Australia without her. Anna Rose couldn't be found, and Ella Rose has been feeling guilty about it all these years. Their father (our great great grandfather) had loved growing roses, and he had named them both — Anna Rose and Ella Rose. There would be at least one rose plant in front of their house. Ella Rose continues with that tradition — of growing roses. And she wears a rose in her hair too.

But there is so much to tell you! Call as soon as you can. Maybe you could get some lead about Anna Rose in India now. I am so happy, and I feel from now on that we will only get good news. It has already begun! A new set of cousins. A new freedom. A new life — for all of us!

The two send their love, of course — and prayers for your wellbeing. And yes, Ella Rose and her family also send their love to you. We have more family to love us and more to love, as you would have said!

Take care!
D

Part 2

July – October 2015

2.1

Rose Haven was a haven for us all including Benny who was a hero. Elaborate food arrangements and his preferred drinks would be readied for him whenever he visited. He often joked that he had no competition and loved the attention being the only man among women.

Ella Rose often singled me to speak about her past.

One day, when Benny was present, she invited him to join us. She pushed her wheelchair into the furthest corner of the lounge room and asked me to pull a chair and sit close to her. Benny pulled a chair too, and soon, Ella Rose was sitting in between us.

She began with a story she remembered at the Balachadi camp.

Ella Rose had fond memories of the Indian king, Jam Saheb, who welcomed Polish children like her and Anna Rose to India, which was part of the British Empire at the time. He built a children's camp at Balachadi, close to his summer palace.

From experiencing acute hunger in the earlier camps, the children at the new camp were well fed and looked after. But some habits continued due to fear.

'Many, like Anna Rose, hid bread or fruits and ate them in their beds at night. Many of us worried whether there would be food for the next day. So, the idea was to eat as much as one could. Some didn't like to eat the same food every day and preferred to go hungry some days,' she said.

The king was upset by this. He had special cooks and chefs brought in from Goa, India, which was a small state under the Portuguese rule for hundreds of years. Goa was culturally different from the rest of India, as its people had embraced Portuguese culture. Most of the local population were Catholic. Chefs from Goa would cook European dishes for the children at Balachadi.

She particularly remembered eating fried fish and coconut chicken curry on the first day the new chefs arrived at the camp. Being older than the rest of the children, the twins' opinion mattered.

Benny was shifting back and forth in his chair, looking disturbed as Ella Rose continued with her story. Sharp as a blade, she saw him too and asked, 'Some memory trigger for you?'

He nodded.

'Do tell us then,' she invited. The way she said it, it sounded more like a command than an invitation. Benny hesitated at first, gave a quick nod and began his story.

'I was raised in Goa, Old Goa, and in Portugal … Sintra,' he said. 'My great grandfather was also a popular chef. Papa said he often stayed at royal households and palaces throughout the empire in those days, cooking in their kitchens, travelling with them and training royal chefs. The way he cooked meat was a secret he didn't share — seems the meat melted on the tongue.' Ella Rose and I noted the pride in his voice; Ella Rose encouraged him to carry on.

'He visited internment camps, had a team of cooks and helpers, and cooked for the Portuguese army and naval commanders.'

For a man who just said cryptic words like 'nice', here he was talking ceaselessly. Did he single me out for minimalistic words?

'He may have cooked in the Balachadi and Valivade camps,' he added.

Ella Rose seemed to consider Benny's words. She wheeled herself to her bedroom, motioning us to remain where we were.

'I should leave,' he said to me. 'I've spoken too much already. It was wrong of me to add my story here. I must apologise to Ella Rose.'

'I loved listening to you,' I responded.

He raised his eyebrows.

'I mean, you hardly speak about yourself. Nice to hear you talking of your great grandfather.'

'I must get going, though. Ella Rose's stories are meant for you.'

'Or equally for you too,' I said, adding, 'We'll both stay and listen to her. Isn't she amazing?'

Ella Rose wheeled herself back in the lounge with another old photo. She handed it to Benny, saying, 'This was taken in the kitchen, at Balachadi. The chefs had come from Goa.'

Benny looked at the photo. His hands were trembling, and his lips were compressed. 'Yes,' he said, pointing to a man in the centre of the photograph.

I moved closer to look.

There were five men, all wearing aprons and chef hats. They were all grinning.

'That's my great grandfather,' Benny said, pointing at a smiling man in the centre. 'His old photo hangs on the wall in my ancestral home in Goa.' His voice was unsteady. He brushed his hair with his right hand as he handed the photo back to Ella Rose. His dark eyes were misty. 'I can't believe this. After all these years, I see his photograph here. Right here,' he said.

'Make a copy and return the original back to me,' said Ella Rose.

'No. I don't want it. I must get going.' He then left abruptly without saying goodbye.

I took a photo of the photo and saved it on my mobile.

'There is a deep, secretive pain he carries,' remarked Ella Rose talking to herself. 'As we all do. There are no clear winners in any war. Wars among countries, or wars in families. I wonder what his war is about.'

I felt sorry for Benny. *What was going through his mind?*

Placing the photo on the side table, Ella Rose picked up an ornamental wooden box. The box held her precious wealth, she said, which included her hair pins. The Indian rosewood box was intricately carved with a floral pattern and had two brass elephants inlaid facing each other. 'I loved Arthur because he reminded me so much of my papa. And he understood my pain of being parted from Anna Rose. He understood other things too,' she told me. 'War pain is unbearable. Maybe not so much for the ones who have gone, but for the ones who are left behind. The things we do to survive. Arthur was also an orphan. He came to the camp after we arrived.'

The seven pins were not the only contents of the box. Under the red, velvet-lined tray was a small red drawstring pouch. She gently tugged at the string with both her hands, and opening the pouch, she removed two beautiful red bangles. She gingerly picked them up, saying, 'Before we moved to Valivade camp from Balachadi, we were given gifts by the king. Being the older children, Anna Rose and I were given two of these each. I took these red ones, while she took the pink ones, and—'

'I love pink too,' I promptly said. 'Sorry. May I?'

She gave them to me without hesitation.

The thick bangles were covered with red silk thread, tightly woven. A string of pearl-white beads went around in the middle, and there were cut diamantes stuck all around. Both were identical and very light, although the silk thread had paled with age. I returned them back to her, saying, 'They're so pretty.'

'They've been lying here all these years. I don't open the pouch without painfully remembering my Anna Rose. I touch the pouch sometimes and feel for her presence …'

I shivered. Could anyone feel someone's presence by touching certain things? I had no idea why that thought came to me, but it did make me think back. Back to Ewa's letters — she spoke to me through those. But I hadn't felt her presence when I'd touched the letters. I'd been more interested in the contents. Back to her things at home — we had still not emptied her room.

'Have you heard from your brother?' Ella Rose asked suddenly.

I shook my head. 'No, not yet. He was to go to another village this week. So, we're hoping to hear soon from him.'

2.2

We met Rosebud finally. She was just like Mum: shy, doing things quietly — preferring not to be seen or heard. She was also slim, her shoulders drooped; she wore a printed, blue A-line dress. The only difference was the hair — Mum's was cut short, while Rosebud's hair was tied in a neat bun, with a red rose in it.

Rosetta, the ever flamboyant, made up for her daughter, Rosebud's silence.

Her current partner, she said was amusing and went on to talk about an incident when he'd tried to order drinks at a self-help machine of a juice bar.

'An *order here* sign was displayed, so he went on punching keys. Nothing happened. He turned to me, saying it didn't work and could we go somewhere else. I shook my head. I pointed at another hand-written sign stuck above the machine. It said: *out of order*. How silly,' she said, laughing aloud, her eyes twinkling and clearly awaiting our reaction.

We all laughed.

She seemed satisfied. '*Order here. Out of order.* Funny,' she said.

These were her small, everyday stories, she told me later, where she tried to bring some liveliness into the lives of Ella Rose and Rosebud.

Would it have worked in my family? I didn't think so. Ewa would've asked us to shut up.

Sometimes, Rosetta and Rosebud would visit us, but Ella Rose was confined to her own home.

Many stories were being shared — happy and painful ones, and silly and serious ones.

I basked in the novelty of Ella Rose sharing her stories with me — the new feeling of being wanted was strong.

She'd been a young mum in pain when she landed in Australia, even though she had Arthur and her baby, Rosetta, with her. She missed her twin.

'Mama died of an unknown illness before the war, when we were very little,' she said, 'but Papa lived with us, until one day some people came and took us away. Anna Rose and I were taken to a children's camp. We didn't see Papa. He must've died walking into the wilderness of the cold, frosty landscape of Siberia all those years ago when Poland was seized,' she said and then lapsed into silence.

'Tell me about Anna Rose. What was she like? What did she like?' I asked.

'Ah ... she was kind — too kind. I remember once, when I had stolen bread from a dying boy at the first camp and given it to her, she was most upset. The boy was sick and dying anyway. So why waste bread? But she said it may have helped the boy live one more day. Such was my Anna Rose. She didn't think of herself; she had been growing weaker and I had to feed her. Even if it be stolen bread.'

I smiled, already liking Anna Rose and admiring Ella Rose — both so very different from Ewa.

'I had to reassure her every time she felt emotional or teary that we'd always live and die together.'

Ella Rose lapsed into silence.

I did not prod her. Maybe she felt a promise was broken.

But then she continued with her story. 'We promised Papa we would always have a rose in our hair and not shorten our long hair. We had cut a flower each from an old scarf and pushed it in our hair bun because there were no fresh flowers while at camp or travelling in between camps. We kept our promise to Papa.'

I loved listening to Ella Rose speak of the past. I got to hear wonderful tales of a bygone era sometimes, when Ella Rose would return to the 'bring back the memory' cycle.

Hitler's harrowing horrors were unknown to the children at camp in those days, she said. 'We knew nothing. Why were we put into camps away from home? Why did we travel by trucks on treacherous mountains to reach a strange country called India? Where were our families? We were ordinary Polish Catholic orphans made to believe we were lucky to be alive.'

I felt her pain. Yes, I knew about the Holocaust, had read books and seen films documenting that shameful, shocking time in history. But I hadn't come face to face with anyone who had experienced first-hand about war times. This wasn't about merely feeling sorry. The wound was deeper, more personal. The wound that bled across continents and festered.

Did I need to take sides — between the Polish side of my nana's maternal ancestry and the German side of her father's? The fear and shame, the cruelty and pain and ill-gotten gain swept my senses. I had to confront things at deeper levels than just the hatred I'd felt for Ewa. My bloodline was heavily tainted — even without Ewa's revelations added to the mix.

Our visits to Rose Haven continued.

One day, I overheard Rosetta saying to Ella Rose, 'Mum, if you know more about what happened to your *siostra*, tell Daphne. She needs to know.'

After a pause, Ella Rose seemed to say, 'Yes. I will. But only to Daphne.'

And I made myself known. 'I heard someone say my name, and here I am,' I said, smiling.

'Mum's remembered something about her twin. Maybe we'll get to hear about the men in their lives,' she said and winked.

Ella Rose's bring-back-the-memory moment had arrived again. She was in her wheelchair, and I sat opposite her on the leather sofa in their lounge, curious to know more.

She said her twin was the quieter one, the shy and the scared one. They were different in behaviour and emotions, but physically, they weren't too different. Some people saw the similarities at once.

As usual, Ella Rose's story began in the camp.

Those days were idyllic, she said. The good king was like a father to them and helped preserve Polish culture. They had cultural shows, sang Polish songs, played on the field, learned to swim and were happy, although they missed their parents. The chaplains and older Polish caretakers ensured they all learned their prayers and stayed out of mischief.

'All Polish children were transferred to the second camp at Valivade. I don't remember when exactly. We couldn't go back to Poland. The camp was like a little Poland for us. There was a chapel and a church, a school, a post office … everything. Those were beautiful days, but sad too, as we missed our parents, our families,' she told me, and then she fell silent as if she had transported herself there.

When she would lapse in silence, I could do nothing to prompt her back into her tale. Rosetta or Rosebud would then wheel her away and put her to bed. But in this way, I began to get answers to some of my questions.

2.3

I had to learn patience when Ella Rose lapsed into long silences midway. At times, the silences would be shorter.

'Sometimes, the occupants of the camp went to the crowded marketplace,' she said. 'Sellers and buyers flocked for bargains.'

I struggled to imagine how an Indian marketplace looked like, and so I asked her.

'Think of our Sunday marketplace in your school's open grounds. But not as organised. Nor as dull. Think of vibrant colours, of Indian costumes, of bare feet, of noise, of distinct spicy aroma filling the air and people sneezing or coughing. And freedom,' she said.

'They displayed all wares and produce on mobile carts. There were fruits and vegetables, spices, toys, fabrics, and women's fineries, such as colourful bead necklaces, dangling earrings and bangles, secret medications, and herbs.'

Now it was easier for me to imagine. 'And the Europeans would be easily recognisable,' I said, smiling.

'Some vendors even secretly sold lethal poison,' she blurted, her eyes narrowing, her frail hands gripping the hand rests of her wheelchair. Alarmed, my hands lightly touched hers.

But she brushed them aside and continued like as if the interruption didn't happen.

'Yes. Many Europeans — soldiers, spies, maids, and teenagers alike. It was a good outlet for us from the camp.'

'Did you meet Henri there?' I asked. She nodded.

'Who introduced you? Was Anna Rose there too?'

'No. I stepped out most times to buy fresh produce with the cook. No one introduced Henri. Our eyes met across a tomato cart — a full cart of bright, big tomatoes and we smiled. That was all.'

That was all. Yet, so much happened after that.

It was at the marketplace that she met Henri. The marketplace attracted many Europeans — soldiers, spies, servants, and ordinary people. There were always whispers in the camp, and that's how Ella Rose learned about spies and their world.

Young Henri told her that he worked for a large company in its research and development division in France. He was preparing to trade with an independent India. But he was a German soldier collecting information for his bosses. Henri began to ask details about how many people were in the camp and who lived there and how things worked.

'He was a Nazi spy,' Ella Rose whispered. 'Some lived in India, hiding their real identities. In those days, things were secretive — not talked about.'

'He must've been very ... attractive,' I said.

'Yes. I was a teenager, and the most good-looking young man with blonde hair and blue eyes was interested in me. I liked it.' *So had Ewa.*

Ella Rose had continued to meet him in the marketplace. The locals weren't affected by what the Europeans did among themselves, she said. There were bigger things at stake. India was on the cusp of freedom from the British Empire, and all energy was concentrated on that one goal.

But their chaplain was informed about a few young girls from the camp and other young men meeting in the marketplace, and he had confronted her. She had been banned from leaving the campsite thereafter.

'It was a sad day for me,' Ella Rose said. 'Not just because of Henri, but meeting secretly at that age, because it seemed to be a rebellious freedom, of sorts. But we agreed to do what the chaplain asked of us.'

When Anna Rose learned that their chaplain was upset, she became upset herself. She had pleaded with Ella Rose to listen to the chaplain. Ella Rose had promised her that it would be the last time that she would go to the marketplace at night — just to tell Henri that they couldn't meet again. She had shown Anna Rose the opening in the fence through which she could escape from the camp and return without anyone knowing.

'Anna Rose was impressed. She said I was very brave and that she was proud to have me as her sister. But it had been Henri who had made the opening in the fence and covered it with vegetation so no one would know I could come and go as I pleased. I did not tell her that.'

On that fateful night, Anna Rose had said she wanted to learn to be brave and have an adventure by herself, and so instead of Ella Rose going to meet Henri, Anna Rose went!

She never returned.

'And since that day, I've never forgiven myself, nor stopped thinking about her. My dear sister. It should have been me,' she said.

Ella Rose desperately tried looking for her, and next day, she told the chaplain. Everyone, considering the circumstances at the time, joined in the search. No one could find her. It was assumed that she may have drowned in the river, which was in full spate due to heavy monsoonal rain. Henri, too, was never to be seen again. And no one could recall any young man by that name.

I imagined that would be very scary for any young girl. Ella Rose must have died a thousand deaths, filled with guilt for having let her shy twin go on her own. But was Henri merely her friend, or more, I asked. She didn't answer. Instead, she began to talk about the time and place.

India gained Independence in August 1947, but the horror of partition — the painful process of the Hindus crossing into India and the Muslims into Pakistan — happened, and blood and gore, pain and chaos reigned.

Ella Rose said, 'We would hear about stories of rapes, killings and madness. But there was little anyone could do.'

Ella Rose left the camp one night to go looking for her twin. She had got on the train from Valivade train station and headed out. However, she got on a wrong train and was almost dragged into a one-off riot between Hindus and Muslims in that area at the time.

'From the moving train, I could see people shouting, yelling, and fires burning. Bodies flung everywhere. Yet the train moved without stopping, until it reached a remote area, and then it stopped suddenly. The rioters didn't do anything to Europeans. It was based on a religious bias between Hindus and Muslims. But who could tell about opportunists?' She stopped as she sipped water from the glass close by.

'Luckily, a man who had seen me at the Balachadi camp was also on that train. If not for him, I'd have not survived. The train I was on would be returning to Valivade station, as it was too dangerous to go ahead. And so, the man offered to escort me back to Valivade.'

She stopped and looked at me, as if memorising my face. 'Do you believe in the stars? I just remembered a Hindu man who kept our gardens at the camp, once told me our fate was linked to the stars.'

I merely shook my head, uneasy but willing her to carry on.

'The man who saved me was Benny's great grandfather. He was on that train, and he recognised me from the Balachadi days. He had come from Goa to the Valivade camp.'

'Oh! A small world. I must tell Benny. He will be so happy,' I said, feeling happy myself.

Ella Rose nodded and continued, 'My Anna Rose was kidnapped and ra-raped and … it was Henri, I'm sure of it! Oh my God!'

Ella Rose had been close to Henri — either in a flirtatious way or had some affection for him. Ewa had loved Henri. Henri had played with both Ella Rose and Ewa. But he had raped an innocent Anna Rose! Why? What had she told him? That Ella Rose could not meet him again?

Poor Anna Rose! She would've been clueless.

Months later, when the Valivade camp closed, Ella Rose, Arthur and baby Rosetta, along with other displaced persons travelled by ship from then-named Bombay to Australia.

What were the chances, I thought, that Ewa with Nana as a baby and Ella Rose with Rosetta may have been on the same ship? One got off in Australia and the other continued to New Zealand, to then end up in Australia.

It could have been synchronicity. Parallelisms of a weird kind.

'Promise me, you will find my sister. I know she is still alive and somewhere out there. I can feel it. I've always felt it. I'll wait for her. Promise me.'

'I ... yes, of course,' I said, without thinking. 'But did you try to find her after you landed in Australia?' I asked.

She nodded. 'My husband said she too would be looking out for me, and if it was planned by the heavens, the day would come. When the stars align, it will happen.'

'Stars?' I asked, feeling uneasy again.

She nodded. 'Like the Bethlehem star which shows the way.' I ignored that.

'Do you have any of her belongings? Her pink bangles?' I wanted to touch and wear the pink variation; it was as if they naturally belonged with me.

For a moment, Ella Rose looked into my eyes with fear. 'You sound so much like my Anna Rose. But no, I don't have her bangles. A few days after her disappearance, her little bag with the pink bangles and some of her personal belongings disappeared from our dormitory. I was too scared to report it. But I also thought that it somehow meant Anna Rose was well and in hiding for reasons best known to her. Besides, I was dealing with pain and confusion myself.'

Anna Rose's belongings had disappeared? Who took them? Why?

The silence stretched, until she almost screamed, 'I am alive because I won't die until I know what became of her. I won't!'

Rosetta wheeled her back to her room. Ella Rose was upset, she said, and needed to sleep.

My thirst to find out if the other 'rose' woman was alive, increased rapidly. I craved to know her, to see her for myself. I now had a stronger desire to travel to India.

I'd talk to Benny. He'd keep an eye out for Nana and Mum, who were now in Rose Haven every weekend. They both had decided to grow their hair — just to see how long it could grow and how quickly, they said. Secretly, I decided that I'd not cut mine either. It was not very long, but I too wanted to see if it would reach below my waist. Such simple desires.

2.4

Our beach bird's eye, meant to be a shrub, had grown into a tree between two big gums. It was quite tall — almost five metres. I loved to feel its smooth, firm bark. What always fascinated me was the fruit. When the seed cracked open, it revealed a shiny, hard black bead partly covered in red. With two together, they looked like drunk, swollen red eyes, and appeared to look straight at me, questioning. Always questioning and asking me, 'Now what? What'll you do next?'

I don't know, I'd say to the eyes and sigh.

Wearing my old jeans, a jacket over a loose white T-shirt, walking shoes and a scarf around my neck, I stepped out one day. The Sunshine State, as Queensland was known, lived up to its name … most days. Even in winter months, when nature was in hibernation.

Today, the sun was playing hide and seek as some puffs of white clouds glided lazily across the bleak skies. It was a winter, August-month rainy day.

As I walked, I thought of Kevin.

Kevin had finally got in touch. He said that he was busy, and that village life was so unique there. He was glad we were able to get in touch with Ella Rose and her family. And while the 'rose' connection was a big event in all our lives, Kevin didn't find it too huge.

Strange that such a monumental event, which had the potential to change our lives and the connectivity we were finally experiencing, could have a minor impact on him. Of course, he did say once that it was not blood, not nature but the love and nurturing aspect that mattered more in a family.

But it did mean something to Benny. He did his sleuthing to help us reconnect. He helped Kevin to reach India. Did family ties mean so much to Benny? And if so, why did he insist he had nothing to do with his own family?

Kevin. Was he all right, I'd asked him. Enthusiastically, he'd told me about the village children again. I told him to record a video of them and send it on my phone.

The following day, there was a short video from him. It was self-filmed.

'Hey, folks …' he said, smiling. 'Look at me …' He was wearing a loose long shirt, which I assumed was a tunic, and dark trousers. His eyes were twinkling through his glasses. I noticed his fresh haircut and his clean-shaven face. He looked so happy! On his shoulder hung a sort of bright-coloured cloth bag, and he wore an odd pair of sandals — leather ones with a one-sided toe ring flip-flop kind of look. Dusty.

The landscape was almost barren except for a huge tree, its leaves covered in dust. Brown dust as that of the earth below. Suddenly, voices sounded, and Kevin was enveloped by a dozen or more children. He was laughing, and his camera was moving without any focus. At times, I could see little boys wearing colourful half-pants, some with their chests bare, and little girls with tiny multi-coloured beads strung around their necks, in colourful skirts and short blouses, their hair tightly plaited with multi-coloured ribbons. All laughing.

His face came in view as he said, 'Hi … can you see them … so happy and carefree. And now, see the magic.'

As soon as he opened his bag, the children shouted with glee. They put their hands in and began to remove what looked like cellophane-covered candies. Kevin's camera focused on the candies: red, blue, green, yellow. A boy opened a wrapper, popped the candy in his mouth and unfurled the red cellophane wrapper. He brought it up in front of his eyes and began to look through it. The surroundings of his little world must have all lit up in red.

Kevin focused the camera on another little girl who had a blue wrapper. She did the same as the boy. Soon, everyone was looking at the view and at each other through assorted colours. Where I could see brown earth, a big tree, and some dusty thatched huts in the distance, I imagined every child could see the same view, but in a colour of their choosing.

After viewing with his own wrapper, the first boy exchanged it for another and looked through to see the world again. Green. Red. Blue. Yellow. 'Did you see the magic?' he asked the camera. He then placed a blue cellophane in front of the camera and showed the landscape. Everything appeared blue. He changed the colour to red, and everything appeared red. Then he showed the real landscape, and I could see the dusty yellow-green leaves of the big tree, the yellow-brown thatched roof houses and the dry brown sands or dust further down.

'The magic of childhood,' said Kevin. 'Happy, carefree, and simple. Bye ...' He waved.

Oh my! He's a local now. And after only a few days in that village.

Kevin didn't give us any news about his own search about Anna Rose. I didn't think he'd even begun it. He was more interested in how he could serve people who were needy. Was the need to be needed so strong in some of us that we crossed continents to achieve it? Were we aware of this need? Inwardly I was scared that he might never come home.

Nana and Mum didn't show any emotions when I showed them his video, although Nana remarked about his happy face. Kevin wasn't of this world. He was given to God, so God would care for him. If God willed him to be placed in that service, so be it, she said.

Benny, on the other hand, seemed concerned. 'It's not the best of the villages to be in,' he said.

'What do you mean?' I asked. I had called Benny to voice my uneasiness about Kevin.

'It's remote. Little access to amenities. Leave it with me. I'll find out more,' he said.

I left it with him.

2.5

I went to see Benny at his office, unannounced the next day.

I waited in the reception area. Among a pile of magazines on the centre table, I saw a manila folder and picked it up. It had neatly filed pictures. The pictures were of a beautiful, palatial house. But the house was in Lisbon, Portugal.

I was flicking through the pages, when Benny came and sat beside me on the sofa, saying, 'Beautiful, isn't it? I bought it.'

'In Portugal?'

'Yes. There's one more property I need to call my own,' he said.

He really was a property tycoon, and being a lawyer was a ruse.

'Benny, I've a favour to ask. That's why I dropped by.'

'Okay. But let's step out for lunch first.'

We were out of the building and walked a few metres to the nearest Thai restaurant. Having ordered our food, which was just rice and green vegetable curry for both of us with a green salad, we sat at our table and sipped some water.

Benny smiled, as if he were pleased with himself. 'So, what is the favour you want from me?'

'Benny, could you please keep an eye on Nana and Mum for me? I'm travelling to India.'

His eyes almost popped out. 'Why are you going to India? Is it to do with Kevin?'

'No … I mean, yes, in a way.'

I quickly told him about my own restlessness and what Ella Rose had told me — about Ella Rose believing that Anna Rose was alive. I also told him about his great grandfather's role in helping Ella Rose all those years ago.

'Dad would have been so happy to know that about his grandfather,' he said.

'Do you think it's strange that you united my family with Ella Rose's but in doing so, also learned she had met your great grandfather?'

'Yes. I've been thinking about it too. So, I will come with you,' he said as he placed his half-empty glass of water back on the coaster.

'What? To India? But you've not been there since you migrated here. Why do you want to go there now?'

'To settle some unfinished business. And Ella Rose's family can keep an eye out for your nana and your mum in the meantime,' he said.

Curt. No explanation. Just a decision made on the spot.

2.6

The fortnight frantically wheezed past us in between the spate of tears from Nana, as she worried sometimes of being left alone; the connived convincing for Ella Rose and family to keep an eye out for her and Mum; the packing; the need to keep Kevin out of the loop; and the several related arrangements that needed to be in place.

Finally, Benny and I were ready to leave.

Benny arranged for a cab, picked me up, and we headed to the Brisbane International airport.

I remembered the last time we came to see Kevin off. There had been the mystery of him going into the unknown. And the hugs and the pain and the excitement that we would soon hear some good news from Kevin relating to our ancestry.

Little had we known that night that Kevin would enter another faraway world. A world where he would justify his take on how things should be and why. And remain there to learn more of himself.

Tonight, it was not like that at all. The tears, the hugs, the instructions were all left behind at home. Finished. Accepted by all.

We were on the plane via Singapore to Mumbai.

The flight itself was not eventful. Benny closed his eyes and was fast asleep. By now, we were in tune with each other's mood swings. We left each other alone when that happened to either of us.

The Singapore airport fascinated me. It was like a little city within itself. The shops, the lights, the crowds. Everything looked amazing. Of course, it was my first step out of my own birth country.

I said sorry to my old self for not giving it a chance to see the rest of the world.

I had been filled with the 'Ewa risk and mitigation strategy' all throughout my life. Life had passed me by without knowing about me, just like the rainwater that passed through Cassowary Creek and then into the river and from there into the sea. Would the water know which pebbles had touched it when it landed in our creek? No. It just played its role of moving on. As we all were doing now.

The flight from Singapore to Mumbai was again not eventful. I was tired when we touched down in Mumbai and grateful that Benny took charge. More than eighteen hours from home to a hotel in another country did that to me.

Benny had booked us into a hotel next to the famous Taj Mahal Hotel. Ours was called Seaview, an imposing modern fifteen-storey structure facing the sea, categorised as a 'four star'.

Our suite was on the seventh floor. Opulent and impressive. The paintings on the walls were rich, local village home interiors of men, women and children in colourful clothes, relaxing, which I loved the moment I saw them.

Benny noticed me looking at them and asked, 'Like them?'

'Yes,' I replied, my tone overbright, excited. 'No wonder Kevin loves the village he's living in.'

'Sorry to disappoint you. But those are views of a village chieftain's house, most likely. Not those of most homes the poor live in.'

'Yes, I understand that. Brisbane has its own mansions ... and units too.'

'Your place in Brisbane is a mansion.'

'Yes, and I love it! It's my home,' I declared.

He nodded.

I wished I was back home, almost. The trip had not even started.

2.7

Being in Mumbai seemed surreal and exciting.

Unlike Kevin's route and his wish list, I wanted to find whatever I could about Anna Rose. When I wanted to approach the Polish Consulates in Australia and India, Nana and Mum said Ella Rose hadn't done it and would have had her reasons and that we all should respect those. I had to agree.

Benny appreciated that as well, as he too had his own list of things to get done; he was visiting India for the first time since he'd left these shores for the shores of Australia. But in the meantime, he said we would visit all Christian cemeteries in Mumbai and look out for any Polish gravesites — for clues, and to avoid attention.

The colourful chaos that was Mumbai hit me all at once as we stepped out into a waiting cab. I could see scenes float by as in a movie. A sea of people moving. Vehicles moving. Buildings, shanty residences, hawkers with an array of wares and produce. Huge Bollywood movie boards. Heat and dust, although in the airconditioned cab, I hadn't yet felt the heat nor the dust. I turned and noticed that Benny, who was looking out on his side of the street, seemed solemn and tense. The only movement he was making was pressing his big hands together, fingers opening and closing. The ring was gone.

It was overwhelming. I'd see something new, take it in, and at once, I'd be confronted by another view. I expressed this to Benny, who assured me that that was what every first-time visitor felt. That I should take it easy.

We stopped at the Christian cemetery. The driver got out and ran towards the entrance. Benny and I continued to sit inside. We would get out once the driver got back with some news. Through the cab window and through the old open gate of the cemetery, I saw the usual tombstones with angel statues and crosses, some greyed and worn out, broken and derelict, green shrubbery weaving through weather-aged crevices on most of them.

I didn't want to go in there, I told Benny. It was a bad idea to just come directly to a cemetery and look for a tombstone bearing Anna Rose's name. And what would that achieve? Just her existence once upon a time. Or her remains could be in an unmarked grave somewhere — anywhere in the world. *Why did we come here all this way? And why assume she's dead?* I felt disappointed and uneasy. Gravesites opened new chapters for me. Benny said there was no point in thinking about those things, as we were already there.

We thought differently. He assumed death; I assumed life.

Why look for the living among the dead?

The driver came along with another man and spoke with Benny. 'Sir, this man is the caretaker. He knows someone who could help. Many Europeans contact him to learn more about their relatives and war soldiers who were buried in Mumbai when the British left. If you ask any questions, I can translate,' he said, helpfully.

The caretaker was an old man, bent, wearing a long white tunic and loose linen pants. His glasses perched on his nose had the thickest lens I'd seen.

Benny began to speak in Hindi. I should have known he'd be able to speak the national language.

I didn't understand what was spoken but gathered we were heading to another place without getting out of the cab. I heaved a sigh as the driver got in the cab, turned around, and then we headed in the opposite direction.

Benny, in his cryptic tone, said, 'Very few marked Polish graves are here. He said there's a couple living close by, who can give us more information. We're heading there now.'

'Can we just show up unannounced?' I asked.

He smiled. 'In this part of the world, we can.'

He looks so different when he smiles, I thought, surprising myself.

The drive from our hotel to the cemetery had taken us a good one hour and a half. Jet lag was creeping on me.

2.8

Zubin and his wife Fehroza Mistry lived in a two-bedroom flat in Khulaasmaan Baug Colony. The name translated to Open Sky Garden Colony.

While Benny rang the doorbell on the third floor of the building, I turned in the corridor to watch the street below. Cars were lined up and people were getting in or out. The site was different from what I had seen so far. Less noisy. Curious, older residents peeped through the windows of their lace-curtained homes. They were looking up at me.

The door was opened by an elderly woman with light-brown eyes, short grey hair, and wrinkled fair skin, wearing a sleeveless blue cotton dress. She introduced herself as Fehroza. Benny quickly explained the reason of our visit.

'Come in. Sit, please,' she said and went into one of the rooms to get her husband, Zubin.

A maid got us refreshments served in old chinaware, which delighted me, as it reminded me of home — the blue and white China crockery, which Nana loved to display and use only on special occasions. I sipped milk tea and admired the dainty shape and colours of the teacup and saucer, smiling, loving this moment. Natural light entered through the rooftop skylights.

The small lounge area was tastefully done and had the normal seating space — brown leather sofa set, a tea table, a corner table, and further away, a four-chair dining table. The walls were covered with many framed family photographs. I noted the colourful floor tiles, which belonged to a bygone era.

Benny sat erect, ignoring the refreshments.

A man walked in, followed by Fehroza. He wore spectacles and a plain loose white tunic and bottom pyjamas. A skull cap covered his head. He appeared old but walked steadily.

Benny extended his hand.

The man then looked at me … and fainted.

Instead of attending to her husband, Fehroza stared intensely at me, and her eyes nearly popped. 'Oh my God,' she said. 'Sit, sit, sit. He will be all right. Just a shock looking at you.'

She sprinkled water on the man's face, and he was now sitting on the sofa opposite.

Benny's gaze switched between me and the couple. He shook his head. I was nervous. But we both knew we were about to learn something significant.

'You look like her. Sorry. In this age, shocks are not very good for me, you see.' Zubin smiled as he came back from his fainting spell. 'I will show you something,' he said as he walked back into the room from where he had come out earlier.

A few minutes later, he returned with an old biscuit tin that was wrapped in a now-yellowed khadi cloth. The moment I saw the box, my heart began to beat faster. My mind went back to the day Ella Rose had opened her old box.

Zubin opened the box. Looking at me, he said, 'Mother had brought home a young girl, who lived with us for some time. I was maybe seven or eight years old. She couldn't speak. After a few weeks, the girl was taken to another place. That was, I think, in late 1947. These are her things. Just before Mother's death, she gave me this box. The girl, Mother said, had been pregnant at the time.'

Inside the box were pink bangles and a copy of the photo that Ella Rose had.

'You look like her,' Zubin said. 'That's why I thought of the box. I've not opened it in many, many years.'

It was Anna Rose. Her belongings. I was touching sacred things. My eyes welled up.

The world is a queer place. One open box led one to another.

'Do you know where she is … or if she …' Benny asked.

Zubin didn't reply for a long time. He looked to his wife and a silent communication passed between them.

Benny told them that another woman in Australia had the same photo and showed them the photo he had on his mobile.

'Very fascinating,' Zubin said. 'No one will believe this tale. But I do.'

'Mother had said this box was given to her by a young man who had brought the girl to our house after a few days. They thought giving her some of her old things might revive her memories. But she remained silent. And we continued to hold her things. She is alive. Old and ailing in a hospital for the mentally ill in Poona. Fehroza and I visit her often, as we promised Mother. She doesn't talk, shows no emotion,' he said.

The silence stretched until I noticed they were all looking at me. It had to be Anna Rose! She was alive! What more could Zubin and Fehroza tell me?

Zubin instead asked me to tell him about myself.

I told him — about Ewa, about Nana and Mum, and of course about Ella Rose and her family. The basics.

Zubin got up suddenly, saying, 'Let's leave tomorrow early morning. All of us. To see Arzoo Mistry. Your Anna Rose.'

Zubin and Fehroza Mistry belonged to the Parsee community, Benny told me. Their lineage traced back to the Iranians — Zoroastrians — who had fled Persia centuries ago to head to India because of religious persecution. It was truly puzzling how religion divided deviously when it was meant to unite unanimously.

'There's a nice story of how they were welcomed in India.' He winked.

I smiled, nodding. 'Yes, I could take one more story,' I said.

'Nah. You can travel the internet for that.' He actually giggled.

2.9

I wore a loose white salwar borrowed from Fehroza. No shorts and T-shirt to the hospital, she'd said. It was a conservative place. I just wanted to meet Anna Rose. But it gave me a chance to wear something different than what I was used to. Benny regarded me thoughtfully. So, I tried my best to ensure the long cloth, called a *dupatta*, stayed on both my shoulders, but it kept slipping.

Fehroza took some safety pins and pinned both sides. 'There. It will not slip anymore,' she said, clearly pleased with her little manipulation.

'My wife has a solution to every problem — big or small. It's the way her mind works,' said Zubin as he grinned with a look of summation.

It wasn't a quiet ride in the airconditioned car that Zubin was driving us in. Benny sat in the front with him while Fehroza and I sat behind.

Through Fehroza, I learned Anna Rose had been smuggled out. Zubin's mother had been working as a nurse in those days, and young people were under her charge at the Valivade camp. A European officer — Henri — had asked her to look after a young girl who had had a terrible experience. In those days, European girls didn't go about on their own. They were always chaperoned. Zubin's mother took her in, hid her without realising she was pregnant. When she did, she thought it could be an Indian man who may have raped a young white girl, avenging whatever be the reason. These were all suppositions. Nothing could be proved, but the Second World War had ended, and there was chaos all around the globe. Amid this, a newly independent, proud India was adjusting to new life, freedom, equality and religious animosity. Helping a pregnant white girl suffering from high trauma, and who was unable to speak would be dangerous.

'My mother-in-law told me that the baby was born in a bullock cart. She was to deliver the baby at home because a hospital delivery would invite investigations. However, being a nurse, she knew there would be complications and decided to take her to the hospital. She called the local milkman, who agreed to take them in his bullock cart. My mother-in-law delivered the baby in the bullock cart, as the baby was in a hurry to be born. They returned home afterwards, but Arzoo didn't even look at her baby.'

Goodness! Rosetta gleefully announced to the world about her brothel birth. Would Nana, upon learning of her bullock cart birth also do likewise, or would she hide it?

Fehroza continued with the story.

Zubin's mother had been relieved the baby was European. She waited for Henri to come and take them with him, but he didn't return immediately. And while his mother had tried to find out both within the camp and from visitors about his whereabouts, no one could find him. So, Zubin's mother had to keep Anna Rose and the baby hidden with her in her home.

One day, Henri returned and said he'd take the baby first to her aunt and return for Anna Rose later. Seeing the child would have a better life with her own relatives, in the absence of Anna Rose, whose condition continued to show no improvement, Zubin's mother handed over the baby to him.

He never came back for Anna Rose.

He hadn't returned for Ewa either!

With no improvement in Anna Rose's condition over the following months, Zubin's mother had her shifted to a mental health asylum in Poona, which was run by the Parsee community trust.

That's how Anna Rose became Arzoo Mistry.

After his mother died, Zubin and Fehroza took over the role as her guardians. Arzoo was a special patient whose benefactors donated financially to the institution in exchange for her wellbeing.

'Except for her eyes, she doesn't look European at all now,' she said to me. 'She may remember something when she looks at you. Maybe. Let's see.'

'Or she may not be the Anna Rose we're looking for,' I said.

Fehroza gave me a strange look, and so did Benny.

'Although I do hope it's her. It will be a big relief for Nana and Mum,' I said quickly. 'Do tell me more. Does she engage with anyone at all?' I asked.

'No. But she recognises us. She brings two glasses of water whenever we visit her. In the past few years, she hasn't been able to walk well and uses a cane. She has never allowed anyone to cut her hair, and she always places a rose or any other flower in her hair bun. That is something she's always done, and the chief warden has no issues with that.'

Benny and I looked at each other. It was that trait again — the hair and flowers.

'She's not a burden to anyone. The only thing is that she doesn't talk. She's Arzoo. Arzoo — care of Mistry family. Not Anna Rose. Her name was changed so the authorities wouldn't ask any questions about her,' she finished.

Zubin continued to drive, showing Benny various landmarks that we passed.

'She doesn't remember being pregnant and giving birth,' said Fehroza. 'It will be difficult ... we don't know how she will react seeing you but let us try.'

2.10

Four hours later, having stopped midway for a short break, we arrived at the facility.

We parked beneath the shade of a big neem tree where a few cars had already been parked. It was a bright sunny and hot, dusty day. It hadn't rained in this part of the town and there were visible signs of a stressed environment where every little green leaf had dust settled on it, even before it uncurled.

As we got out of the car, stretching our limbs, I looked up at the neem tree. It was dense, and the smallish green leaves covered every tiny branch, which accounted for the denseness and the shade underneath.

'It has medicinal uses,' Fehroza said to me, looking up the tree. 'Some use its twigs to brush their teeth with. It's very bitter though. And they say some of the neem's properties include contraception too,' she whispered.

The huge deep-brown painted corrugated iron gate to the facility was closed. A side entry showed people could walk in, and that was where we were headed.

I'd come face to face with my great grandmother and that made me both excited and nervous. After all, I was instrumental in finding our maternal side of the family here. How I'd love teasing Kevin about it!

I shared this with Benny, thanking him, for it was all happening through him.

'Maybe, it was written in the stars. Maybe, like Fehroza, your mind also works towards solutions,' he said.

Huh? Could it be true that I didn't park potential problems? I smiled.

'At last,' he said.

'What?'

'You smiled. You don't dislike me anymore.'

'Too early to decide,' I said, but I didn't hide my smile.

'Ah! You'll keep me on my toes.'

'I intend to.' He raised his eyebrows.

Led by Zubin, we followed through the side gate and walked into a compound. There were a few tall trees, shady ones too, and little garden beds and pathways. These would have been continuously watered, as they looked green and fresh with no dust on them as the ones outside.

There were a couple of marques around with a table and bench and several canopied wooden swing chairs. Some people were on these swinging, staring steadily into nothingness — moving from a high to a low but nowhere in between.

The main residence was a pink-coloured, single-level building, which had a corrugated iron roof, and it occupied half the area. A dozen steps led to the main entrance. On either side were small rooms, some with open doors and windows. It was no modern building but clearly had been repaired and repainted over the years and belonged to a different era — pre-Independence days, as Zubin informed, British influence.

'They grow vegetables on the land behind the building,' Fehroza said as we began to walk along the pathways towards the main entrance to the building.

The place looked neat and well-kept, and there were no immediate signs of neglect or unhygienic conditions. That was because the facility was privately managed. I was told that it made a lot of difference, as there was no government interference.

Zubin went directly to a room, knocked on the door, and without waiting for an answer, he then opened it. 'Arzoo,' he said softly.

Benny and I, as agreed, remained outside until Zubin and Fehroza talked with her and informed her about us.

After about fifteen minutes, we went in.

A woman in a cotton green and white sari sat on the only bed in the room. Her grey hair was tied in a loose bun pinned with a pink rose. She smiled and stood up, carefully holding the bed.

I was staring into the eyes of an eighty-plus-year-old me! My eyes widened. No wonder those who knew Anna Rose, screamed or fainted when they looked at me. I took a step back and bumped into Benny, who steadied me. I stayed like that — my back touching his chest and his hands on my shoulders.

Anna Rose moved backward and slumped on the bed. Her eyes were questioning, pleading with the Mistrys. She slowly stood up and came towards me. I ran to her from the doorway, my arms stretched out.

The tears came then.

At that moment, I understood why I had never been able to hold Ewa and feel what I was feeling now, with this woman. I was overcome with feelings, emotions, absorbing everything like a piece of sponge. Blood called to blood. The sisterhood of generations.

Arzoo. Anna Rose. Did it matter? We all had touched history again, this time in Mumbai.

I hugged my great grandmother and wept. It was a new feeling for me. For until then, I hadn't known the feeling of a never-let-you-go type of a physical touch, even when I had hugged Ella Rose. Language barriers existed, but not body language.

I was overawed. *Ewa had dared to keep my family away from such overwhelming feelings.*

Later, I connected with Ella Rose, and handing my phone to Anna Rose, I left the room with the others. Benny called Nana and Mum in Brisbane and gave them the news and promised them that once Anna and Ella Rose had finished talking, he would dial them through his number. They would have to wait their turn, he said.

Anna Rose recognised Ella Rose at once via the video call, and the two sisters smiled and wept continuously. Ella Rose used soft tissues to wipe her tears; Anna Rose used the ends of her sari to wipe hers. None of us felt the need to intrude on those precious moments.

Before leaving Anna Rose and promising to see her again soon, I saw her wearing her own bangles, which Fehroza had given her. *Had she remembered something?*

Back in the car, curious to know how Anna Rose had reacted, I asked Fehroza how she had broken the news to her.

Fehroza said that Anna Rose, after the initial shock, appeared calm as she digested what she was being told.

'Did she remember anything?' I asked.

Fehroza was quiet as if reliving those moments. 'I don't know ... she didn't say ... she kept touching her forehead. Maybe her head hurt? I thought it best not to probe too much. Besides, you were waiting outside, and she wanted to see you first.'

I nodded, remembering those moments.

But Fehroza broke my thoughts and said she didn't have good news.

The trusteeship of the facility was changing, and older occupants would be transferred to old age homes. This meant, those inmates who wouldn't display any acute signs of mental illness would be transferred. Anna Rose was almost normal, Fehroza said, except that she had lost her voice.

It's not fair, I thought. Anna Rose couldn't be left there, as if she was without family. She had two homes to welcome her in Brisbane.

Could we take her with us?

2.11

There was an agreeable silence in the car as we drove back. My mind was racing. It was an emotional race.

Kevin called me and broke the silence. I began to cry and choked on my words.

Benny took my phone from me and began to speak with Kevin. 'Kevin,' he said, 'we're returning from visiting your great nana. She's fine. Yes, Daphne's fine too, but unable to talk with you now. Yes, later, once we reach our hotel. Yes, you can stop your search.'

Was that all they could say at such a momentous discovery? I grabbed the phone from Benny's hand. 'Ke ... Kevin,' I said, wiping my tears and sniffing. 'Leave everything and fly to Mumbai as soon as you can. Please. We found her. She ... she's beautiful. Not like Ewa at all. You've got to meet her. I ... I can't even begin to tell you what I felt when ... when I hugged her. She—'

'Yes, yes, Daphne. As soon as you disconnect, I'll book my ticket and be there. I promise.'

I switched off my phone.

After that, silence gripped us all again. Benny held my hand, and I let him. Several minutes passed until Fehroza commented how amazing it all was, that she never could have believed their own Arzoo was our Anna Rose. She went on about coincidences and how pleased she was that it all happened during Anna Rose's lifetime.

Zubin suddenly stretched his hand towards the car radio button, saying, 'Too much tension inside. Let's listen to some Bollywood oldies.'

'How can you think about Bollywood just now, Zubin?' asked Fehroza, seemingly surprised.

But Zubin's finger had already touched the button, and as soon as the song started, Benny said, 'Oh no! Not that one. That will set the battle of the sexes debate.'

'So what? Happens in my house every day,' Zubin said, winking.

'The lyrics are true. You refused to leave until I had said yes to marrying you. Remember?' Fehroza asked him.

It was a friendly banter of 'you said, and I said' between the two of them. Until I asked Zubin to translate the lyrics.

'Oh no! Please no!' Benny begged.

Was he embarrassed? 'Why not?' I asked. 'Especially if it's so funny. And after having cried so much, I'd like to laugh, please.'

'It's not exactly funny. It's just too, too …'

'It's Bollywood romance. What else would you expect?' said Zubin. 'But I'll translate for you … Boy pleads with his lady love not to go out alone in the beautiful spring weather. A storm of dark clouds may stop her.' Zubin translated.

'I remember this song was filmed in a green valley, maybe in beautiful Kashmir then. Anyway, the lady responds that no dark clouds can stop her as they themselves are held spellbound under her long tresses.'

Love and romance were new to me. But this was supposed to

be fun and funny. So, I forced myself to join in. 'Ooh … that's so beautifully expressed,' I exclaimed. 'Tell me more,'

'And she haughtily replies, "My footsteps mark out the pathways of spring, and every bud looks at my face. Every flower and bud know me as they all get their bright colours from my lips." But,' Zubin continued, 'the last part is even more interesting.'

'Trust me,' Benny whispered, 'you don't want to know. Let's talk about something else. Daphne isn't into romantic foolishness. She's practical. Like me,' he said.

'No, Zubin,' I said, 'Benny is a good friend, but he doesn't know me. Please continue.'

'Boy concedes, "I should hold your hand and claim you as my own. You are going your merry way. The call of my own love will stop you." Fehroza, did I translate correctly? At least close to the lyrics?' Zubin asked Fehroza, who nodded.

The song continued, and she said, 'No more translations. It spoils the beauty of the original lyrics, and Zubin doesn't always get it right.'

'But you just said that I translated correctly,' replied Zubin. 'Told you.' He looked at Benny and said indulgently, 'I can't make the missus happy all the time.'

'You two men can talk now,' Fehroza said. 'We will close our eyes and take a short nap.'

As I closed my eyes and began to fall asleep, I was wondering if I was as unfeeling as Benny thought me to be. A realistic, reasonable, rational woman, or an idealist, ingrained, ignorant woman who only knew and felt 'Ewa-notions' to the exclusion of all else. I had steered away from romance all throughout my life. No wonder I wore my virginity as a boulder sometimes. But then, no one knew about that. Still, I began to wonder how my tresses, if they grew long enough, would hold onto anyone?

Benny's face swam before me.

Kevin arrived in Mumbai looking worn-out physically, but his eyes had a new light in them. I told him non-stop about Ella Rose and Anna Rose.

He acknowledged my role in finding both the 'roses' before he could. 'One more to you, little sister,' he said. 'Now, as soon as you land back home, let's find a boyfriend for you.'

What on earth was he on about now, I questioned him.

'There are some gaps in our family history, and no doubt they will be filled over time. From now on, it's going to be all about you, little sister.'

I blushed. Benny had heard every word of this conversation.

2.12

When Anna Rose saw Kevin for the first time, she almost recoiled.

'I'm Kevin, Daphne's twin,' said Kevin.

After a few moments, she nodded and hugged him tight, and inviting me to join in, she hugged both of us together. All were teary-eyed.

I had bought a new mobile phone to give to Anna Rose. Both sisters could use the phone's messaging app, see each other and talk whenever they wanted to. The rest of us could also remain in touch with her.

We gave her the new phone, with Zubin explaining to her patiently how to use it. We connected her with Ella Rose, and it was a tearful, happy reunion again, but this time, Anna Rose didn't have to hand back a phone after her call. Anna Rose didn't use words. Ella Rose did all the talking. But Anna Rose placed her phone on the table, resting it in front of an old glass vase, and she began to communicate with hand gestures. They understood each other.

We also called Nana and Mum, who were curious, teary, but Nana didn't say 'Mama' to Anna Rose even then.

Kevin said we should all give them more time. Nana had been impacted more than anyone else. Because, he said, it was Nana who was the child of a rapist.

'Do you think Anna Rose was truly raped?' I asked Kevin.

'Ella Rose told me. She and Anna Rose have talked about it.'

'Anna Rose can't talk,' I said. I then startled and added, 'That means she remembered!'

He nodded.

'She doesn't have to use words to explain what happened to her all those years ago to her twin. Ella Rose already suspected. It was Henri. Henri must've been angry because Anna Rose had taken Ella Rose's place that night. Henri was already on the radar for deportation because other officers had reported on his spying activities. He had to move out and had been vengeful. Anna Rose endured his motive.' He was silent for a while. 'It's intriguing,' he then said to himself.

'What is? Tell me,' I urged him.

'Henri didn't disappear by himself. He took a stunned young girl, whom he raped, along with him. When he learned she was pregnant, he hid her with a family whose men lived closer to Mumbai. No one knew what Henri did for work. To some, he was a soldier, others a spy, and some believed he worked for a big organisation. But he was a Nazi in hiding. When the war ended, most internees were sent back to Germany. But Henri must have stayed back somehow. Anna Rosa had had a complete memory loss, and the assistant nurse — from the Mistry family — took her under her wing. The rest, we know.'

He fell silent while I tried to understand his summary. I was still puzzled. *Had Henri been disgruntled or was it because Ella Rose did not give him what he'd wanted and that angered him so much that he hurt and kidnapped her sister?* Then, I laughed.

Kevin looked confused. 'Seriously? You're laughing?'

'Ah … um … I was just wondering … if there were sophisticated mobile phones in those days, this story would have been rewritten, and we wouldn't have existed. Which reminds me, Ella Rose didn't want either you or Rosalyn to meet on a video messaging service. Wonder why she relented?'

'She's strange. I'll go see her when I'm back in Brisbane. Anyway, coming back to your earlier question … we don't choose to be born. Others manage our birth, our nourishment. After that, our destiny is the one we create,' he said.

'The stars take their positions,' I replied.

'What stars?' he asked, puzzled.

'Never mind.'

After some moments of silence, I asked Kevin, 'Do you know why Anna Rose had a frightful face when she saw you?'

'Think. If you look like Anna Rose, I may have brought her memories of … Henri …?'

'Oh no!'

'Yes, sadly. I didn't want that to happen to her. Again, we don't choose our genes. I can live with "looking like Henri", but thankfully, I don't have his traits.'

'Along with a mix of convict history from Granddad and Dad. Don't worry. You're the gentlest, most caring person. No wonder she stole you.'

'Stole me? Who?'

'The Church. That's why you serve her.'

'She didn't steal me.' He laughed. 'I went to her of my own free will.'

Yes, Kevin was a perfect priest. Nana, Mum and I always admired him. So had, unfortunately, Ewa in her own twisted way. And he treated all four women with utmost love and respect. But would he continue to live this way throughout his life? I asked him.

We were walking on sacred, sentimental grounds. Kevin, I knew, wanted to speak with someone close. And I was the closest to him.

'After coming here, living among all these people, your experience in Kolkata, do you think you will continue to remain a priest? You will return to Australia, won't you?'

He was clearly thinking. I knew he was uttering a silent prayer. 'I will always remain a priest. Whether here, in Australia, or any other place in the world. This is the life I've always wanted, and I will continue to serve the Church in whatever capacity I can. No … the Kolkata experience was too … too intense. It's not for me. I can do anything else but that kind of work.'

Some other time, I'd ask him about his Kolkata experience. But time, like the stars, didn't wait. It simply moved forward.

In the meantime, practicality demanded we get Anna Rose's documents readied so she could travel to see Ella Rose. It would be a big ask, but I was determined to do it.

The following day, we did a quick sightseeing tour of Mumbai. Benny didn't join us, saying he had to prepare for our Goa trip.

The first place we visited was the beautiful Gateway of India, which was walking distance from our hotel. We poised for photos in the archway. Kevin said it reminded him of the Romans when they would have entered that ancient city of Rome, after sacrificing thousands of Christians. I asked him to stop thinking of the Church just for the day.

I learned from Fehroza that Anna Rose had deft fingers and had learned to embroider the Parsee saree — the Gara — an exquisitely hand-embroidered motif showing rich flora and fauna, the elements, with silk threads of rich colours. It took long, laborious hours to finish one such saree. She made them, and Fehroza sold them in her community. That way, she said, Anna Rose paid for her own personal expenses. Anna Rose had embroidered scarves for me and for Ella Rose's family too.

The Taj Mahal Palace Hotel was our next landmark for photos. Looking at the onion domes, I told Fehroza they reminded me of pictures I'd seen of Russian churches. We could ask Anna Rose to fit in onion domes in the Gara, I said.

'Yes,' said Fehroza. 'What a wonderful idea! Take some more pictures and we can send them to her.'

No trip was complete without seeing the Mahalakshmi Temple and the Haji Ali Dargah, said Zubin. 'The temple is very old and is dedicated to Lakshmi, the Hindu goddess of wealth. And just a short walk away is the Dargah — a Muslim floating shrine. Yes,' he reflected, 'the Hindus and the Muslims can live in peace and harmony. The partition after independence should never have happened. Families are still traumatised today. Independence came at a big, big cost.'

'Let's not start about that part today,' interrupted Fehroza, and Zubin stopped. But not before reflecting further, 'If God is one, wonder why wars and destruction continue in the name of religion?'

No one answered and we continued with our tour, had a quick late meal at a restaurant and returned to our hotel.

2.13

The remaining two days passed quickly, and it was nearly time for Benny and me to leave for Goa, and for Kevin to leave for the village from where he'd come — again.

On our last day in Mumbai, Fehroza and I decided to visit Anna Rose — it was a 'say our goodbyes and see you soon' kind of trip. Benny, Kevin and Zubin decided to have a men's day out.

We went directly to Anna Rose's room this time. She was happy to see us and handed me two black silk hand-embroidered scarves, in the Gara style. The border lines were set in red and white on the two shorter sides of the scarf, and in between the two rows of the lines were red- and gold-embroidered onion domes. The main pattern was a rose creeper — roses of all shades of red and pink. There were two separate creepers coming from either side and getting meshed into one. It was simply gorgeous, and I could see it would have taken her hours to finish one scarf, let alone two.

She pointed out that one scarf was for me, and the other for Rosalyn.

I was tearful, and the wetness showed in my eyes. It was a very special, unique moment. I stretched out my arms and hugged her. I don't know when our positions changed, but after a long time, I noted that her arms were hugging me and mine were closed around myself.

This is what I have missed all throughout my life. The thought came out of nowhere. Suddenly, there was this urgency where I wanted to speak with her, tell her all about my past, my hurt and pain, and my hatred of Evil Ewa. I needed to do it.

I was also waiting for an opportunity to ask her a few questions that had been bothering me.

Fehroza, the wise woman that she was, seemed to understand the scene before her. She said, 'Talk with her. She can't respond verbally, but she can hear you. She understands English. I can help, if needed.'

The flood gates then opened. I told her how Ewa had treated me all throughout my life, all the little incidents I could remember. I told her about how neither Nana — Anna Rose's daughter — nor Mum had sided with me, that they both wanted only to please Ewa. That as I grew up, I hated Ewa and made sure she knew it and rebelled about anything that Ewa wanted. That Nana didn't call Ewa mum, but just 'Muh'. That I didn't know why Mum rarely showed her love for me or Kevin and always had that lost look about her. I told her about Dad and how I still missed him.

Every incident that I could remember, right up to the time of Ewa's death and the letters that followed, were covered in those two hours I was with her. Anna Rose wept too, and so did Fehroza.

We wept for our destinies, for the wars that had brought people to their knees and made some people act like savages; for those who strove for freedom and sacrificed their lives. And for those like Kevin who, despite it all, would choose to remain faithful to their personal callings and serve humanity — especially humanity that didn't deserve their pure, sacred sacrifice.

I wanted to stay with Anna Rose. I asked her if anyone she knew had ever tried to get in touch with her; did she try to reach out to anyone, except the Mistrys?

Fehroza filled in the gaps. Anna Rose, it appeared, had been ashamed. For many years, she lived with amnesia. Then, one day, as she sat watching the live Indian Republic Day celebrations at the Red Fort on TV, her memory returned, because she had remembered the celebrations in the camp on 15 August 1947, the day India became independent and the Poles had joined in, encouraged that they too would regain their own homeland someday.

But she lost her voice forever.

A confused Fehroza asked her why she didn't let the Mistrys know about her memory returning.

Anna Rose took Fehroza's hand and looked into her eyes, seemingly willing her to understand her thoughts.

By that time, Anna Rose didn't want to be found and be sent back to Poland to have her story told to the authorities. She had simply accepted her fate, relying on the kindness of the Mistry family, and she became a well-respected member of the facility, doing her bit to survive and help others to revive. Her life would be here at the asylum where she would die. She had expected nothing more, just longed to be reunited with her parents in heaven.

What about Ella Rose? Did she not want to know about her, I asked.

She assumed Ella Rose had her reasons for not trying to find her at the time, and she was content with that knowledge.

But it was different now. Now that she knew she had her own blood family, she wanted more from life.

Promising to visit her soon again, before I returned to Australia, we said our goodbyes and left. She promised she would have more scarves ready for me by that time.

Who would have known that Evil Ewa had been watching from the clouds far away, wanting to extract her own promise of what she had wanted?

We had been invited by the Mistrys for a quick supper before we took our flights to Goa, and Kevin to Raniganj.

As Zubin poured red port wine in our glasses, he commented that the wine was a product of Goa. 'You will get plenty of it in Goa,' he said.

Benny nodded.

'So, what did the three of you do today?' I asked the men.

They looked at each other.

Winking, Zubin replied, 'I showed them how to be a little naughty. I took them to Mumbai Studios to watch a Bollywood song being filmed.'

'No ... was it an item song?' asked Fehroza, clearly pretending to be offended.

'Don't worry. It wasn't all that bad, but yes, it was an item song.'

'What's an item song?' I asked.

'You don't want to know,' responded both Kevin and Benny together.

'An item song in a Bollywood movie,' explained Zubin, 'is a song filmed where a young, beautiful, skimpily dressed female dancer dances provocatively. Because of the sexy scenes, the movie goes on to become a box-office hit. That's all.'

'Oh, I wish I was there to see Kevin,' I said.

Zubin winked again, saying, 'That's the moment I will never forget. The dancer came to where we were sitting and did a lap dance on him!' He clapped his hands, looking pleased with himself.

He was laughing heartily, and Benny and Kevin were obviously trying their best not to be embarrassed.

'Harmless fun,' I said to Kevin. 'At least you weren't wearing a cassock. Relax! No one's condemning you!'

'Did she do a lap dance on Benny too?' I couldn't help asking, an image coming suddenly to mind.

'Oh, she almost kissed him!' Zubin gave another hearty laugh.

Benny shook his head, looking embarrassed.

'I hope it doesn't go anywhere beyond that studio and this room,' Kevin muttered.

'Cheers,' said Zubin, and we all raised our glasses of port wine.

I didn't tell Kevin about what happened during my meeting with Anna Rose. I'd tell him back home in Brisbane when we would all gather for a meal. Time, like the stars, would move on.

2.14

In Goa, Benny had booked us two separate rooms at a resort, which was close to the beach and had an appealing, relaxing feeling around it. The sound of the crashing waves and the coconut palms as they swayed in the wind added to a lethargic feeling. Because the crashing happened farther away, close by, everything was fine.

The day after we arrived, Benny and I set off for his ancestral village and his childhood home.

He appeared tense and thoughtful. He faced the window as the cab took us through narrow bitumen roads climbing higher, and which were lined up on both sides with all manner of houses, gates, and rock fences covered in red dust. Maybe, he was unsure why he'd made this trip to his old village where he was brought up as a child and left when sense returned to his senseless world. So, I asked him.

'To see the house I grew up in, and to buy it now,' he explained.

Oh. So, it's one of those things. An overlap between revenge and arrogance; a powerful powerplay just because one could. Or is there more to this seemingly secretive mission?

The cab stopped on the top of the hill on the roadside of a stately colonial, Portuguese mansion, which was stunningly beautiful. *Casa Barreto*, read a small plaque on the right-hand pillar of the iron gate.

We got out.

The mansion had an elaborate entrance and several concreted, red-coloured stairs leading to it. The colour theme was blue ribbed and white, with red roof tiles. I noticed the leafy green gardens within the compound walls.

Benny stood in front of the gate and looked at the house without saying a word. He'd forgotten I was with him. Eventually, he tapped on the latch of the gate and waited.

A frail woman was walking slowly down the dozen steps. She was bent, her thin hair tied up in a bun, her skin wrinkled. She looked sad, overburdened, like a person who had had a painful life.

She took reluctant steps to answer the tapped latch. Her brown apron was in front of a pale-blue cotton dress that reached her knees, and she wore worn-out sandals on her feet. As she came closer and opened the gate, she looked at Benny, and continued looking at him. 'Benny?' she whimpered.

'Yes. We speak in English,' he replied. Curt.

'Please … oh, please come in … Oh my good Lord! It has been so long … so long …' She moved closer as if to hug him, but Benny moved away and began walking beside her.

I followed behind; I was either unnoticed or ignored by them.

'It's been so long … we tried our best to contact you, but you simply vanished.'

'I went away because I didn't want to be found. And you know why. Anyway—'

'You don't know what has happened since you left?'

'No. And I don't want to know. I've just come here to … show you these …' He removed his folder, which contained pictures of various houses. 'These are my houses. This one is in Portugal. Yes …' He looked at the woman. 'I will soon own this big house in Lisbon. Does it look familiar? Look at those stairs — just like Casa Barreto's. But it's bigger.'

I was stunned. The man was showing off and belittling the woman. Why? And we hadn't even entered the house.

'I want to buy Casa Barreto. Name your price. And I want everyone's signatures, including your three sons' and their wives. But I want it all done as soon as possible.'

An old man limped towards us. 'Benito …' he said.

Benny glanced up and looked at him. Then he ignored the man. 'If you don't sell, I'll get it my way. We all know it. But let's try it this way.'

'Benito … you truly don't know what's happened since you left?'

'No, I don't. And as I've said, I don't want to know. When are your sons returning? I can wait or come back later.'

His words were met with silence. By then, we had entered a large lounge.

Benny looked around the room. 'Don't think you've looked after this place well. Mama would be so hurt to see this. Are your three sons all wasters?'

The woman shrieked then, '*Mai de Deus!* Don't say anything anymore.' She walked crookedly to a mahogany table, opened a drawer and returned with what looked like a booklet. I could see smiling faces of three young boys on the cover of the booklet, which looked like a Mass booklet. Below, were the printed words: *Forever in our hearts — 15th death Anniversary.* She handed over the booklet to Benny.

He took it, looked at the pictures and dropped it abruptly on the table. He stood up and walked to the long, elegant window and stood there with his back turned to all of us inside as he peered outside.

After some time, he came back to the table, collected the photos and brochures he had placed there, put all the papers in his bag, gave a quick nod to me and began to walk out the door.

I quickly hugged the woman, who was clearly deeply upset and was weeping, shook hands with the man, and then I followed Benny outside.

He ran down the stairs, opened the gate and stepped onto the kerb. The cab driver appeared at once, opened the door and ushered us inside.

'Back to the hotel,' Benny instructed the driver.

As the cab slowly went downhill, I wondered if I should break the silence and ask him if he was okay. The driver braked suddenly. A rooster had crossed the road, and the driver cursed. I glanced at Benny. He stayed static. This was not the right moment to ask him anything. Not even if he was okay. Wow, I was more introspective than impulsive.

Benny had been rude. Very rude, I thought. The death of three young men would be heartbreaking for any parent. It was a lifetime of mourning. But who were they?

Back at the resort, Benny walked to the bar and ordered a whole bottle of neat fenni — a locally brewed strong alcoholic drink made of cashew fruit. Fenni was to the Goans as was vodka to the Russians, I remember Zubin telling me when we had port wine two days ago in Mumbai. Fenni had a distinct stink and burnt one's insides.

Seated at a corner table in the bar, Benny poured half a glass and drank it in one go.

He was reaching for another pour when I decided not to hold back anymore. 'Great! Not only have you forgotten your manners, but you've also reached a stage of desperation,' I said.

He stared at me as if he was seeing me for the first time. 'You don't know anything. I shouldn't have taken you there.'

'No, you shouldn't have. But you wanted to show me that grand palatial ancestral home of yours. You wanted to see it again through my eyes, maybe?'

He remained stubbornly silent, starring at the fenni bottle.

'I'll tell you what I saw in those short minutes we were there. The Casa is grand. The stairs leading to the porch are the same as the house you will soon own in Portugal. The façade, the arches, the pillars, and the tiled roof too, as well as the courtyard are similar. The long, open-arched windows look beautiful, and I noticed the mother-of-pearl-shelled windowpanes, with lace curtains too.'

I took a quick breath before I continued, 'Inside, I noticed Italian ceramic tiles and the mahogany, old furniture, including the sofa we sat on, the centre table, the chairs, the desk, and corner tables. Old, framed photographs. The oval one resembled the man in the photo Ella Rose had shown us — one of the chefs — your great grandfather, I'm sure. And antique paintings. I noticed fresh flowers in a vase too, in that room. I—'

'The *sala*,' he said. 'That's the *sala* — the hall. The porch — that's the *balcao*. It catches the breeze.'

'And I loved the exterior painted in white and blue,' I replied.

'Colours of the Madonna. My mama's favourite colours,' he said softly.

'I noticed the altar in the inner room at the side,' I said.

'We'd gather at dusk to recite the Angelus and the Rosary there. At the chime of the chapel bell,' he said.

I realised then that there was nothing more I could do. He wanted to be in pain, feel the pain and hurt himself. I got up from the chair. It made a screechy sound.

It helped him come out of his reverie, and he blinked as if he'd just realised that I was still there. 'Where are you going?' he asked.

'To the beach. For a walk.'

'No. Not by yourself. It's not safe.'

'And I'm safe here? With a drunk man?'

Suddenly, Kevin's remark about finding me a boyfriend came to mind. 'A walk by myself is not a bad idea,' I said.

'Leave your passport and bag in the room. Take your ph-phone. I'll ask se-security to … ah … to follow you, and—'

I took his face in both my hands, and looking into his half-shutting eyes, I said, 'No. I'm going by myself. I overheard some women talk about male strippers in the shacks out there. I want to see some.'

'No!' screamed Benny, pulling me out of my own trance. He got up, promptly slumped into the chair and was sick.

The waiters came running to clean up. I told them to help him get to his room and get him washed up. He muttered 'Sorry' continuously.

2.15

It was a balmy afternoon when I walked to the nearby beach. People were in the sea, and some were sunbathing. I didn't go into the water. After a while, I placed my towel on the sand and lay down beneath a tree and closed my eyes.

I thought of home, Brisbane, Nana and Mum. About Ewa and how I was shaped because of Ewa's attitude and negativity towards me. I began to feel sorry for myself, more so today, when I could've easily slipped to the beach without drawing Benny's attention to seeing half-naked men. I felt silly, stupid.

And then I remembered an embarrassing incident of almost having had sex at school.

Shy John hadn't seen me with any of the boys, and so, he befriended me. We had stayed back in school late one day, chatting, and when the sun had begun to set, we had walked in a quiet lane at the back of the school and begun to kiss clumsily. Neither of us had liked it, but we tried for the sake of trying. Earlier that day, there had been toilet talks among girls that guys didn't have enough money to buy good quality condoms. Sometimes they broke, and the fear of pregnancy lurked. In the end, I had muttered a hurried sorry and left. John and I avoided each other after that, and my virginity stayed with me.

That was yet another definite defiance decider due to Ewa's so-called prediction that I'd be no good, fall pregnant and die disgracefully.

Recollecting those moments, I fell asleep on my towel. When I opened my eyes, I found Benny lying next to me and watching me intently. The shadows had come, lengthened, and the beach was readying itself for a night party.

'I'm so sorry. I've never been sick this way,' he said.

I got up without a word, folded my towel and began walking towards the resort.

He followed and caught my arm, saying, 'Daphne. I need you. Please.'

'No, you don't. You're full of yourself,' I retorted.

'It's a façade. I'm alone. I need you.'

I looked at him, his intense, pleading eyes. I pondered over his words. *I'm alone. I need you.* Did I whisper them too?

Silently, we made our way to the lifts and towards our rooms. He guided me towards his room, his eyes questioning. I understood what he was asking. I nodded. I could feel my heart race.

Silently, he unzipped me. Silently, I let him. We kissed. Unhurriedly. His eyes were dark, focused, and his hands were all over me. Mine were all over him. I didn't want to let go of him. We shed our clothes. I tried to cover my breasts, but he gently removed my hands, shaking his head. Raising my eyes, I too looked at his torso. Carved to perfection. I touched him, marvelling at my own courage.

Naked, we walked to the bed and lay on it. We smelled, tasted, felt free like the salted sea. Heard the crashing of the waves on the distant rocks. Deep-brown eyes bore straight into frenzied light-green eyes. Light-green ones allowed the scorching and did some of their own.

He reached for a packet of condoms.

My heart racing, I whispered, 'Is that strong enough ... um ...?' I regretted the moment I asked him that. Dippy, dizzy Daphne! Embarrassed, I looked away.

'You've not done this before.' It was a statement.

I looked away.

'Daphne, tell me to stop now.'

'I want you to do this ... to continue doing it to me,' I whispered. Pleaded.

There were no more words, no declarations. We muttered each other's names. It was as though we needed to be sure we knew who we were with. Who was reaching out to whom and who was accepting that outreach, who could tell? That was all.

We came together gently, conscious of shielding each other unknowing from what. A need was felt. And we responded to that need. Instinctively, I knew what to do. Benny encouraged me with soft words, moans, guiding me, asking me if I was okay, all the time. I felt treasured. My first sexual experience. Painful physically; exhilarating emotionally. Sweaty bodies. Teary eyes. I licked a tear from his eye.

'Do they taste different?' he asked.

'No. Tears taste the same in every eye,' I responded. 'Not that I've tasted anyone else's except my own.'

'Thank you,' he whispered after a few moments. 'It was your first time. How do you feel?'

'Some discomfort. But I'm not questioning myself.'

'Are you saying you're ashamed?'

'Ashamed? I feel free. I'm wondering why I didn't do it all these years.'

He looked away and smiled. 'That's not very good for my ego,' he said.

'Is … is sex about ego? And what took you all this time … to come to me, I mean?'

'You're Kevin's sister. And a lot younger than I am.'

'Then why now? I'm still his sister. And I'm still younger than you.'

'I couldn't control my need for you any longer. You pushed it when you talked about the male strippers.' I had to smile at that.

'Was it because I was easily available — known face, right time, right place?' I asked.

'No. At Ewa's funeral. In the graveyard. That was the time but not the place. I felt uneasy with my thoughts,' he said, playing with a tendril of my hair.

'I don't believe you. You didn't know me then.'

'But I knew of you. Then I saw you. I had already lain with you. In my mind's eye.'

I was shaken. 'What … what uneasy thoughts did you have?' I whispered.

Again, deep-brown and light-green eyes bore into one another. Tongues fused. Heartbeats quickened.

'That I was inside you. That you took me in willingly. Just like that.'

'Oh! You always get what you want, of course?'

'I want what I get.' *What's the difference?*

We were whispering. He told me he had noticed my mutinous eyes the first time. I said I had noticed his dark and mysterious eyes the first time too. That was the moment we lay first with each other, he said. I smiled. I had noticed his hands too, I told him, and caught them in my own as we lay talking. He said that was the moment when he had clasped my hand and known he'd never forget my touch.

'By the way,' he said, 'I used the strongest available. For extra protection.'

I knew what he meant, as he laughed softly, while I punched him.

I had never been playful. Now I wanted more. It felt … heavenly. He gathered me back in his arms.

Outside, the sun sank, and bright electric bulbs lit up the entire resort. Further outside and up above, there was a starburst. That which had been written had happened. I lay in the arms of the man the stars had brought me to.

Afterwards, I thought of Kevin and what he was missing, curtailing his own needs. Physical touch is so, so unique. I wondered why the Church insisted on celibacy in her priests. If it believes procreation is vital to the continuance of humanity, if it agrees human touch is necessary for human sanity, why deny her own men the only way towards redemption on earth? Why expect so much self-giving from those who continue to give so much of themselves in terrible circumstances — all over the world? Because some people avoided mere thoughts of reform.

There were no right or wrong answers. Deep down, I felt guilty thinking about such questions.

'Um … Benny, this morning at your ancestral home,'

'No. Not now, Daphne. Please. Nothing of that now.'

'Okay,' I said. 'But there's something I need to find out soon.'

'And what might that be?' His breathing was heavy. So was mine.

'I wonder what this falling in love is about.'

He grew still.

Stupid thing to say, Daphne, I thought. 'Don't worry about it. It's for me to find out,' I said as I drew him closer.

The next morning, we both moved into a suite at the same resort.

I wondered what Benny planned to do about his ancestral home, and who those people were who lived there. Benny wasn't ready to talk about anything. His need, he said, was only for me.

More than twenty-four hours in the suite made me want more, and I grew restless, breathless. Each time Benny kissed me, I said the word 'more'. The last time, before I dressed and headed downstairs, Benny asked, 'More?' and I said, 'Yes, please,' very politely. He gave me more. So much more. I told him I hadn't been greedy, except for him. He said greed just between us was good greed.

But after we had showered, Benny winked and said he was exhausted and needed some sleep. I said it was because he was old, and I slipped away before he could catch me, saying I was going downstairs to the pool area. And maybe to the shacks to see half-naked men.

2.16

Half an hour later, I finished drinking cool coconut water and walked towards the restrooms, which were at the furthest end of the pool area. Thinking I'd order another cool drink before I headed to them, I turned and walked towards the restaurant. At the corner to the entrance, I heard voices and stopped. One was Benny's, and the other was a woman's voice. I hid behind the wall and listened.

'You said you'd wait.' Benny's voice.

'For how long, Bena? You didn't write nor call. No one knew where you were, what you were up to. You simply disappeared.'

'How long did you wait? How old are your boys?'

'Ten and seven and—'

He laughed softly. 'Not even five years. And whom did you marry? An old widower! Just because you could be the mistress of his estate. You're no different than any other woman.'

'Bena, please listen to me. I was alone myself. Granny died, and I had to vacate the house and give away the block of land, which never had belonged to us anyway. We were squatters, as you know. I had to do what I did, anyway.'

There was silence.

'Why do you blame me? You fared no better. You ran away.'

'Yes. I ran away. But I always knew I'd return to claim what was rightfully mine. Casa Barreto. You knew that too.'

Again, there was silence.

'What is the point of talking about all of this?' the woman asked.

'Why did you come to see me then? To gloat? To let me know that you have the two boys you always wanted to and to show that you are now a mistress in your own right?'

'Why do you accuse me? You're no saint! Who knows how many women you've slept with? At least I've been faithful to the one I'm married to!'

'Faithful? The word should never have been invented. You wanted to be mistress of Casa Barreto more than you wanted me. Failing that, you walked into the arms of the next best thing.'

Had I been in that woman's place, I'd have slapped him and walked away. But this woman didn't.

'I am happy, Bena. My husband loves me and the boys. We've made our little world. Someday, I'm hoping it will also happen to you.' She was speaking softly, as if her carefully chosen words would penetrate her listener's ears and remain there.

'Maybe it's already happening to you.'

'What are you talking about?'

'I hear you're with a girl.'

'Leave her out of this. She's nothing like you. She's ... nice.'

I had heard enough. There was that word again — nice. I had to bring myself out of hiding. I walked out and stopped at their table, feigning surprise. 'Oh! Benny! When did you come down? I thought you'd still be asleep.'

'Hi. Just a few minutes after you left, I guess. Uh, Daphne, this is Veronica ... Vera. Vera, Daphne,' he introduced us.

I extended my hand in greeting, and so did Vera. We were both sizing each other. I felt a pang of regret.

Vera was very beautiful, sophisticated — a dainty lady. She wore a sleeveless royal-blue silk dress with a lace collar. Her short, wavy black hair sat perfect on her head. Her skin glowed, and her makeup was flawless. Her gold earrings dangled each time she moved her head. She also wore a gold chain with a cross. She had slim arms and long, thin fingers with pink nail varnish, and her ring finger had a thick gold band, plus a diamond ring.

I wore a cotton top and black shorts. My hair was tied in a ponytail, no makeup. I was the opposite of Vera. I had to run away from here. My mind was playing fearful visions.

I excused myself rudely, saying I would pick up a drink from the bar and head towards the shacks. Benny said he'd join me soon.

Having ordered my drink, I had to pass their table. But Vera had already left, and Benny was lost in his mobile. I quickly made my escape and headed towards the restrooms.

There, the fearful vision reappeared. I could clearly see Benny doing everything he had done with me in bed, with the beautiful Vera. They looked perfect. My insecurities had returned; they had never left me. They were merely hiding playing dead. What would I say when Benny told me about Vera? Would he? I walked back to the pool area and slumped into an empty easy chair, feeling uneasy and lacking.

2.17

Sometime later, I saw Benny striding quickly to where I was.

'I've been looking out for you,' he said.

I looked at him over the rim of the glass I was holding. I didn't go to the shacks, I told him. I tried to finish my drink. The drink was cool through the straw, but pushing aside the straw, I licked the froth from over my lips. I'd ask for another glass soon.

'Do you know where Kevin is?' he asked. He was obviously agitated.

'The same village he was at last week. He was to leave, but he said he'd stay a while longer,' I said.

'Have you been watching the TV? News?'

'No ... I've been here. Just lazing and drinking this heavenly ... Wait. What news?' I got up from my lazy chair, placing my glass on the pool floor. I then hurried towards our suite, but Benny directed me to the common lounge area, which housed several TV sets mounted on the walls. A popular news channel was blaring breaking news. Amid the dust, I could see images of people running and shots being fired by police. It was in a village.

'There's been rioting in Raniganj — one of the smaller villages where an Australian missionary visited occasionally.'

My face was blank. I wasn't interested in missionaries. Unless Kevin was involved.

'You do remember? Born in Palmwoods — the town of the Big Pineapple … Sunshine Coast? Queensland folks?' he asked.

I shook my head.

He gave a long, exasperated sigh.

'Benny, when you sigh like that, you make me feel stupid. Just as you did when you noticed more about Rosetta that first night and I hadn't. If it's important, just tell me, instead of asking me to jog my memory.' I was annoyed.

He mentioned a name which made no sense to me.

'An Australian Christian missionary who was killed along with his children — their vehicle set on fire at night in this country. There's a plaque in his memory in Queensland. It's somewhere on Mount Lindsay Highway. Don't you know? I don't believe this!'

'No. I don't remember. But what's it got to do with Kevin?' I asked, fear taking over my annoyance.

'Locals might think Kevin is a missionary too.'

The moment he said that, I understood the horror of the possibility.

The Church was a suffering, martyrdom-inspiring Church. Even today. But Kevin was my brother first. I said to Benny that if Kevin was anywhere near the rioting, I had to be there.

'No way,' he said.

'You can't stop me. Kevin is my brother, not yours.'

'No. You've no idea. It's dangerous.'

He was agitated, but so was I.

'If you can't come with me, I'll go by myself.' In my mind, I had already started packing.

He must've seen my determination. 'I shouldn't have told you.'

'Too late. And if you hadn't, I'd have hated you for the rest of my life.'

'All right,' he said. 'Leave it with me. We'll both go.'

Kevin couldn't be contacted. The TV was on continuously. No further updates were available.

Did Bishop House in Brisbane know what was happening, I wondered, and called them. No, they said, they didn't know, but they thanked me for informing them.

'What help ... I mean, is there any diplomatic help you can provide? Maybe contact the Australian Embassy — anything at all?' I asked, desperately.

There was silence at the other end.

Then the voice spoke. 'We shall contact the Department of Home Affairs. But Kevin is on a personal holiday, not on official business of the Church.'

'For God's sake! He's your priest, and he's getting an experience of a lifetime that will help you train others. All at his own expense. Does that mean nothing to you? Are you saying Home Affairs will deal with it? Are you not his family?' I yelled across the line, distraught. I then disconnected abruptly.

The suffering Church. And its suffering people. Its godmen in rich red and gold robes ruled royally in diplomatic missions and dictated to the select faith-hungry men and women on the ground. I was scared and gave free reign to my emotions. Benny and I left for the airport soon after.

We arrived at the main township late that evening but weren't allowed to go into the forest through which ran a dirt road into the village. The district collector — a stocky man of medium height in his political gear: a white cap, tunic and loose pants — informed us that this was for our own safety. So far, no one had died in the riot, he said. The young foreigner was safe in the house of the village chieftain, but the situation was still tense and therefore, he had a twenty-four-hour police vigil in place.

We spent the night at the district collector's government quarters.

Early next morning, the district collector took us under police escort to the chieftain's house.

Kevin was embarrassed to see us and reassured us of his safety. He looked pale, as if he had had nothing to eat nor drink.

There was a misunderstanding, we were told. The rioting began because some youth had ogled some young women, and the men from both sides had a fight. A comment was made about Kevin that he too was party to the ogling men. Luckily, the chieftain confirmed Kevin was living with his family and had not stepped out that day, as he was unwell due to a stomach bug. The police would continue to be there, but they asked Kevin to leave. The orders had come from Delhi, and as Australian citizens, we would always be welcome anywhere any time, but only after the current news about Kevin and the rioting had died down.

Reluctantly, Kevin agreed to return to Goa with us.

I called Bishop House in Brisbane and thanked them. They said they had 'gone through the proper diplomatic channel' to ensure Kevin's safety and wanted to know if Kevin intended to cut short his trip and return. I didn't know, I said, but once things normalised, Kevin would call them and let them know himself.

Kevin didn't know of my talks with Bishop House. It would have embarrassed him, had he known his sister had intervened on his behalf. Neither did I tell Benny. He would conclude I didn't trust his abilities to look after Kevin's wellbeing. Whatever they would think and believe, we all could do without another argument. No one at Rose Haven or at Somerfield knew what had happened either.

In the meantime, the local news would simply die a natural death. We would all go back to living our routine lives.

Or so I thought.

2.18

On our way back to Goa from Raniganj, we flew into Mumbai to surprise Anna Rose with a visit.

She was delighted to see us, but her eyes rested for longer periods on Kevin. Did she know about the riots? Had she watched the news? I didn't ask and instead, we talked about mundane, touristy things Kevin and I had been doing in India. She was working on the scarves, as promised, she said.

When Benny asked her if she was now familiar with using the phone's app and chatting with her twin in Brisbane, she nodded, thanking me again for gifting her a phone of her own.

When Anna Rose turned to look at me, I realised she had caught me looking at Benny. Her eyes moved from me to Benny and back to me again. I felt she understood.

She took Benny's hand and handed him a newspaper clipping. It was in English and informed that a group of Polish people were planning a visit to India to remember their time spent while being sheltered as children in Valivade and Balachadi camps. Many did that periodically, Benny said. They visited familiar sites and the monument of remembrance.

Anna Rose opened her contact list on her phone and signed to Benny when she got Ella Rose's profile. She asked if Ella Rose could visit India at the same time.

'No. Ella Rose is not strong enough. What do you think?' Benny asked me.

Anna Rose looked a little sad but agreed. While she walked with the help of a walking stick, taking small steps, Ella Rose was in a wheelchair.

'I agree, Benny. But Anna Rose could be taken at the monument site, and she could give Ella Rose a video call at that time?'

Anna Rose nodded.

I made a mental note of getting in touch with the Mistrys and asking if they could help Anna Rose.

I phoned Fehroza while we were driving back to the hotel. Kevin sat next to the driver; Benny and I were seated behind in the cab.

'That wouldn't be ideal. She's been living in a mental health facility and has remained hidden all this while. I don't think it would be wise to remove her from there,' Fehroza said when I called to speak to her and Zubin.

Benny agreed. 'It wouldn't be ideal,' he said.

Kevin agreed.

Zubin, however, wasn't convinced. He said he'd find a way to take Anna Rose to the event. She never asked anything for herself, and it was only fair that he fulfilled this wish of hers. As it was, she couldn't speak, and clad in local clothes, no one would be able to recognise her or give her any attention. She had asked something for herself for the first time. She would recognise some people in that delegation, and Ella Rose could reopen those relationships. 'What a reunion that would be,' he said.

'Zubin, you're my hero,' I said. 'I'd have given you a tight hug just now! But as we're talking on the phone, here's a flying kiss for you.' I blew him a kiss, laughing. 'Thank you again, Zubin. All expenses on me, of course.'

'Don't worry about expenses. She has been my responsibility all these years. I won't give up now.'

We concluded the call, promising to be in touch.

Benny held my hand in his, across our seats. When I turned to look at him, his eyes held mine as he whispered, 'I want real kisses, not the flying ones.'

I caught Kevin's gaze in the mirror and slowly removed my hand.

I wondered whether Benny had talked to Kevin or given any sign of the change in our relationship. Up until that point, I hadn't given it a thought. And neither had we discussed anything, as other things had got in the way. It had been only a few days since we had begun our sexual relationship.

Soon, we all were looking out the windows.

2.19

Benny, Kevin and I flew back to Goa the next day.

We sat next to each other on the flight. Kevin sat a few rows ahead of us. Benny asked me if it would be awkward if Kevin found out about us. I joked, saying I'd tell Kevin that Benny and I had taken one job off his list — that of finding me a boyfriend, as I had now done it myself.

'Your boyfriend. That's teenage stuff. But let's talk about Kevin,' Benny said.

'Not yet,' I said, wondering what Benny was thinking about our relationship. *Will he call me his partner? Will I do it too?* 'If you're not my boyfriend, who are you?'

'A friend,' he said, adding, 'but more than a good friend.'

I let out a breath. 'Okay. That sounds fair.' I remembered the panic I had when I realised Kevin was in danger. 'Had it not been for you,' I told Benny, 'I'd have lost him there in Raniganj.'

'Hmm ... leave it with me. I'll tell him about us,' he said after a while.

I sighed. We were back to our personal, very physical relationship. He shut his eyes.

We had another thirty minutes by the time our flight would land.

The lights had been dimmed inside, and seeing Benny had closed his eyes, I got up and walked to where Kevin was seated. The seat next to him was empty, so I sat in it.

'Sorry for all the trouble, again, sis,' he said as soon as he saw me.

'No trouble at all, Kevin, but you had me worried. We've always looked after each other's backs,' I said.

After some time, he said, 'I need to ask you something.'

'I need to tell you something,' I said, and we both smiled. I turned behind and saw Benny still slumped in his seat, his eyes closed. 'Kevin, Benny and I've become more than friends,' I said without trying to cover it all nicely or break it gently.

'I thought as much,' Kevin said.

It surprised me. 'How did you know?' I asked.

'I saw the two of you looking at each other ... ah ... differently.'

'And? Are you okay with it?'

'Yes. I was hoping ... He's a good man, and you're my sis.'

'You didn't pray about it?' I asked, noting he used the word 'hoping'.

He laughed. 'I may have,' he said.

'We've come a very long way in all of this, haven't we? That day, when we buried Ewa, little did we know what life would unfold ...'

We began to reminisce.

'I can't wait for you to meet Ella Rose and the others. They're all lovely,' I said. He didn't hear me. He was clearly deep in thought.

I never felt any closer to my brother than I felt during those thirty minutes. I was simply glad to be with him, listening to him and talking with him.

'Love him, sis. Ben needs love. Yours. Allow him to love you too. Because you need love as well.'

'Love?' I laughed. 'Relax, brother dear. We're with each other because we each fulfil a need in each other. Love — or whatever that means — has no part in what we share. It just happened.'

'The day you realise you're in love and are being loved in return, will be the day you know how potent its power is. It makes you do things you wouldn't otherwise do.'

'You mean ... like what Ewa did?'

'Yes. Love makes the best of us fools. And the worst of us astute.'

'In that case, I don't want to know what it is.'

'We're never in control of it. It walks in and humbles the proudest of us. Beware. I've warned you.'

'Looks as if you've experienced it too. Have you?'

'My willpower is schooled to choose what is right for me.'

'Your Church ... your training ground.'

'Our Church. Our grand mausoleum,' Kevin said, thoughtfully.

So, love has power? I needed to explore that for myself, as simple things seemingly made life easy.

Ewa was gone; Nana and Mum were safe and getting on well with Ella Rose and her family; Anna Rose was safe, and so was Kevin; and I had a boyfriend. It piqued me knowing Benny hadn't yet told me more about Casa Barreto and its occupants. When I had mentioned it to Kevin, he said Benny would do so when he was ready. I returned to my seat, and we landed soon after.

Tired, Benny and I retired to the suite, while Kevin checked in in another room.

2.20

Next morning, Benny and Kevin decided to leave for Old Goa to see the Bom Jesus Church, which held the mortal remains of Saint Francis Xavier, the Spanish Jesuit and the patron saint of all Goans. I didn't join them.

I had a strong coffee and was reading the local newspaper when I saw a waiter coming towards my table, followed by an old couple. It was the same couple who lived in Casa Barreto.

The woman was clad in an abstract-designed black and white dress, and her short, wavy grey hair strands were neatly tucked behind her ears that had gold studs. She wore light makeup and light-pink lipstick, and she was carrying a purse. Her feet were covered in black closed shoes. Her hand held onto the man's elbow. The man himself was moving with obvious difficulty, with the help of his walking stick, his glasses perched crookedly over his nose. He was fully suited. They looked like an old Goan couple going for Sunday Mass.

They came towards me smiling uncertainly as the waiter hovered. I stood up and requested them to be seated and asked if they would like to have a cup of tea or some soft drink. They both requested warm drinking water.

I told them Benny wasn't in, and looking disappointed, they peered at each other, clearly wondering what they could do.

'I'm Bruno Barreto, Benny's uncle, and this is my wife, Angela.'

Oh ... so that's the relationship!

Benny left abruptly that day, he said. They had been shocked to see him. Someone had mentioned that Benny was staying at this hotel, and they came to see him here. Could I please listen to what they had to say?

Uneasily, I agreed, aware that Benny would be annoyed.

'We've been punished,' Angela started, with tears in her eyes. She looked so forlorn that I began to feel sorry for her. I offered her a face tissue from the little bamboo woven basket, which was on the table. She shook her head, and opening her handbag, she removed a pale-blue handkerchief with white lace. Opening it with trembling fingers, she ignored the corner that had a square of lace, and taking a middle option of the cloth, she wiped her tears. She folded it and held it in her left hand.

'Benny's father, Bernardo, was older than Bruno,' she said, nodding towards her husband, 'They lived in a village by the sea. One day, Bernardo left the shores of Goa for Lisbon, in Portugal. There he met Estella.'

Oh ... I felt guilty; Benny wouldn't want me to know of his family history.

'I don't think you should tell me,' I began, but she carried on as if I had not interrupted.

'Casa Barreto, at the time, was Casa Lavanda. Estella's family bought it and gifted it to Estella and Bernardo as a dowry. Estella was very beautiful, and they were happy, living partly in Goa and partly in Portugal. Benny was born here. When we married, both Bernardo and Estella asked us to live with them. I went on to give birth to three boys, but Estella couldn't conceive any more after a difficult pregnancy and birth to Benny. Everything was fine, until I thought we should have a home of our own, as we had three boys. We didn't mention this to Benny's parents, of course.' Angela began to weep, and Bruno held her.

It was painful to see an elderly couple in this state.

'Bernardo and Estella died in a car crash in Portugal, leaving Benny with us. It was all my fault. I wanted Benny out of the way. I drove him out.'

Two years later, their three boys drowned in a freak accident at a popular beach.

'No one understood our suffering. Suddenly, the Casa stood alone and frightening. We tried to find Benny but couldn't.'

Several minutes passed as we sat there, listening to the waves of the sea and the ceiling fan whirring as it threw warm air in the partly open dining hall. Lips trembled, eyes watered, and the lace handkerchief came out again.

'Seeing Benny that day was so good,' Bruno said. 'He looks exactly like Bernardo when he left for Portugal with Estella many years ago.'

'I'm so sorry to hear all of this,' I said. I really was.

'Casa Barreto is Benny's. It was never ours,' Bruno said.

'I don't really know anything about any of this. Benny hasn't told me anything. He and my brother Kevin have gone to Old Goa and will be back later in the afternoon,' I said. 'Kevin's a priest and wanted to celebrate Mass in Bom Jesus.'

'Your brother is a priest?' Angela asked, her eyes wide, smiling for the first time.

'Yes, he is.'

'Oh … that is wonderful! How blessed must be your family, to have a priest!'

'Maybe,' I replied.

Angela turned to her husband questioningly. Bruno shook his head.

I didn't understand this short exchange.

'No, Angela, not again,' Bruno said, his eyes looking deeply over his glasses into the eyes of his wife and reaching out to hold her hand.

Seemingly disappointed, Angela looked down.

'What … what is it?' I asked, looking from one tear-stained face to another trembling one.

Bruno sighed. 'Over the years, since we lost our boys, she has been asking every priest we meet to come and bless the boys' gravesites.'

'Yes ... more priests praying for their souls is always good,' she said. 'And from heaven, they, in turn, will pray for us and Benny. That is our Catholic faith.'

'Oh,' I said. I knew I had to answer carefully. 'I'm sure Kevin won't say no but let me ask him and get back to you.'

'Thank you. Thank you so much. God bless you,' they both said.

I walked with them to their car, said goodbye and then took the lift to my room, thinking of what I'd learned. *Oh, Benny! How our lives have formed. We both have complicated pasts. Both have tried to move on in life as best as we could. And what strange stars have lined up to line us up!*

Now my immediate problem was getting Kevin to help Benny's uncle and aunt. I was a cynic; the Pope was infallible, and the chain below followed the same path. Faith was a gift from God, as Kevin reminded me often. Because he loved his Church so much, I was careful not to argue with him about the supposed errors of the Church, her priests, all those who refused to believe in anything else than what they had been taught to believe. And those who refused or refuted any truth or reform.

Benny's folks, who believed in the immortality of the human soul, also believed in being accountable at the last judgement seat. A very Catholic upbringing — I knew. I understood this was their way of redemption, of atonement, and all they wanted now was forgiveness from Benny and restoration of that relationship.

Forgiveness could be very tricky. *I should know. I'm what I am mainly because of Ewa. Had I forgiven her? I felt indifferent.*

For Benny, the perpetual pain penetrated deep within. The outlet was obsession with property purchases — something tangible to soothe an intangible revenge. Or thirst. Or need — which was for me, at this point.

I wondered what he'd say when he'd learn of his uncle and aunt's visit.

2.21

Benny and Kevin returned from their trip to Old Goa in time for lunch. The intercom buzzed, and Kevin asked me to join them downstairs for brunch.

As I walked towards their table, I began to wonder how I'd break to Benny about having met his uncle and aunt. When Kevin saw me, he got up, pulled my chair for me and began to speak. He had a glow about him, as if he'd experienced a strange, spiritual phenomenon.

'I saw the mortal remains of Saint Francis Xavier! How blessed was I to have said Mass in the old church! The stones speak! You should have come, Daphne,' he said, his eyes shining.

I smiled too. 'Next time,' I said. 'And I'm sure you loved the place.'

'Thanks to Benny, here. Truly, I can't wait to tell my fellow priests in Brisbane about all my experiences here.'

I turned to Benny. He too was smiling. Indulgent.

Kevin continued talking about his trip to Old Goa and stopped abruptly, clearly realising he had been talking for too long. 'Sorry. How was your morning, Daphne?'

'Um ... I met Benny's uncle and aunt. They came here to see you, Benny,' I said, turning to him.

He was alert at once. 'Why?' he asked.

'To tell me what you refused to tell me,' I retorted. I had begun to feel sorry for the old couple, and there was no need to be gentle, so I dropped the news.

He was quiet, reflective.

'And Kevin, they want you to go to the cemetery tomorrow morning,' I said to Kevin. Quickly, I explained to him what they wished him to do. Kevin, of course, at once agreed and asked Benny if he would like to join. He nodded. I said I'd come too. Benny said he'd send a word to let Bruno and Angela know, so they could be at the cemetery.

Soon after breakfast the following morning, the three of us left in a cab to the cemetery.

Bruno and Angela were waiting at the entrance. Angela greeted Kevin first, and Bruno limped towards Benny, who stood aloof before accepting the hand Bruno extended to him. It was a solemn procession inside.

From the entrance itself, it wasn't difficult to find the three marble stone graves. They had hundreds of lit candles and were decorated with strewn rose petals and marigold. They didn't occupy a prominent place. They were in a faraway corner.

We stood at the three graves. There were no elaborate words written on their graves, except a long white arch that read: *Taken too soon*, with the names of the boys and their birth and death dates. All heads bowed, and Kevin said the required prayers. I didn't raise my eyes to see what the others were doing.

Afterwards, Kevin hugged everyone.

Bruno then began to lead us towards the centre, where there was a shaded cover, a kind of a marque with a red tiled roof. There were two stone benches facing each other under the roof.

Kevin smiled. 'You'd like me to bless another grave?' he asked Bruno, as Benny reluctantly followed.

Bruno didn't answer.

There was a foot-square white marble stone that read: *Mr Bernardo and Mrs Estella Barreto — soil from their gravesite in Sintra, Portugal. RIP.*

Angela opened the large black bag that had been placed there, I assumed, earlier by her. She removed a plastic bag full of rose and marigold petals and two big white scented candles. Offering them to Benny, she said, 'Benny, would you please … please …?'

Benny trembled. He looked at Angela, then at Bruno. Suddenly, reaching out, he hugged them both and sobbed loudly. There was a lot of crying. From Kevin and me too. Sometime later, Benny emptied the bag of petals on the site. He placed both the candles in the candle holders and lit them. Kevin said the prayers again.

Later, we all sat on the two benches — Kevin and me on one, and Bruno and Angela on the other, with Benny between them.

Like me, I suspected that they were all wondering about life and death and what could have been if death hadn't intervened when it did — in the lives of the many who were close to us.

Each of Benny's hands were held by Bruno and Angela. He was no prodigal son.

2.22

'Whom will you buy it from, Benito? It's yours. You own it,' said Bruno.

'Free? Everything has a price. Name yours. I'll pay,' Benny replied.

'You don't understand. Your uncle and I are planning to move to the agile. This house and everything in it, is yours ... Always was and always will be. We only want your forgiveness,' said a tearful Angela.

'My forgiveness? Have you forgiven yourselves?' Benny asked with obvious anger. It was sinister, sarcastic and scornful. He turned and walked away, while his uncle and aunt collapsed weeping.

I rushed towards them ...

My feet twitched, and my eyes opened wide. I was in bed. I'd been dreaming about them.

I settled down more comfortably, adjusting my pillow, thinking how little I knew of another's pain. *What lies before me, is not what lies within another. What I get to see is not what is.* Life is strange, and we all live in that strangeness, knowingly or unknowingly. We must make the most of what is laid before us. Or we die inside before we die outside.

For the first time last night, Benny hadn't reached out to me. Neither had I to him. Perhaps his need for me didn't exist anymore. I felt sorry for everyone. An alien feeling. It played in my head.

Benny remained in silent combat. He was contemplating bigger things. The mirror that reflected reality, or a fantasy that vanished like a pin pierced in a balloon. Yet, whenever I asked him what he was thinking, he said, 'Nothing.' It was the 'nothing' that contained everything.

It meant I shouldn't get involved with whatever he was combating with. I didn't understand his stubbornness to remain disconnected, especially with me. My expectations were changing too. Because we understood our body language — the physical need that had to be assuaged. Or was there more? Did some people first fall in lust and then in love? Or did they simply drift into either of the 'Ls' as placing one foot forward followed by the other and continued because that was what it took to walk?

Besides, my own pride stood like a pillar between his indifference and my longing.

I left him alone, as he asked me to. He'd said he needed to get things sorted first in his head before he made further decisions. I understood that. Who better? The thoughts in my head had always intertwined with the feelings in my heart, but in those days, I hadn't deciphered them.

And so it happened that Bruno, Angela and Benny began confronting their past, contemplating their present and shaping their future silently and independently, while I stood as a bystander.

Benny refused to visit Casa Barreto anymore. Kevin told me Benny had visited the cemetery again with him. This time, Benny had taken the flower petals and plenty of candles himself and placed them at the memorial stone of his parents.

Benny had done the same at the gravesites of his cousins.

That afternoon, I visited Benny's village. The cab dropped me off at the start of the village — just at the three-arched stone bridge over the back waters. The red mud and the pebbles reminded me of country roads in Australia.

Clouds had been floating off and on throughout the day, and it could rain. I wanted to feel the Goa rain, which somehow, I thought, would be different to the Brisbane rain. As I walked, I took in the tall coconut palms, the various fruit-bearing trees, which I could identify: cashew, jackfruit, mango. I passed by both small and big houses with red-tiled roof tops, stone fences and ornate iron gates, and the striking red-brown cemented, built-in seats on either side of the steps leading to the main foyer of larger palacios.

On the street, some houses had a white-washed, stone-built cross with a little crevice to place burning candles in worship. Some others had a structure built in with a live *tulsi* plant. Both edifices signified religious symbolism.

The paddy fields were vast, and the hills rose in a distance. It was siesta time; the younger folks were at work, the children at school, and the grandparents napped in their homes.

I continued my walk, taking in the freshness of the afternoon cool breeze. Soon, I came across a little chapel and went in to sit in the *balcao*. The chapel door itself was locked.

I began to imagine how life would have been in this little village, which Benny called his ancestral hometown. I could see a little boy running in the paddy fields or kicking a football on the vast football field. He had everything one moment, and suddenly, nothing in the next.

It began to drizzle, and I quickly turned to go back the way I'd come. But places and streetscapes looked different in the rain. It was getting darker, and my wristwatch showed it was past 6pm. My phone had died on me. I'd have to walk to the place where I'd got off before, and hopefully, a cab would be waiting. I began to walk. The light drizzle became stronger, and there was no way I'd remain dry. It was good to get wet but being alone in a place unknown made me uneasy. How I wished Benny would suddenly appear. Of course, he'd be annoyed and give me the silent treatment, but at least I'd see a familiar face.

He did appear suddenly, driving a car, and the joy I felt when I saw him was inexplainable. I wanted to hug him, kiss him, and tell him how grateful I was to see him.

However, the look on his face as he lowered the window glass stopped me. His eyes were blazing.

'Get in. Quick,' he said.

I opened the door and got in. Not a word was spoken. No looks exchanged, either. After a few minutes, the car spluttered and stopped.

Benny cursed, but the car wouldn't start. 'No fuel, of course. I borrowed a waiter's car, as there were no cabs ready. What made you go out without letting me know? Luckily, someone saw you taking a cab and overheard you mention Casa Barreto.'

'I wanted a nice walk by myself, and my phone died,' I explained, feeling silly.

'Looks like we're stuck here,' he said.

'Let's go to that house,' I said, pointing to an old, almost falling apart house porch. 'We can wait there instead of in this stuffy car.'

Without waiting for his answer, I opened the door and rushed outside, running straight to the porch, and I sat on the concrete seat. I watched the sheets of rain followed by thunder and lightning. Benny followed me. I met the thunder in his eyes. The joy I felt earlier had disappeared.

An old woman dressed in a worn-out pleated brown dress, her spine bent in half, appeared out of nowhere and began to talk with Benny. She gave me a quick glance and ignored me thereafter. I didn't understand what was being said, but I noticed whenever I turned to look at them that Benny uttered monosyllables or nodded or pretended to ignore her. The woman continued talking at times in a conspiratorial manner and at times in an abusive tone.

A cab came by and stopped across the road, and Benny said we should move on. I followed him. The woman yelled something. I thought she was asking him to stop, to listen to whatever she had been telling him, but he didn't respond. As I was walking behind him, she turned to me, caught my hand, almost twisting my wrist. It hurt. Her black eyes were blazing, and she pointed a finger at me as if in warning. I brushed her aside forcefully and was in the cab before I knew it. She frightened me.

Settled in the cab, my mind still thinking about the old woman, I dared to ask Benny, 'Who was she? What was she yelling about?'

'Nothing. A mad village woman. Every village has a local gossip, a drunkard, and a mentally unstable person. They're harmless, and after some time, they become part of the landscape.'

I looked at my hand. There were ugly red marks where she had held me, and my wrist hurt.

Benny noticed it and took my hand in his. 'Are you hurt? Did she do this to you? Why didn't you tell me there and then?'

'So many questions, Benny. But no ... I'm not too hurt, I can manage. Yes, she did this to me. And I couldn't tell you at the time because you were already in the cab. I was following you, remember?'

'I'm sorry. I'll get some ice cubes for it, once we are back at the hotel, and I'll call for a doctor.'

By then, my eyes were smarting. For a thin, bony woman, she had put a lot of strength in trying to stop me. 'What did she say to you, Benny? I want to know.' My mind flew to that moment again. Benny had appeared shocked, but soon had decided to ignore her.

'I told you she was a mad woman. She told me a silly story and cursed me. I think she was more annoyed with me — for not believing her. Forget about her.'

'Do ... do you know her? And why would she curse you?'

'Because she's mad. And yes ... I know her. Everyone does. These days, she just roams about the village cursing everyone, I assume. Stop thinking about her.'

My wrist hurt, and I thought it was best to do what Benny asked.

Benny played nursemaid when we got back to the hotel, gently taking my hurt hand, rubbing the ice on it, bringing in the doctor, asking if an x-ray was needed. I didn't need one, and he helped me in the shower. He ordered room service — hot soup first — and then he tucked me in. It felt good to be waited on, and I enjoyed Benny's attention.

I woke up later in the evening to a worried Kevin hovering near me. Assuring him I was well and well looked after, he left saying he'd have an early dinner and retire for the night.

My wrist was healing, and I stayed indoors most of the time for the next two days. But the nights were spent passionately with Benny. We didn't talk much, and I imagined that was how it would be for an old married couple. Just get on with sex at night. Daylight hours were for serious matters.

Kevin visited most churches on his own, and Benny was meeting his old friends and dealing with some paperwork, he told me.

Soon, it was time to fly back home. Home to Nana and Mum.

Later that night, I called and spoke to Zubin and Fehroza, saying my goodbyes and see you soon. I also made a video call to Anna Rose and said goodbye. She showed me the two scarves she'd been working on. There was a pattern appearing, which I didn't follow. I made hand gestures letting her know I was flying back to Brisbane, and we threw flying kisses at each other, promising that we'd see each other soon. She shook her head, gesturing that we never should make any promises. Promises break, she said.

How was I to know at that time that she would be right?

Part 3

November 2015 – February 2016

3.1

I flew back to Brisbane by myself, with both Benny and Kevin having checked on my wrist and both sceptical about whether I should take a long trip with my injured wrist. I reassured them it wasn't that painful anymore.

Kevin returned to Raniganj — 'just for a few more days, before I come back and take my priestly duties in Brisbane,' he said to me. Benny said he'd stay a while and finish pending business. Neither of them worried about me travelling on my own.

When I asked them, out of curiosity, Kevin said, 'You're a big girl now. You won't come to any harm.'

Benny said, 'You'll be fine. You know what to do. I'll be back soon.'

Both were right. I oversaw my own life from now on. I closed my eyes. I visualised a starlit sky. And one lone shooting star whiz past.

Home, sweetest home, I said to myself as I walked into Nana's arms first and then into Mum's arms.

I briefed them about all that had happened in India and showed them the two scarves Anna Rose had made. Nana slowly touched the fabric, and her eyes filled.

At breakfast the following morning, Nana asked me how Benny was and when he'd be returning to Brisbane. After telling her as much as I knew about his past and what had recently happened in Goa, Nana — astute as she always had been — knew I was dying to tell her about something else altogether.

'Your mum's outside.' She winked. 'Tell me, did anything happen between you and Benny?'

I tried to smile while I sipped some tea.

Nana took my hand in hers and said, 'You can confide in me,' she pleaded.

I nodded. 'It's sexual, Nana.'

'And it's good?' I nodded.

'Well, I can't tell you much about that. I've not had sex since I fell pregnant with your mum.'

'Nana!' I exclaimed, but smiled when she winked, and we both shook our heads.

'It's temporary too — for both of us. I've much to learn. He's my first, but I'm unsure if he should be last … or even if he thinks the same about me. Oh … and I'm not his first, of course … he had been in love with a woman in Goa. I met her. She's married and has a family of her own. I don't know anything anymore.' The words just spilled out.

'None of us do. Look at Ewa. Or Anna Rose, me, or your mum. We've all had broken or incomplete relationships with men, one way or another. Who can we blame? But that doesn't mean you've got to be like one of us, Daphne. That is what I want the most — for you to be different. For you to experience everything in completion.' Nana stressed, looking deeply in my eyes.

'Mum did have a good life … until Dad …' I said, feeling annoyed.

'No. Look at her. Dull and lifeless. Always sitting out the porch and waiting.' She seemed as startled as I when she said that.

'Waiting? For Dad? But he's dead!'

'What's the point in hiding anything now …' she said, as if she was speaking to herself.

'Nana, what do you mean?' I insisted. 'I've heard so many stories from so many people that one more won't make me wonder.'

'Well, there's no story as such, but it's high time you knew more about your mum.'

I was enveloped into another story. My mum's.

'Your mum had a childhood sweetheart — a boy in her class. They grew up, promising to marry each other. I was okay with that, and so was Ewa at the time. But he disappeared for about two years. When he returned, he was … different. He said he'd spent time with his birth mother and her family on Country. He was a child of the Stolen Generation and had been adopted by a good English family in Brisbane. His adoptive parents hadn't told him about his adoption. When he learned accidentally, he decided to go in search of his roots and left.'

'And he never came back?'

'Oh, he did. But when Ewa learned about his background, she was critical.'

'Of course, she was,' I said, anger seething in me. 'She was never happy and could never see anyone else happy. But go on.'

'I'm not sure about this, but I believe Ewa visited his adoptive parents and learned more about his background. She told me that I had to ensure your mum stayed away from him. Or else,'

'Or else?'

'Or else Ewa would kill herself.'

I laughed. 'That, she would never have done. But what an opportunity we all missed, Nana.'

'If she died, the boy would have been blamed. He would sit in prison for the next twenty years, at least. She would ensure that.'

There was silence at the table.

This talk was serious. Why had Nana not intervened? We had all lived the best years of our lives in the shadow of a dangerous big brown snake.

'Aren't you now glad you're not her daughter, that Ewa's blood is not in our veins?' I asked Nana after a while.

She shook her head, saying 'Who knows? The other part … I don't even know who the horrible man was who raped my mother. All of us were tricked into being who we're not.'

'Oh, Nana!' I said as I got off my chair and knelt beside her.

'Anyway, your father came along. He was visiting our town … and he whisked your mum to a charity ball. The next thing I knew was they decided to marry and that was that.'

'But she wasn't unhappy with Dad,' I said.

'He wasn't happy with her. He thought she simply tolerated him because Ewa and I liked him. He was a good man, mind you.'

'Then he was no more.'

'He was no more,' repeated Nana, 'and Ewa ruled us all. She said we women were all cursed. That men weren't happy with us, and somehow, nature took care of them by removing them from us.'

What a cruel, typical Evil Ewa thing to say.

Suddenly, Nana caught hold of my shoulders, her eyes bright, her lips trembling. 'That is why you must defy her. You must find a man you love, who loves you, and make your own little successful world — a family! Bring an end to this silly curse nonsense! You must! Oh, you must! Can't you see it, Daphne? Ewa saw the fire in you. You defied her and everything she stood for. That's why she asked you … you, Daphne, to find her jilted lover who deposited his baby with her … Me.'

I was stunned. I had never seen Nana so emotionally charged. But three words stayed with me.

'Silly curse nonsense. Yes, Nana, it is silly. So, how does one fight it? It's not a thing in my hands that I can smash it. And why should I do what she wanted me to do?' I asked.

'She chose you to finish her job because she couldn't do it herself. She feared for her own self if discovered. Who knows? She may have killed or been a party to some killings during Hitler's reign! Who knows what secrets she had? Don't do what she asked you to do. Do what your heart tells you to — fight for the love of your life. If it is Benny, so be it! If not, move on.' Nana was rambling at a feverish pitch.

'Oh, Nana!' I said, 'Benny's got to fight his own demons first. And I'm not sure what I feel for him. All I know is … I'm confused.'

'There is a way. It will find you,' Nana said.

3.2

That night, I called Benny.

He said he was about to call me, and wasn't it amazing that I happened to call him at that very moment? He sounded cheerful.

His next question threw me off. He asked, 'So ... are you missing me as much as I'm missing you?'

What? I gave nothing away. 'Are you drunk, from ... fenni?' I asked.

He didn't answer, but replied, 'My uncle and aunt have said hi and a big thank you to you.'

My uncle and aunt ...? 'Oh, well do say hello to them from me too. Hope they're well?'

'Yes. They are ... and ... long story short, I've decided to preserve Casa Barreto as a heritage home. It means that a small part of the house — the western wing, which also houses the rooms my parents lived in — will be private quarters. Uncle and Aunty are to live in one of those rooms along with a live-in caretaker couple who will look after them and that wing. I talked them out of living at the local aged care. Instead, they'll continue living at the Casa.'

I smiled; Benny was showing his human side. He was not alone anymore. He had his uncle and aunt. He had blood family.

'The other major part of the house, the grounds, and gardens ... I'm handing over to the government. I've met with the officers, who were eager with the idea. There are plans to convert that wing into a tourist visitors' part and showcase tourists with the history of the place. That way, the whole property will be looked after and generate its own income.'

I could feel the excitement in his voice. He had finally laid down all his past ghosts. 'Oh, Benny, that's wonderful news! I'm so happy for you and for your uncle and aunt,' I said. 'Well done, it's perfect!'

'Thank you! I was hoping you'd be as excited as I am ... but I do need a favour from you. I'd like you and Aunty to coordinate together and document the history of the place, create a website — that sort of thing? You game?'

'Yes, sir! Any time, sir.' I laughed.

After more talking along the same lines, he asked how Brisbane was and how Nana, Mum and Ella Rose and family were faring.

'Brisbane's getting hot,' I said, 'as can be expected at this time of the year. The others are all good. They miss you, Benny. Nana wants to go to Suncorp with you for a rugby match again.'

He laughed.

'When are you returning?' I asked.

'I'll return when you say you miss me.' He laughed again.

I grinned widely.

'No need to answer that. I … I'm sorry about our last few days … nights in Goa. No excuses, but there were too many things on my mind. I was rude. I'm sorry.'

'And you should be. But I'm glad that's out of the way. When are you returning?'

'I'm flying to Portugal, where I'll visit my parents' gravesites, see the recent property I bought there and visit the suburb where Mama lived before marrying Dad. See if I can unearth some relatives,' he said.

I felt disappointed. It meant he wouldn't be returning to Brisbane anytime soon. 'How strange. Or maybe not so strange,' I said.

'Uh?'

'Somehow, we both have been looking for our long-lost relatives.'

'Yes. It means we have at least that in common.' I felt his smile.

'Have you heard from Kevin? Anna Rose? Mistrys?' I asked.

'Kevin is fine. I've not heard any untoward things happening in Raniganj. As for Anna Rose and the Mistrys, I plan to visit them when I'm in Mumbai. I'm in Goa for a few more days to settle paperwork. And—'

'And?'

'I … uh … I'm living with uncle and aunty at Casa Barreto. Being fattened by them. Fattening them too. Sharing stories …' His voice was heavy, as if he was trying to hold back his emotions.

I felt his joy, the burden of wasted years, of misunderstandings and the freedom of forgiveness. 'I wish I could hug you tight,' I said as my own eyes were welling up. 'Will a flying kiss do instead?' I heard a long sigh.

'It must. Until we meet again. Anyway, I must go now. I'm taking them to the movies and dinner later.'

'Wow! All right … take care …'

'I'll be here for some time … text me a list of things if you want anything from here.'

'Don't forget to bring my scarves,' I said; it was the first thing that came to my mind.

'Scarves? What scarves?'

'Anna Rose will hand them over to you.'

'Ah. Okay. Anything else?'

I said no, wished him well and disconnected the line.

Five minutes later, I texted him: *I miss you, Benny. Travel safe and return soon. D.*

My phone pinged. *Thank you for that. I will. B.*

I didn't respond. Not even with an emoji. But he did. He sent a winking smiley.

I lay in bed that night, reading our text messages repeatedly. Smiling. And feeling silly.

At last, I was ready to concede that Evil Ewa did do something good after her death. She gave me freedom. And she gave me Benny.

There was something good in every evil person and vice versa. Kevin would say things along those lines. Not me. And yet, this thought had come to me.

I remembered Ewa's letters — how she had wanted me to learn bit by bit rather than all at once. How she could believe that I'd do what she wanted me to do — about Henri. Surely, he'd be dead by now.

I sat up straight in bed! *Oh my God! The Polish reunion!* Anna Rose wanted to be there. She would recognise some of her friends, as Zubin had mentioned. She would recognise Henri if he were there. Another mystery waiting to be unfurled.

3.3

In the meantime, Kevin's enthusiasm to be among the poor villagers in Raniganj, the way he had accepted them and was accepted by them had reached a point where he was hesitant to leave, and so he sought one pretext over another to stay.

His request for a money transfer didn't surprise me. He talked enthusiastically of all that he planned to do to help the villagers.

'If only more people had bikes, it would make their lives so easy. And they're cheaply available. I'm planning on buying half a dozen,' he told me. Or he'd say, 'Some of them have no footwear, and they could do with flip-flops even.'

It started with these simple, everyday individual needs.

Then his enthusiasm moved towards sustainability. He began to buy milch cattle and tools for farming and road building. Everything started happening and began to move at a very fast pace.

He even started drawing attention to himself — both in Raniganj and the main district, as well as in Brisbane. While one part of the world drew accusatory lines pointing towards proselytization, the other gloried in philanthropy.

Both worlds were wrong. But Kevin got caught in both.

I hoped he would have somehow inveigled his way out of both worlds and come unscathed.

He was a dreamer. Perhaps, growing up within an all-women household had something to do with it.

Kevin seemed to glory in the heady days of heat and dust in Raniganj, in the nights of dry, open, sometimes starless skies. He dreamt of greenery, of the sounds of bleating cows and goats and chooks. Of local government grants and overseas funds to help build a school and pave a pathway of successful employment to the villages. And for himself, a pat from his Church leaders — not for commendation, but to enable his continuity in living in India and continuing with his dream.

His occasional telephone calls always spoke about these matters, and his emails were full of them describing how he felt his calling was more suited in Raniganj than in the walls of an elaborate cathedral at home.

Nana and Mum said nothing of it. For them, Kevin was a man dedicated to God. Where he went and what he did, it didn't matter if he was safe, and they heard from him as and when he was able to.

He was getting on with his simple life, which he believed to be an illuminating one, in Raniganj. I'd wait for his next call or email, where he would ask for fund transfers to help people there. This time, I decided I'd send him more than what he'd asked for.

Ella Rose had told me that she would also contribute to the good effort of the only priest in the family. She had $5000 already and would ask everyone to contribute so they could give a neat sum of $10,000 to Father Kevin.

One day, he called from an unknown number. It was 2pm in Brisbane, which meant it would be around 10am in Raniganj.

'I was hoping you'd pick up your phone, Daphne. Thank you. Hope everyone is well?'

The line was bad. I could hardly hear him, but I picked up some words.

'My mobile … dropped it in a puddle. Yes. We had some rain here … phone's stopped working …'

The line died.

I hoped he would go into the little store and email me, as he was already in the closest town from where he'd called me. Or call again from the phone booth. I waited, but there were no further calls. When I opened my email, I was happy to see one from him.

Hi sis,

So very sorry. We had some rain, and I too joined the village folks in dancing outside. They were so happy. You should have been here — the joy on their faces as they freed themselves and welcomed the thunder and fat drops of rain hitting a tired, thirsty and hardened land. All people — young, old, children, sick people who had not left their little beds — got up and danced the night away.

And amid all of that, I dropped my phone again and didn't miss it until I returned to my room. Had to go back outside and find it. But of course, it's dead and useless now. Anyway, the reason I'm emailing you is mainly because we need some money. My head is full of ideas, especially now that it has started raining. The villagers say the famine is broken and there will be plenty of rain for the next few years. No more heat and dust. But they don't have anything.

If you could send me — I know this is a big amount, but — if you could wire $1000, it would help. I didn't feel it right to ask Benny, because he's already done so much. Did you know he's arranged a new motorcycle for me? I'm picking it today as soon as the store opens. A bike will make my job so much easier. I leave it to your imagination.

Love to all — and please respond.
K

I hit reply.

Kevin — so glad to hear from you. And happy about the rain too. Of course, money transfer is no problem. Doing it today itself. $1000 from me.

Guess what? Ella Rose and family want to contribute to your one-man mission in Raniganj.

Another — hold your breath — $10,000 will soon be with you. All from Ella Rose and family! Merry Christmas!

Take care.

Love you aplenty. And can't wait to see you.
D.

I hit send, very pleased with myself and very proud of Kevin.

God reigns from heaven, and all is well with his world, I thought. But the Church, as an institution, was nobody's friend. It set its rules and regulations — the ancient imagery of heaven and hell — as well as set limits to the roles of the men and women it employed.

Fear, retribution, and the inability and extreme hesitancy to encourage open debate to bring reform, perhaps were the very reasons it stood its ground, wearing its magnificent buildings and tall edifices inspiring awe. And the will to continue was a suffering, sacrificial institution, which accepted nothing less, but just that — sacrifice — not of itself but from its servers. Yet, this institution had given some high-calibre men who had propelled the world through the centuries into waking up consciousness.

This was not the reason Kevin had joined the priesthood. Kevin's reasoning was giving of himself but under the protection of this institution, which meant he was bound by its dictates. It was called 'taking a vow' or several vows.

He'd do everything to stay longer in Raniganj.

3.4

Ella Rose and Anna Rose saw each other every day via their phone video service. They were like schoolgirls smiling and giggling, although Anna Rose didn't speak at all. And yet, they both communicated and clearly understood what the other wished to express. A mobile phone was a necessity for most, but for these two, it was a holy element, and they guarded theirs as they would guard their lives.

On one of my visits, I casually asked Ella Rose if either she or Anna Rose would recognise Henri — if at all they'd see him.

Ella Rose didn't respond immediately. She closed her eyes and after a while said, 'I am sure we would. And we would kill him with our bare hands.'

This was illuminating to learn, given the event that was going to be held in India. And I admired them for the fierce fire they still carried against him.

As the day drew closer, I learnt that the delegation of Polish people, together with a few other Europeans who had been refugees in India during the Second World War, would be visiting India to remember old times and to thank the people of India. This was advertised in the local newspapers in Kolhapur. Ella Rose mentioned it to me, saying Anna Rose would be attending a little ceremony at the Monument of Obligation built there by the Polish ex-refugees and would recognise some of their old friends.

Fehroza and Zubin were to take Anna Rose in a wheelchair. A few office staff, who they knew over the years from the facility, would also join, as Zubin thought it would be nice for them all to have a day out. They would all go out for lunch afterwards. That was the plan, he said.

Zubin had booked a big van. They would video call me on the day. *Dear Zubin. Such a lovely, dear man.*

Ella Rose did not want to watch the ceremony on video. She said she'd told Anna Rose that she'd hear all about it from her twin later. All other women in both families thought that was quite odd, but Rosetta said that was fine. Each to their own. In the end, it so happened that it was just me who'd be watching the ceremony.

The day came and I closed myself in my room, hoping that I'd get a glimpse of Henri — if he was there for the reunion. I was keen to see the face that had made Ewa love-sick, put stars in the eyes of Ella Rose at the time, and raped Anna Rose.

Nana and Mum had left earlier that morning for the community centre, for a group meeting to discuss Christmas hampers to be donated to their local charity. Nana said she had promised to be there, and it would be rude if she backed out. But as they were leaving, I overheard Nana say to Mum, 'I don't want to see Henri even accidentally. If I do, I'd be remembering him as the man who raped Anna Rose and caused me into being. Nah. Let's run away.'

Fair enough, I thought.

I greeted the Mistrys on video call and then saw Anna Rose. She was wrapped in a lovely grey sari with a shiny pink border. Her hair was in a neat bun, and it had a garland of pink roses around it. She wore pink bangles. She looked more like a Parsee woman — more like Arzoo Mistry than Anna Rose. I told her so. Fehroza agreed, clearly pleased with herself. She had chosen Arzoo's sari for today's special occasion, she said.

Anna Rose nodded, smiling.

As Fehroza was our translator, I asked her to let me know if Anna Rose would give any sign if she saw Henri at the reunion.

There were six of them in the van as they travelled through part of the Sahyadri mountain range, Fehroza explained. Zubin said the monument had been built on a hill. There were about thirty steps leading to the pillar, but there also was a wheelchair access from behind. It would be quite a climb, but they would all take turns in pushing the wheelchair. Or he would arrange for a palanquin. He turned and asked Anna Rose if she would like that. She in turn hid her face in the corner of the covering of her sari and shook her head. Of course not. She wouldn't want to draw any attention to herself.

But Zubin said it was high time she was treated like a princess. He obviously quite enjoyed himself in the role of an organiser, and they all let him take the reins. Watching them all chit-chatting and happy, I thought they were all going for a picnic somewhere. In a way, it was.

Zubin had made up a story. He told the guards at the gate that he was at the event on behalf of one of the descendants of the Polish children who had lived in India during the Second World War. The rest of the group were also all friends and had only come for an outing and to be with the Mistrys. Some more explanation on similar lines, and the guards had allowed them to enter the gate.

The Monument of Obligation was a simple perpendicular stone pillar with a black plaque at its foot which had gold inscription. They were all at the foot of the monument and looked at the surroundings. Anna Rose was moving the camera, and I could see the bright sunlight, the various greens — dark, light, yellowed — everywhere. The place of the monument amid the mountain range was as close as it could be to nature. I could hear cuckoos continuously cooing. Often, Anna Rose would show herself on the camera, reconfirming if I was able to see what she was showing.

People were gathered below the edifice taking in the beauty of the surroundings before they would slowly make their way on the steps, stop mid-way for photographs and continue again. Zubin and his group also stood and looked around. Anna Rose pushed herself to stand up, and the phone fell to the floor. Zubin quickly pushed her back into the wheelchair.

'If anyone sees you're able to walk, they won't allow you to be taken in the wheelchair. Let's not draw any attention,' he said.

The others agreed, and Anna Rose shook her head, smiled and settled down.

They were slowly making their way to the top, and I could see some people had already gathered there and were waiting. The dignitaries and VIPs would make a late entrance, as it was fashionable to be late on such occasions. The Polish delegation of about a dozen people was already there, talking and laughing with each other. Some were in wheelchairs, like Anna Rose. There were more people slowly climbing the stairs, stopping for photos and making their way up again.

I heard Fehroza murmur that Anna Rose shouldn't waste her phone battery and space and wait until the speeches began. But it was said and taken lightly.

Anna Rose was looking at and videoing the people in the wheelchairs. I was waiting for a sign from her about Henri, if at all he might be there.

Nothing happened for quite a while.

And then, everything happened at once.

Anna Rose zeroed in on a particular wheelchair.

I could see an old man wearing gold-rimmed glasses, suited in grey, complete with a tie and a hat, as he slowly began to make his way towards Anna Rose from the opposite side. As he came, Anna Rose moved her own wheelchair towards him. She stopped our chat and switched off her phone.

What happened? Anxious, I called her back. No answer. I called Zubin and Fehroza. No one answered.

If only someone could confirm he was the man we all were hoping to be Henri, I too would have given him a few choice words. But where was everyone? Why was no one answering their phones? I was frustrated. Giving up calling after multiple times, I went and sat outside on the front patio.

Nana and Mum returned from their community centre visit. Nana was grumbling. She rarely did that, and I asked her what the matter was.

'Well, the least they could have done was to tell us that the man had died in England,' she said as she slumped in her chair.

'Who died?' I asked.

'From the past few weeks — three weeks — we were asked to pray for Mrs Wilson's son-in-law, who was in a comma following a car crash. Today, as I began to pray loudly for his healing at our prayer meeting, I was interrupted by Mrs Davies, who said he had passed away last Saturday evening. I was stunned. Then she took over and prayed for his soul and the family he left behind. Why were we not told? We were praying for his wellbeing long after he died! I felt like a fool! Imagine praying for a person to be healed when he's already dead! Some people!'

Mum was quietly reassuring Nana that it was all right. Such things happened, she said.

'All those wasted prayers! Huh! People have better things to do.'

'Nana, did you really?' I asked her. I hadn't ever heard her pray for anyone loudly. During family rosary time — when Kevin was home and insisted, we pray together — she would rattle her Hail Marys, and so would I.

'I hadn't prayed for him,' she whispered to me, 'except this morning, in front of them all. It was my first time — to pray loudly. And that silly Mrs Davies interrupted me.' She winked.

I smiled.

We understood and accepted the light-heartedness and her imaginary outrage.

Mum stood quietly, wringing her hands.

Nana stood up and began to walk to her room.

'Did you see him?' Nana turned and asked me.

'No,' I said. 'We lost connectivity. I'll call again soon.'

'Oh well. I didn't miss anything then.'

3.5

An hour later, Fehroza called. She was upset, crying and could hardly speak.

Alarmed, I asked her to calm down and tell me what had happened.

Haltingly, still crying, she said, 'Oh, Daphne! I'm so very sorry. I ... our Arzoo, Arzoo, Anna Rose is, is ... no more. There was an accident. Two wheelchairs tumbled down the steps and ... and ...'

Anna Rose was no more? How?

Everything had been going on well, she said, after she had cried for a while on the phone to me.

I wanted to interrupt her but knew I could do little. Anna Rose was dead.

Fehroza had seen Anna Rose wheeling herself towards a man who was also in a wheelchair. Suddenly, Anna Rose had sped up her own wheelchair, bringing it more towards the edge of the platform, and she had wheeled it into the old man's wheelchair, instead of moving to the side. The man in the wheelchair tumbled from the top, followed by Anna Rose herself in her wheelchair, down all the thirty-two steps below. Both wheelchairs had made terrifying scrunching sounds as they hit one step after another or missed some altogether as they plummeted down.

'It was horrible, horrible. The noise … like swords clashing,' Fehroza said.

There was mayhem. People screamed. The guards had begun shouting orders, restricting everyone.

Without thinking, Fehroza had run down the steps to reach Anna Rose, followed by the guards and several other people.

'When I reached Anna Rose, she was breathing very heavily. She was alive. I saw her move her head towards the man. He was already dead. Then, she too closed her eyes. She … she died in my arms, Daphne, she died in my arms, and there was nothing I could do. Nothing anyone could do.' She sobbed.

'There was blood everywhere. We shouldn't have taken her there. I don't know why we agreed to this stupid plan of Zubin.'

'Stop, Fehroza. It wasn't your fault. Nor Zubin's,' I said, my mind churning many questions.

'I think she recognised that man and wanted to meet him. Because he too was coming to meet her. Only thing is that she fumbled with her wheelchair and instead of moving away from the edge, she moved towards it. She wasn't used to being in a wheelchair. It was her first time, after all.' Sobbing and talking some more, she said she would disconnect me and call Kevin. He would know what to do.

'Kevin? What will he do?' I asked.

'She always reminded me that she wanted a Christian burial. Kevin will know what to do and how. We must give her a Christian burial and have her buried in a cemetery. Would … would you be coming? We could hold off the funeral until you do.'

'I don't know, Fehroza. I'll call you later. Uh … Fehroza, do you know who the other man was?'

'No. Not yet. Zubin will find out. Both bodies are at the hospital morgue awaiting post-mortem reports.'

We disconnected after telling each other to take care. It was distressing for the Mistrys to lose Anna Rose this way. Two generations had responsibly looked after their Arzoo — Anna Rose. Now she was no more. Their community would be in mourning as well.

As I stood looking at my phone, shocked, in pain, I felt that this was no sudden accident. And only Ella Rose would have some answers. I shook myself. I had to go and inform Ella Rose what had happened. A phone call wouldn't do.

Nana and Mum had to be told too. I'd also need to call Kevin and Benny. Giving death news was never easy.

Nana's reaction was, 'I must go to Ella Rose and comfort her. Anna Rose was her twin.'

'But Nana,' I said, 'she was your birth mother.'

Mum, as usual, didn't say a word, except joined in echoing about her going with Nana to Rose Haven.

Soon, all three of us were on our way.

It was late afternoon. In the car, Nana and Mum were quiet, contemplating. I was trying hard to control my tears and remembering the brief times I had spent with Anna Rose. Nana understood what I was experiencing, because of the three of us, only I had met Anna Rose, held her, hugged her. And now she was dead.

Ella Rose was in her rose garden in her wheelchair, and Nana and Mum left it to me to relate to her what had happened.

Ella Rose listened silently. I had an uneasy feeling that she had almost expected to hear about Anna Rose's death.

After a few moments, she said, 'No more video messaging from India …' Then she added, 'At last, it's over.' She was clearly talking to herself. 'I was called the brave one. But in the end, it was Anna Rose. She lived her bravery all these years and died a brave death too.'

She knew.

'My Anna Rose recognised Henri. She did what she had to do. We both wanted it,' she said.

At last, it dawned upon me. The survivor-victim had killed her rapist. *Good on her!*

Ella Rose was trembling. Alarmed, I asked, 'Ella Rose, are you okay? Should I call Rosetta?'

She seemed to be struggling to get her words out. I felt she wanted me to understand something truly important, which she wanted to express. She shook her head violently. 'Listen. It was Henri. We both hid from him all these years, in our own way. Yet, we both wanted to kill him. He was a fraud, evil. Because he had had both of us.'

Had had both of us. What did she mean?

The hair on my body stood, and I couldn't bear to hear another word. This story had a bizarre, unbelievable, significant gap to be filled. One part of me wanted to know it. Another wanted to stay out of it. But I realised Ella Rose was my only living relative who knew everything. This moment was important for everyone. Keeping aside my own fears, my own shocked and saddened state, I forced myself to listen to her.

'Henri and I were meeting each other in those days. What no one, including Anna Rose, knew was that Henri had been seducing me. I was flattered, young and silly, as I was at the time, not knowing the consequences of this dangerous path I was taking.

'Just two days before Anna Rose disappeared, I had lain with him. It was all a game to him, but he hid it well. Years later, I understood that he was one of those young Germans — misguided, brain-washed and arrogant, a spy seeing his future as a saviour of everything clean and majestic, while he indulged in the nastiness of every evil that politics stood for at the time. It was expected of him. He was a product of the Hitler Youth, disguised as a young salesman based in India.' She paused slightly to clearly compose herself. 'He said he worked for a multinational; he was also a soldier. In truth, he was evil. Evil.' She grew silent.

I tried to make sense of all that I was being told. *No, please don't go into your silent mode now.*

'Juliana and Rosetta are not cousins. They're sisters,' she finally concluded.

3.6

Shocking!

'What? How?' I asked, my eyes growing wider, wilder.

Ella Rose said she too had fallen pregnant, and as soon as the chaplain was informed, she had been whisked away secretly to live with an Indian family in the north — Dehradun — where she remained until she gave birth. She was quickly married off to another young man from the camp — Arthur — who had to be sent away too. Otherwise, she was told, her baby would be put up for adoption.

That was how she started her new life — married to a young man who took her child as his own. Over time, they had genuinely fallen in love and begun their lives in Australia. Ella Rose and her Arthur.

It could have been possible that Ella Rose, with baby Rosetta, and Ewa, with Nana, may have been on the same ship that had left the shores of Bombay.

My head was hurting. The turns and twists of Evil Ewa's death had generated more mysteries and family histories, and they were as alarming as they were unbelievable.

My great grandmother had been raped by my great grandfather. My great grandmother killed my great grandfather. And herself.

Nana and Rosetta shared the same father.

Ewa was right where she said in her first letter that such were the stories that movies were made of, even though she hadn't known what had happened and why. Ewa's fate was also written in the stars.

Ella Rose asked that Nana and Rosetta be called to her in the garden. I ran to call them.

Ella Rose took Nana's hand in one of her own and Rosetta's hand in her other hand. She was trembling, yet she looked at both and said, 'Listen, carefully. Juliana, your mother Anna Rose is dead. Rosetta, your aunt, Anna Rose, my twin, is dead. And both of you ... Juliana and Rosetta, your father — Henri Stein — is also dead. You are sisters.'

'What?' Rosetta screamed.

Nana looked confused.

'Are you saying that Dad ... uh ... Arthur wasn't my father?'

'Arthur was your father because he married me and brought you up as his own. He ... he couldn't father any children of his own. He ... he had been injured. We only had you.'

'Did you tell Anna Rose about Rosetta ... that she too was Henri's?' I had to know.

'No.'

'Then why are you telling us now?' Rosetta asked.

'Because she told me to.'

'Who?'

'My Anna Rose. She was here a moment ago. She asked me to tell everything to you all.'

Nana understood. She said Ella Rose was shocked and needed to rest. She was wheeled in and put to bed. She waved us all a quiet goodbye.

Late that night, and alone in my room, too tired and sad, I tried to understand what had happened.

Anna Rose and Ella Rose had certainly talked and confided in each other about the visit to the monument. They had been hoping all along for Henri to show up to that event.

I checked my phone. Zubin had sent a link to a video to a local news channel.

'Two people died at the foot of the Monument of Obligation. A man and a woman who were both in wheelchairs. The woman was a local. The man, Mr Andrew Bajek, was not part of the Polish delegation. He had travelled by himself from New York. Both bodies are lying in the hospital morgue and will be released only after the enquiry process and post-mortem formalities are completed. No one is sure why Mr Bajek, an American citizen, had visited the monument. This was sadly, a terrible accident.'

Bajek, I wondered. Would it just be a coincidence that Ewa had changed her name to Bajek herself? Or, had Henri known of it and changed his own name to match with Ewa's? No one would know.

I'd go again to see Ella Rose and learn more. She wouldn't deny me any more family secrets.

Little did I know that one couldn't learn all secrets of another family member, however close. Some had to be imagined.

Ella Rose didn't wake up the next morning. She died quietly in her sleep.

As usual, when the pain became more acceptable, as it usually did, another sinister trait became visible.

Henri Stein had sex with two sisters. One who went to him willingly to experiment an experience. Another was a victim of his instant retaliation. No wonder Ella Rose had lived with an insurmountable guilt.

I could visualise an alert but excited Anna Rose walking in false confidence in the marketplace at night, looking out for a young man who she had no idea her twin had had sexual relations with. She was on a mission to let the man know that his friendship with her twin had to end because the camp chaplain thought it wasn't right. Would she have been distracted with the wares on display, as she walked? She might have. She'd have bought a little trinket. No. She'd have bought two. One for herself and another for her twin. Then she may have waited for Henri.

She may have told Henri the reason for her mission, and Henri would have felt tricked. But ever the cunning, calculative young man that he'd have been, he'd have felt the need to play the role he was familiar with. That of luring with vengeance.

Taking a naive Anna Rose to a secluded place wouldn't have been difficult. Coercion, certainly, and the use of force would have been made. Poor, gentle Anna Rose. Broken, confused and in pain. Once that was achieved, he'd have had hidden her because she would talk, and he'd be caught. Luckily, because his victim had lost her voice and was fit only for treatment of insanity, he was safe. Was that how it must've played?

Henri had successfully separated the twins. History would have mapped its road, and circumstances would have pulled the victim into a vortex of no return. Trying to safeguard his own skin, Henri — the smart operator — would have played a sympathetic card and somehow ensured that Zubin's mother, who was a nurse, cared for a frightened, young, white pregnant girl.

That was a likely story. How awful. He then would have taken Anna Rose's baby and handed her over to Ewa. *But why? Had he hoped to reach Ella Rose via the baby?*

I had called Benny last night to tell him about Anna Rose and how she died. I also told him about what Ella Rose had told me. Sometime today, I'd also call to tell him that Ella Rose too, was no more.

From the lips of the now no-more-alive Ella Rose, we had learned more about our weird and wonderful family.

All that we could say was that both sisters were born on the same day and died on the same day. Both had given birth in the same year, and the children's biological father had been the same man. The father too, died on the same day.

3.7

Nana insisted we all go to Rose Haven again the next day and be together with the family.

Seeing that Nana and Rosetta were in the same room, I entered and locked the door behind me. Rosetta was crying, and so was Nana. They were holding each other. I heard Mum in the kitchen — the safest, most uncomplicated place for her to be.

As best as I could, without showing any emotions, I asked them what they thought about Ella Rose's revelations yesterday. Had it been only yesterday that we lost them both? And wasn't it odd that each side of our family had similarities? None had been lucky with the menfolk.

There was silence first. Then Rosetta started to laugh aloud, tears running down her cheeks. I was stunned. Was it the shock? But Nana soon joined her in laughing too.

'Well,' said Rosetta, wiping her tears, 'I wonder how many more secrets remain to be unveiled. We share the same father. That means we share the same DNA. Yes. You and I are sisters. Our mothers were twins. Our father slept with both. There. All ends tied.'

They laughed again.

'Cheats. All of them. They tricked us into being.'

'Look at the funnier side of life, Daphne,' Rosetta said to me. 'Don't be so serious. How many families would you know with such an intriguing story?' she asked.

'None,' I said. 'But I hope there's no more to come. I don't think I can cope.'

'Well ... I hope not too,' said Nana. 'But it doesn't bother me anymore. I mean, look, whatever may have happened, Muh — Ewa — did look after me, and one could say she gave up her own life in doing that. She ensured I wasn't a demanding child. Maybe, she picked me up from my cot when I cried, fed me when hungry, cleaned and bathed me when needed. What more could she have done?'

There was a brief silence before Nana continued, 'When I held my first born — my only child — I held her and saw everything minutely. Her mop of soft golden-brown hair, her eyes, nose, lips, ears, toes ... and marvelled that she came out of me. I hugged her and smothered her with kisses. Muh — Ewa — didn't do that to me,' Nana whispered. 'That's why I didn't expect nor demand anything. I must have lain in my cot and let her do what she pleased. I let life pass by. Until both my mums died.'

It was a sudden, silent, serious moment.

'Does that mean you're going to do something now?' asked Rosetta, clearly sensing the seriousness, and deciding to break it.

'Maybe,' Nana replied, her teary, swollen eyes suddenly twinkling.

'The ones who caused all these stories are all dead and gone,' said Rosetta. 'Let's start preparing for the funeral. Uh ... funerals?' she asked.

'Yes. Let's,' said Nana.

But Rosetta held her hand and stopped her. 'There's another secret that you need to know. Mum had forbidden me to tell you ... especially, when she learned that Kevin is a priest,' Rosetta said, including me in the conversation.

She was sharing yet another secret story.

I had a dull headache since yesterday and it had slowly been increasing. I didn't think I could take in another secret. But who could resist wanting to know more when the seed was planted?

And suddenly, I could hear Ewa taunting me — on the one occasion that I had had a dull headache. It had been on my first day at work and the first thing I mentioned when I reached home. She had come near me and whispered, 'You've had a dull head all these years. Perhaps the dullness will go away now that you've managed to get a job.'

Now, I willed the headache to go away. *Why aren't I letting go of Ewa?*

'Rosebud didn't have just Rosalyn. She also had Raymond, who was a year older than Rosalyn.' She paused for effect.

We all gasped.

'Until his teens, we didn't have any problems with him. Unfortunately, he got into bad company — drugs, motorcycle racing, break-ins too. You get the picture. He was in and out of prison. He missed his father — who died by suicide — and didn't get over that grief. Rosalyn left for Melbourne when she could no longer cope with her brother's prison spells. He died three years ago. Succumbed to a prison fight.'

'Rosalyn had a brother who died in prison? How awful for Rosalyn!' I exclaimed, thinking about my own twin, Kevin.

Rosetta nodded.

'Mum would never accept that Raymond had issues. She believed he was naïve and got into trouble and wasn't understood by anyone. I tried to intervene, but Rosebud sided with Mum, and among our own misguidance, the boy grew up to be a confused, perfectly eccentric individual who refused to learn the difference between the ugly and the brash. My handsome grandson.'

The silence grew and grew. Our weird and wonderful family.

Three years ago, Kevin left the world to become Father Kevin Brown to serve God's kingdom on Earth. Three years ago, Raymond left the world for God's home above.

I voiced my thoughts comparing them. Nana and Rosetta were looking at me as if I was a seer and were amazed at how I concluded this tale.

'Weird. Very weird,' Rosetta said, dismissing the probabilities.

There was a knock on the door, and I opened it. Outside stood Rosebud and Mum carrying a tray each of teacups and biscuits. They hesitantly entered and placed the trays on a little table.

Rosetta said to Rosebud, 'Relax. They know about Raymond now.'

Rosebud looked at Nana and then at me, covered her face, made a distressing sound, and ran from the room. Mum took in the scene and ran after her.

Nothing more was said as we began sipping our tea and eating the biscuits. My headache was gone, and for the first time, I found myself thanking whoever was up there, for keeping my Kevin safe.

Back home that night, Fehroza called, asking me if she should continue to hold Anna Rose's body in the morgue. She hadn't been able to contact Kevin yet, she said. Calmly, I told her about Ella Rose's death. And I requested her to go ahead with Anna Rose's funeral arrangements as best as she could.

Expressing her shock and condolences, she said it was all God's will.

3.8

While Henri's body was flown back to the United States, Anna Rose was quietly buried in the Christian cemetery as she had wished all along. Her meagre belongings were handed over to Fehroza, who said she had got in touch with some of her Christian friends and arranged for a quiet burial.

Fehroza said most people believed that the woman who died had been mentally unstable and that the old man didn't have a supporting person. He had been in the country for only a week. The news died a natural death without causing too much of a ruffle in the media. The media was more engaged with the politics of the state, as state elections were just around the corner, said Fehroza. Her own community was told their Arzoo had turned to Christianity a few years ago and therefore, the Christian burial.

The Rose Lady, as Ella Rose had been called, had many attendees at her funeral service. Her coffin was covered with plenty of roses. All from her own garden — except from her favourite red rosebush that was just outside her bedroom window.

Rosebud had noticed the wilting bush and said, 'Even her favourite rosebush loved her. Now it too is dead.'

'What rosebush?' asked Rosetta.

Rosebud pointed it to her.

'Oh,' murmured a perplexed-looking Rosetta, and taking me aside, she said, 'The morning Mum died, I found a small plastic packet with two or three pinches of green powder in it, lying near her slippers. Thinking it could have been some plant feed, I threw it over the bush. Do you think it caused it to die?'

'I don't know. In any case, it's too late to think about it now. Let's forget about it,' I said.

It all felt creepy.

But what shocked us most was what Rosebud then revealed.

'It was poisonous. I had overheard them talking about it last week,' she said.

We turned to look at her.

'Who?' asked Rosetta.

'Anna was telling Ella that she had seen Henri on the national TV channel and that he was part of the European group visiting the Monument of Obligation there.'

Rosetta dismissed Rosebud, saying, 'You couldn't have overheard them. Anna couldn't talk, remember?'

'But I did hear her talking. I was just outside the door, listening. I know I shouldn't have,' lamented Rosebud, nearly in tears.

'Are you sure?' I asked.

She nodded. 'Anna said she couldn't forget his face as he ruined her life, and Ella had asked her to be careful. But Anna had said that it was the moment she had been living for,' she explained, looking at me and Rosetta. 'Then they talked about some powerful poisonous powder, which they both had with them. It was powerful even after 100 years, Anna had said. And that they both had to keep the powder handy in case something went wrong. What would have they meant?'

There was silence, until Rosetta said, 'Who knows what they meant. But why didn't you tell me this earlier — that Anna was able to speak?'

'I ... I thought Ella would have told you ... including the secret.'

'What secret?'

'I hadn't waited to hear it. I shouldn't have spied.'

Rosetta looked frustrated. 'Never mind. We've got to plan for the funeral. Come along.'

So, Anna Rose's voice had returned. What a woman! She had her revenge. And Ella Rose? Both sisters had managed their secret very well, fooling us all. Good on them!

But none of us would know more about them anymore.

I met the beautiful, sophisticated Rosalyn, who was my age, at the funeral.

And that meeting set me on another course altogether.

Although I had seen her photos, and everyone had spoken of her beauty, in the flesh, Rosalyn was like a model: beautiful, tall, graceful and friendly. She was training to be a doctor in Melbourne. A heart specialist, she winked when she told me. I tried hard to find if there was any resemblance between her looks and mine. Except for the hair and our eyes, there was nothing. I felt so proud being related to her. I wanted her to meet Kevin and Benny too. But Benny was in Portugal, and Kevin was in Raniganj.

How did she cope without her brother?

3.9

Days passed, following the funeral, and Benny and I continued our long phone conversations. I was genuinely missing him — his sardonic smile, his gentle teasing, and the way he would bait me and then ensure I knew I had succumbed.

One day, I said to him, 'Benny, I need to confess.'

'About?'

'Can you guess?'

He hesitated before replying, 'There is a man who admires you more than I do?'

I laughed, feeling free and so very needy. 'No, silly. But do you? Admire me?'

He clearly pretended to sigh at length.

We were flirting.

'All right. What have you done?' he questioned.

'I ... I miss you very, very much, Benny. I'm seriously thinking about flying to Lisbon.'

'Just one more week, and I'll be knocking on your door. Promise.'

But it wasn't to be. Benny had to fly from Lisbon to India instead.

Kevin had gone to bless Anna Rose's gravesite. A few villagers had also come along with him to 'see Mumbai'. I was watching a live feed of the blessing of Anna Rose's gravesite, being videoed by Fehroza.

People there had noticed he was a priest and asked, I presumed, that he tend to the gravesites of their folks too. There was no lack of priests, but the sheer magnitude of people collected — both dead and buried — and the ones left behind must have made it difficult to cater to every gravesite for blessings and prayers.

Kevin followed each particular group, said the prayers, blessed the gravesite, offered his condolences and was then called to another gravesite. The little group of villagers, their eyes wide and curious, followed him.

I was about to say goodbye to Fehroza, when suddenly, there were screams.

The video stopped.

Later, Fehroza said it had to do with the chieftain's daughter. She had come with Kevin and the others from Raniganj, and the corner of her sari had caught the flame of a candle on the ground and burnt. Luckily, someone quickly poured water, and the flames subsided, but everyone had been caught unawares. Kevin, it seemed, had jumped towards her side, his missal hastily handed over to Fehroza. They had all left soon after, the group entirely shaken.

The next day, the whole issue had been sensationalised in the local media. And it was all linked to Kevin — who was a Catholic priest and accused of proselytising in Raniganj.

It had the potential for a diplomatic battle, said Fehroza, who told me that he should return to Australia as soon as possible. An enquiry was already happening. But Kevin had decided to stay and answer all questions.

Next day, he was imprisoned.

I contacted Kevin's community in Brisbane, who assured me they would do everything to free him. I knew they couldn't. The church hierarchy was placid and cautious.

Luckily, Kevin's bail plea was accepted, and he was escorted back to Raniganj.

'I've not done any wrong,' said Kevin.

'Ridiculous,' I said. 'You have no idea how quickly things can change. Please come back home.'

'Daphne, I don't talk about God or religion with the locals. Their faith and belief in the God they believe in, is very strong. How I wish ours was like theirs. They are naïve and sweet, and victims of generational conflicts driven by their own circumstances as well as external invaders.

'I only help them financially so they can help themselves and have fruitful lives. I'm happy to be a mere instrument. I am not afraid because I am not doing anything wrong. And they love me for it. They look after me. Now stop worrying.'

'That's all well, but we all miss you, especially Mum.'

Which was partly true. Mum was lost in her own world. But Kevin was stubborn. After a few more argumentative words, I disconnected the line.

Nana and Mum stuck together. They would be up in the morning, do the routine chores, and then get back into bed by evening. On weekends, they would visit Rose Haven. There too, Nana and Rosetta would get together. Mum remained silently aloof. Rosebud was in Melbourne with Rosalyn.

I quietly told them about Kevin being arrested and released.

While Nana expressed some fear, Mum was quiet. 'Thank God he's out of prison,' was all that she said.

I called Benny. He was exasperated with Kevin's stubbornness. He said he'd talk some sense into him and get him home somehow. I was happy with Benny's assurance.

Apparently, the villagers loved Kevin, and while a court order specifically asked him not to distribute any goodies to anyone there, Kevin couldn't say no. He began doing what he'd been doing prior to his arrest and was promptly rearrested.

This time, the charges against him also included 'behaving inappropriately with young women of the village by offering them sweets and buying them saris', and this was a charge that could be proved to suit political interests. Strangely, this was the charge that bewildered Kevin and made him think that leaving the country would serve his best interest.

A video of him filmed on that fateful day, when Zubin had taken him and Benny to watch a Bollywood filming, was also circulating. This was his proverbial nail.

Once again, his bail plea was accepted but this time with a condition that he never step back in Raniganj. Benny's specific advice had at last prevailed upon him. He was to travel by road straight to Mumbai and catch the flight home the next morning.

At last, Kevin would be back home, and I couldn't wait to receive him.

It was very early afternoon when I heard my phone buzzing. It was Benny.

'Hi, Benny,' I said.

'I've sad news, Daphne. I'm very, very sorry.'

'What's happened? Are you okay? Is it your uncle and aunt?' I asked, feeling sorry for him.

'No. It's Kevin.'

Hearing that, I almost dropped the phone.

'The district collector at Raniganj called me a few minutes ago. Kevin was attacked inside his cell. They don't know who beat him up, but when the guard went to get him out for his release, he found Kevin lifeless. They're investigating what happened. You'll get a call from the Australian Embassy soon. I'm truly very sorry, Daphne. There was no other way to break this news to you.'

The phone dropped from my hands. I collapsed on the floor, and my eyes blinded. My brother had been beaten — to death? We were expecting him back home in less than forty-eight hours! I couldn't even cry; some strange sounds were coming out of my mouth, sounds that I didn't recognise. From a distance, I heard my name being called.

It was Benny, shouting, 'Daphne. Daphne. Are you there?'

'Ye ... yes,' I croaked as I picked up the phone again.

'Look, I've got to go. I'm taking the first flight out of here to Mumbai. Once the formalities are over, I'll arrange for Kevin ... I mean ... for the body to be brought to Brisbane.'

'Kevin ... Kevin is a body now,' I whispered.

'Daphne, you've got to be strong for your nana and your mum. And for me.'

I nodded, not realising Benny couldn't see me. I switched off the phone.

I locked myself in my room. The tears came. I blamed everyone, including myself and the stars. I should have forced Kevin to return with me. Or stuck there by his side. It was easy to blame myself. *Zerah had failed Perez.*

Again, I was facing a stark reality of chances: both Raymond and Kevin died in different countries, but in prison cells. One got into a fight and was killed; the other tried to stop others fighting and was rewarded with death.

Is heaven rejoicing? Had Rosalyn felt the same when she lost her brother?

Coming out of my room after several hours, I walked into the kitchen to find Nana and Mum preparing dinner. Both stood at the stove. Nana was stirring tomato sauce in a saucepan, while Mum was standing next to her with a bowl of boiled spaghetti.

They turned when they saw me. Nana saw my tear-streaked face and walked towards me; the stove was forgotten.

'Kevin is dead,' I said. 'Benny called to say he was beaten in the prison cell and the guards found him dead.'

Mum broke down, covering her face in her hands. Nana went over to her. I switched off the stove, removed the saucepan and placed it aside. Then, I too joined them, and hugging each other, we wept. The three of us felt we were dead as well.

3.10

A week later, Benny returned to Brisbane with Kevin's mortal remains and his belongings. He handed over Kevin's brown suitcase to me and asked me to empty the contents, saying he would return the suitcase to the archdiocese office. I said there was no hurry.

In Catholic circles, there was a brief mention of Kevin's death, 'he sacrificed himself for the benefit of the poor', and in hushed whispers, 'another Catholic priest involved in alleged inappropriate behaviour — in another country'.

Kevin's funeral was a sad but glorious church affair. The cathedral was overflowing with priests, seminarians, laypeople and clergy who I had never seen. My dearest brother was no more. He had been loved by the locals in the village but not by the mischief makers who killed him.

He was a good priest, the clergy conceded — which I read as 'benefit of the doubt; not guilty until proven otherwise'. They knew what Benny and I told them — he had been a victim, not a perpetrator; he was kind and self-giving; his death was an innocent martyrdom.

Just what the Church demanded of her servers.

As we were moving out of the cathedral, a woman with a black-laced veil covering her head and rosary beads encircling her wrist came near me, whispering, 'Can I please talk with you?' I nodded.

She was middle-aged, Asian and wore a simple, black-printed dress. She caught my hand, pulled me aside and said, 'Father Kevin was a very holy priest.'

I nodded, tears welling in my eyes again.

'No, you don't understand. No one understands. He … he had healing hands. Three years ago, I had a car crash. Was badly injured. In a coma. Doctors had given up on me. Father Kevin came to the hospital to give me the last sacrament. The night nurse told me later that he had knelt beside my bed, laid his hands on my head and wept. She said that he had prayed for a long time in that position. He had then left, asking the night nurse to let him know how I passed the night, leaving his phone number with her. I came out of the coma the next morning.'

I wasn't really surprised and thanked her for telling me her story. Kevin was a saint.

'I'm a single mother of two children — both are very young. His prayers gave me new life. I had not believed in this miracle at the time. And today … I've come to say thank you … but it's late. Very, very late.'

I hugged her, crying some more.

Her eyes welled up too. 'Don't believe any lies. He was a holy priest. He died a holy death. I will tell the archbishop. Some other people will also back me — he always helped. Helped by just being with us, praying with or for us and giving some of us money too or bringing us coffees. Was very kind. Very kind. I will ensure the *Catholic News* carries my story.'

I rubbed my eyes, and the next instant, she had disappeared. Benny stood next to me, and I automatically turned into him for comfort. He held me close.

Still, we had both missed each other, and that night — the night of Kevin's burial, after returning home, having small talk with Nana and Mum — he gently pushed me back into his car.

'They need me,' I whispered to him.

'No, they don't. We need each other more. I'll drop you back home in time for dinner. Please, come.'

As soon as we entered his apartment, the floodgates opened, and I wept uncontrollably. He simply held me, let me cry without asking me to stop. When I quietened, I told him about the woman I met and what Kevin had done for her. 'Can you believe it? She thinks he won back her life, duelling with the god of death.'

Yes, there would always be some good men and women in this institution. Because they too, had lived in families of their own before they joined the institution to be moulded.

'Benny, why? Why did Kevin have to die? Evil Ewa! That's it! And here was I … so happy she had died. But she's proving to be eviler after her death!' My face felt swollen. I was experiencing real pain after my twin's death. How would I live without him? It hurt unbearably.

'I thought I held it in my hand,' I said to Benny.

'What?'

'Life.'

'You still do.'

'It's a lie.'

'What is?'

'Life.'

Benny held me, not saying anything more.

Sometime later, he touched his lips to my forehead, kissed my eyelids and tasted the saltiness of my tears.

'Do they taste any different?' I asked him after some time.

'Yes. Because they are a sister's tears for her brother,' he said.

I wept afresh. He let me, held me and consoled me — as if it was a natural conclusion to the closure of the floodgates.

'Just hold me, please,' I begged him.

He did. Held me as if he never wanted me to go.

As time passed, the dam would overflow, and the floodgates reopen.

Now, however, we were both subdued, and we didn't get into any philosophical discussions, nor emotional secret sharing.

As promised, I was back home in time for dinner with Nana and Mum. Benny didn't join us.

On the seventh day after Kevin's burial, the whole family visited the cemetery. The stunningly beautiful and graceful Rosalyn also flew in from Melbourne.

Benny, who I had first met in the graveyard after burying Ewa, also met Rosalyn for the first time in the graveyard.

I introduced them, I must say, self-importantly, even though Kevin's death was still fresh in my heart.

Benny looked at her longer than I thought was necessary. I didn't understand such stirrings within me and felt uneasy. But I was proud to have a cousin who had beauty and brains, and Benny had to be suitably impressed with my lineage.

Later, I asked him what he thought of her. He said she was gorgeous and very appealing. I told him Rosalyn wanted to know if he had a brother or a cousin who looked like him. He laughed. I joined in but grew confused. I began to picture him with Rosalyn and had to concede they looked great together. Professionally, they matched, physically they didn't lack, and their minds, I was sure were attuned.

In comparison, I was still a green girl with a lot of baggage. Benny had needed a female body, when he had turned to me that day in Goa, and I had willingly filled that void, because I simply felt it was high time for myself. That was all. The place, the circumstances and the emotions were different than they were now in Brisbane.

Rosalyn left the next day for Melbourne. We were now without Anna Rose and Ella Rose. And of course, no Kevin. Nana continued to embrace her new freedom, while Mum continued her quiet, aloof life.

Benny asked me to come over at his apartment one day and spend the night with him. It had been too long, he said. So, I went. It was strongly physical — our coming together. Briefly, life remained in me, throbbing life, a manwoman bonding life. I felt a deep release as I wiped the sweat trickling down my neck onto my chest and beyond.

Afterwards, I talked with him about the similarities between the parallelisms of family lineage of Anna Rose and Ella Rose. He said that was interesting.

'Perhaps you need someone as graceful as Rosalyn,' I said, looking sideways. It was something that had been bothering me, and I thought it best to ask outright.

He raised his eyebrows. 'Why?' he asked.

'Why? Well, because you two look so good together. You're more suited, too,' I suggested.

He was silent, twirling a curl of my hair.

'You and I drifted into a relationship. It's as if we had gotten into a boat on a stormy sea and we continued to sail.'

'So ... the storm is over, and you want to get onto a luxurious yacht?'

'No, of course not. I simply don't want you to feel obliged to me. If ... if you wish to, you can go to Rosalyn ... or any of your other girlfriends.'

'I see.'

It wasn't new — this feeling of hurt. But once it was out of the way, I felt I had set him free. I felt less guilty. The noose, however, was threatening to choke me. I imagined Benny and Rosalyn carrying on the 'Rose' line, while I'd die alone, like Ewa. Like Kevin.

I got dressed and left his apartment, my feet feeling like heavy lead.

He called me the following morning.

'Come again tonight.'

'Thanks. But I'm in no mood,' I replied.

'Mood? You're not moody.'

'I always am.'

'Right. Now I'm in a mood too,' he said and disconnected the call.

Then he texted:

Rosalyn contacted me. She's buying an apartment in Melbourne. Needs a solicitor she can trust. Do you want to come with me to Melbourne? B

No. Busy. D

Okay. Leaving for Lisbon straight from Melbourne. Will be a longer trip. B

All the best. D

Between last night and this morning, plenty had happened, including the resurfacing of my own fears of inadequacy due to the constant mental pictures of Benny and Rosalyn together and their perfect suitability. Now, the possibility of that happening was confirmed. Rosalyn had contacted him. And he was stepping in to help her. Just as he had stepped in to help me, all those months ago. *Will I let him go? Is he mine to hold or to let go?*

3.11

'I've been thinking about my illegitimacy. I always felt sorry for such people, but I never imagined I was pitying myself,' said Nana one early afternoon. She and Mum were sitting in their chairs on the porch. The day was neither hot nor cold, but there was a stillness in the air. I don't think they noticed.

'Oh, Mum! Please don't think like that,' said Mum, distressed.

'Not think like that? It's the truth. I was born out of wedlock. Worse, a product of rape. How do you like that?' asked Nana.

Mum was quiet, obviously shocked. Did Mum not remember Kevin — her own son, who was no more? And Nana was feeding her own self-pity. Now it was my turn to be distressed.

'We … we just buried Kevin. Are you still thinking of yourself, Nana?' I asked tearfully.

How I missed him! Ewa had stolen so much from me.

But Nana and Mum needed to be shaken a bit. Kevin was no more, and it was important they understood and believed it and the future of their own lives from now on.

'Yes. Let's all feel sorry for ourselves now. Let's cry and wonder about the unfairness of it all. Let's forget Kevin lived among us. That Grandfather and Dad existed. You know what? Do and think what you want to. I will do what I need to do from now on. For myself. Just for myself.' I could feel their eyes following me as I walked away having had my say.

Such were our days. Dull and drab followed by bouts of silences, tears and self-pity.

Mum held onto her quiet thoughts like a wilting flower stem in a vase of water — not fully alive and not fully dead either.

She continued sitting on the porch, staring into nothingness most days.

Benny was quiet too, and except for his phone calls — which related to how-are-you followed by how-are-things — we didn't say much to each other. If asked by Nana about his whereabouts, my response was 'must be buying another property somewhere in the world'.

3.12

One day, I found Mum slouching in an easy chair on the porch, a teacup in her hand, staring at a fixed spot on the floor. Her pink-knitted shawl barely covered her, and her feet were pushed away behind her. The sun had risen after some rain, and tiny drops of water made gentle sounds of *tap-tap* as they fell to the outdoor tiles below. She was finally coming to terms with Kevin's passing, I thought.

I turned away to leave her when Nana limped into another chair and sat across from Mum.

Mum then sat up straight, her moment of nothingness interrupted. Suddenly, she removed her glasses, wiped them with a corner of her apron, put them on again and stared hard ahead. She got up and began to run, all the way jumping down the steps, her hands outstretched, brown-grey hair flying, unmindful of anything.

A man was running towards her on the driveway. He wore a half-sleeved black bush shirt, a suede hat and brown shorts and carried a tote bag, which was bulging. They caught up in the middle of the long driveway and hugged each other and stood like that for a long time. They were talking, laughing, crying, all at the same time. After a long time, hands holding, Mum was bringing him towards our house.

'Her lost love. Finally,' said Nana from behind me. She too stood watching them, her eyes welling up.

Lucas Harrison was Mum's first and last love. Whatever love meant to her.

'My daughter, Daphne,' Mum introduced him to me. 'Daphne, this is Lucas.'

Nothing more. Nothing less.

Lucas didn't take my extended hand. Instead, he wrapped both his arms around me and gave me a tight hug. I liked him instantly.

'Your mum and I were to marry. Didn't happen. I left. But look at this beauty she's raised! You're like my own.'

I blushed and thanked him for his kind words.

He went to Nana and hugged her too. 'How've you been, Aunty Jules?' he asked.

'I'm well,' she answered. 'What took you so long? Mel's been half-dead since you left.'

'I was forbidden, remember? My condolences, anyway. And for Kevin too — that's tragic.'

'Yes. Well … better be around this time. Pump some warm blood in her veins again and put some flesh on her bones.' Nana winked at him, nudging Mum.

Lucas winked back. 'Ya bet I will.'

I watched this display. Mum looked alive, happy at last.

Lucas was Mum's age, and with his back slightly bent, he carried himself a little crookedly. He had strong, rough hands that had clearly known arduous work.

Mum followed him, looking completely love stuck. There was an urgency in her step. Gone was the forlorn, poor-me look, the worn-out apron that was part of her daily wear.

She took herself to the beauty salon the very next day. She then came out wearing short, shoulder-length hair dyed perfectly to hide all her greys; her nails had been done; she'd had a facial. She had also gone to the shops and bought several dresses and shoes for herself. All paid for by Lucas.

He lived with us for a month. In that month, I too learned not only to know and like him, as a father-figure, but also began to explore what love meant — the kind of love he shared with Mum.

He was — as Benny would've put it — nice. No ... he was more than nice. Quiet and unassuming, he began to help around our house. It was good at last to have a man around the place — a man who worked and knew exactly what to do. He mowed the vast lawns, chopped dead vegetation, fixed broken pipes and hedges, painted walls, fixed broken appliances — a wonderful handy man.

He proved himself in the kitchen too. Barbecuing was his specialty. Meats and onions were barbecued to perfection. Some nights, he would also roast meats out in the grounds in the traditional way of his ancestors, he said, using fire and dry vegetation. Utilising the oven for baking didn't worry him either.

'I'm used to cooking for large numbers,' he said. 'Find it hard to cook just for four. Goes in the fridge for the next day, eh?'

Lucas hugged fiercely whenever he hugged me and called me his sweet child.

We grinned whenever we came across Mum, who blushed at every opportunity. I hadn't known Mum all these years. And now, yes, this woman — a woman in love — was flowering like a new bloomed rose, spreading her fragrance everywhere.

Lucas kept himself busy. In the evenings, he would bring out his guitar, and Mum and him would sing some oldies, laugh, and reminisce about the good old days.

Nana would join in too sometimes. 'I'm joining in the noise,' she'd say and laugh.

I loved to listen to his stories — about his life, his adoptive family, and his birth family.

Lucas had had a good upbringing in his adoptive home. He was more European than Aboriginal, but once he had learned of his mixed parentage, found his birth mother and his maternal family, he changed.

'When I began to search for my birth mother, I found I had many, many cousins and siblings. My two sisters ... we have a lighter skin colour, and so adoption was easy. I was told I was one among the many who was taken from my mama's breast. Three months old at the time.' He paused and whispered, 'My sisters … they were not as lucky as I.'

The White Australia Policy. The Stolen Generation. The sickening trauma of the children as they were forced to adopt a white culture, forced to forget their own culture and language, and worse, experienced abuse and neglect.

While at school, I had known of the whispering stories about the Stolen Generation, but it wasn't a topic we discussed. Many, many years later, the National Apology to the Stolen Generations was broadcast live. I learned more. But it was especially painful to hear stories from the mouth of the one who experienced the pain and learned of his ancestry so late in life.

Just as we — Nana, Mum, Kevin and I, together with our other family — had learned of ours.

'We are all unique, and yet, we are all the same. Members of humanity,' said Lucas. He sounded like Kevin.

Lucas was indifferent to the Catholic clergy for the cruel ways they had treated children in their care. He said, some adoptive parents were worse.

'Imagine this — one of my sisters had to attend church business on Sunday and then was often raped for the rest of the days,' he said, breaking the stick he was holding.

'Still does church business on Sundays. Says it's the best day of the week for her. Even today.'

We had been sitting outside in the backyard after a barbecued dinner one night. It was a full moon; the air was still.

'Didn't know that was happening to her, until very late.'

I squeezed his hand. 'My brother Kevin was a good priest,' I said.

'Mel told me everything.' He nodded and then stood up and took my hand in his.

I stood up too.

We embraced each other. We were wiping each other's tears. For lives lost. For lives ruined. Mum joined us. Together we went to Nana, who stood up and spread her hands wide. It was a group hug. Each hand was wiping every tear in every eye.

Did Lucas marry? Have children, I asked once.

'No. I'm a one-woman man. Me and my Mel. Couldn't have her. Disappeared into the bush and began to help my own people on Country.'

A one-woman man. Was I destined to be a one-man woman? I turned to look at the stars up in the sky, wondering what had been written. 'Do you believe in the stars?' I asked Lucas out of curiosity.

He looked up at the sky and seemed to ponder. 'I do and I don't. It depends,' he said.

'On what?'

'On my mood at the time,' he said and laughed.

'Aren't stars responsible for moods too?'

'They move, lightening the darkness. Moods move too. May not lighten the darkness.'

At dinner time, Lucas would tell us Dreamtime stories, which were very intriguing. Some I knew, and some I hadn't heard before at all. Among these were stories about the black kite, or as he called it, the *karrakanj*.

Lucas explained that in Arnhem Land, as in some other parts of our sunshine state of Queensland, local rangers would burn low-lying vegetation in a controlled way to avoid large bushfires later. It was controlled burning.

But I didn't know about the role of birds during this exercise.

'Smart, clever birds ... the hawks or black kites ... they purposely light fires to bring out food,' Lucas told me.

'For thousands of years, we have known it, but no one believed us. While burning the ground, we look to the sky to see if there is a bird, a black kite. It comes, finds food near a fire, sees movement on the ground, then dives down. It picks up big insects, lizards, reptiles, weak birds, and rabbits too — all running out of hiding to escape the fire.'

I listened intently.

'More black kites swoop down, fighting among themselves for

food. One sees a flaming stick, picks it in its claws, flies away, and drops it elsewhere. This lights another fire.'

'Have you ever seen a black kite doing what you just said?' I asked Lucas, fascinated, imagining the scenario.

He nodded. 'I have. Animals, bugs and insects, they all come out. Fire kills. *Karrakanj*, the fire hawk, spots its meal, picks it and away it goes, happy. Life–death wheel.'

I nodded. Every creature did what it had to — to survive, I said.

He agreed. 'Authorities catch those who light fires unlawfully — some teenagers light fires for fun. They can't catch the *karrakanj*. The fire kites can't be punished. Theirs is a fight for survival.'

I looked forward to our nights, for such talks.

3.13

December 2015 came and so did a subdued festive season for our family and Ella Rose's family. We attended the morning service on Christmas Day. Lucas had cut a pine tree and decorated it as a Christmas tree. We had a simple lunch of cold meats and beer, for which Benny joined us. Then, we all retreated to our own rooms after saying goodbye to Benny.

I heard Nana cry silently. Lucas had Mum in his arms, and I could see she had been crying too. Christmas Day reminded us of Kevin. I went to my room and wept. Seeing Mum and Lucas made me think of being with Benny. But he hadn't tried to talk with me. So, I wanted him to feel as alone and miserable as I was.

On Boxing Day, Lucas and Mum announced they were leaving and travelling by themselves. Lucas wanted to take Mum to Cairns and then to Arnhem Land. They would take his campervan. Mum wanted to see the Min Min lights and other exotic places. Lucas also wanted her to meet his people on Country. They'd be gone for six months at least.

'Go,' Nana said. 'It's high time.'

The big house felt empty without Mum and Lucas. As for Nana, she was a different person.

'What is to be, will be,' she often said. 'I'm not dying before my time is up.'

Some days, she would visit Rosetta, and some days, Rosetta would come visiting us. They became good friends. Rosetta would take Nana out for coffee or to the tavern and play bingo. If Nana won a few dollars, she'd be pleased with herself.

'Who said gambling was a sin?' she asked me when she'd won a hundred dollars once.

'The ones who are miserable because they don't win. Or don't have the guts to try,' I answered. 'Careful, Nana. Don't let it grow on you.'

'Ha. Buying extra bingo tickets won't empty my bank account.'

But Rosetta showed her to play the machines at the local Returned Services League Club, which worried me. They would lose some and win some. 'All, part of the game,' they said.

'We're the new Anna Rose and Ella Rose,' said Rosetta.

'And we're living our lives as we wish. One born in a brothel; one on a bullock cart,' said Nana.

They did a little jig together, laughing.

'Don't think I don't miss Kevin. But I'm still around, although who knows for how long?'

'Nana! Don't even think about it!'

'Oh yeah? And look at you! A dead woman walking! Sort out your differences with Benny. Or go look out for another man! You don't want to live the way your mother has all these years until Lucas returned, do you? What do you say, Rosetta?' Nana asked her.

Rosetta nodded. 'A different man for a different reason.' She winked at me.

Oh my! Nana has developed a sharp tongue. Rosetta's influence, of course. Or was she always meant to be the way she was now — out of Ewa's shadow?

Benny visited us on New Year's Day, and asked Nana if he could take me out to wine and dine. Benny and I had been keeping our distance until then. I tried hard to recollect why I was keeping him away but could not find a satisfying answer. So now, I was glad he asked Nana and not me. It gave me a reason to say I was coerced.

We didn't go to a fancy restaurant by the Brisbane River. We went to his apartment and passionately made up for all the lost time. I was floating. Until he told me he was flying out of Brisbane to Goa and then to Lisbon the next day to settle pending matters. He didn't say where we stood in our relationship. It was just the way it was — we catered more to our physical needs than our emotional ones. I dared not ask him about Rosalyn.

3.14

Two days later, a very official-looking envelope by registered post addressed to Nana was delivered to us. It was from Benny's firm.

I opened it.

It was all legalese, until I flipped the pages and began to read about new ownership details. It said Benny Barreto was now the new part-owner of our house and estate.

I had to read it again. Trembling, I reread that part for the third time.

When I asked Nana, she said she had made Ewa a part-owner of our property, because Ewa asked her to. Ewa had transferred that part to Benny to cover his fees, I presumed.

What a low-lying, super crafty man! Evil Ewa and Mr Lawyer functioned in the same way. The pain was personal, and all my past insecurities came rushing back. I should have never trusted him.

Nana, of course, refused to believe dear Benny would be so crafty. 'There must be an explanation,' she said. 'We need to talk to Benny.'

'No! We won't. Nana, this is an official document. What a cheat!'

And to think I'd lain with this man! The man who taught me to feel other emotions than hatred and dislike, which I'd known before Ewa's death! Were the stars laughing?

But I'd not give up easily. I'd fight him. He wouldn't own even a single tile of our home, nor a baby gum tree.

I called Mum and Lucas. I told them about the document Benny's office had sent. Helpless, I began crying bitterly on the phone, and Mum, for the first time that I could remember, clearly felt my pain.

'My darling Daphne. *Shsh* … I wish I were there to hold you, to wipe your tears. I've not been the best Mum, I know. We can cut short our trip and—'

'No, Mum … I'll be okay. It's just … so … so unexpected. But then, it's all my fault. Ewa brought him in our lives. I should never have trusted him.'

'You love him, don't you?'

'What? No — of course not. And now I never will. I mean … I never will know what love is.' Even as I spoke, I realised I was lying. Benny betrayed beguilingly. I wanted only him — to touch me, for me to touch him, feel his strength, feel … wanted. *But love? No.*

Mum let me weep some more, and then said, 'When you're calm, do talk with him. Find out more. And remember, Daphne, never settle for less.'

I had no idea what Mum was on about.

That night, I looked at the stars. I stared long and hard at the Southern Cross.

I was hurting, hating Benny. I was learning first-hand about pain. Surely, Benny wouldn't have lain with me and treated us this way. Or was I trying to find reasons so I could continue being with him? How pathetic was I!

Assuaging physical needs was different to caring for emotional ones. But the body remembered.

The heart was a strange organ. It felt another's pain. It was helpless against its own. The mind was clever. It knew how to hide the truth — the truth of shame, of guilt, of treachery even. And it justified its actions.

In the end, no one cared. Some feelings were boxed away — or written in memoirs across the waves and forgotten. The world sailed by to create new fault lines and coax new beings into its vortex. It laughed. Because what we thought was new, was not. It had been there, and having completed its rotation, it repeated its voyage. 'Nothing is new under the sun,' Kevin used to say constantly. Nothing was new. Only people who experienced anything for the first time thought it to be new and exclusive to them. As I was experiencing continuously and wondering how others coped.

No one was vaccinated against feelings of any kind. I had no idea what to do. My thoughts and my feelings were both in a free-fall mode.

I heard on the local radio the next morning that there was heavy rain in some parts of our state and flash-flooding too. In other parts, dry and windy conditions prevailed, and controlled burning was progressing.

Rosetta drove to pick up Nana. They were going window-shopping in the rain. For fun's sake, she said. I chose self-pity and spent the day all alone brooding. Well, the depressing weather demanded that.

Rosetta and Nana didn't end up going shopping.

Instead, they went down the swollen Cassowary Creek. The heavy rains elsewhere had pushed the water in the creek to alarming levels and very fast. It went down fast too.

But in those few minutes, the waters rushed with Rosetta and Nana.

They didn't survive.

I called Mum. She and Lucas would be coming home, she said, crying. They would drive to the nearest airport, which was miles and miles away, and fly to Brisbane. I called Rosebud, who got distressed saying she needed to talk with Rosalyn. It was all very sad and unbelievable.

Two emergency services officers met with me the next day. They had found Rosetta's handbag, which was in a larger plastic bag and had her phone.

Rosetta's phone was intact. One of the officers showed me a video clip, which Rosetta had recorded just before the tragedy. It showed a beautiful big cassowary, its long blue and purple neck adding brightness to the green foliage, on the other side of the creek; it was looking directly at the phone camera and seemed stunned. The heavy rain had stopped at that time, and there was only a slight drizzle.

'Get a clear video,' Nana's voice, 'or no one will believe us that we really saw a cassowary at Cassowary Creek!'

'Yes, Juliana. I got it. Now for some stills.' It was Rosetta's voice.

The officer turned to me and said, 'Looks like they filmed, took photos, and then walked a bit further down. One of the ladies must have slipped first.'

The officers had received a distress call from Rosetta, saying Nana had fallen in the creek and both were terrified of being swept away, as the waters were rising quickly. Both had been holding onto a big rock by the side. The boulder was moss-covered and slippery, and both women must've lost grip, fallen and had been washed away in the quick current.

Cassowary Creek had finally proved it had a cassowary sighting. It had also claimed two human lives.

3.15

Little did I know at the time that because of a cassowary sighting and floodwaters, two more people — who were on their way to Somerfield — wouldn't reach it. That yet another bird, and bushfires this time, would disrupt the quietness of Somerfield again.

A draft government report later would say the spread of fire was a result of the windy conditions on the day.

The van in which Lucas and Mum were travelling in had a breakdown on Country when they were trying to get to the airport, and they were trapped in the sudden bushfire. The locals had whispered that they had seen a *karrakanj* flying out from a controlled fire line with a smouldering branch in its beak.

Lucas and Mum didn't return to Somerfield. A black kite — the *karrakanj* — was held responsible for their deaths, according to the locals. It had lit a fresh fire where the van had stopped. Lucas, with all his expertise in managing fires and being proactive, couldn't save them in this, a major fire of his life. It cost him his own life. And that of his love.

'When there is a fire and destruction, the true culprit goes free and repeats the devastation. Like the *karrakanj*. We who are so ingrained in searching for the truth, deny this truth.' I remembered Lucas's words.

In less than forty-eight hours, I lost my nana, my mum, a grand aunt, and a man who had become close to me as my father. The pain was numbing. I wept until there were no more tears.

I thought of the curse that Ewa had mentioned many years ago — about being unlucky with our menfolk. But I also thought with horror how one member each was perishing parallelly in the 'Rose' family tree.

Will it be Rosalyn and I next? Or Rosebud?

My head was pounding. It wasn't a dull headache.

Oh my God! Benny too?

No! I couldn't lose him to the Rose-family curse. I'd have to let him go. If I told him of my fears, he would brush them away. But if I acted as if I didn't want him in my life anymore, blame him somehow and make him dislike me, he would walk away. Yes, I realised and accepted: this was it. I loved him. With all that I had and all that I could ever have. And that was why, I had to let him go. Love was pain. Pain was love.

It was the most painful decision of my life.

I finally called Benny.

'You got what you wanted.' *I won't cry. I won't cry.*

'Huh? What are we talking about?'

'I've seen the legal documents of our estate from your office.'

Silence.

'God! It's a mistake. The documents aren't valid. They weren't meant to be posted. I'll call the office and—'

'It's okay, Benny, I—'

'I'm so sorry, Daphne. I do hope the others at home don't know anything about this. I will—'

'I didn't know the arrangement you and Ewa had. I asked Nana just before she … just before … it doesn't matter.'

'Of course, it matters! Leave it with me. I'll sort it out when I'm back.'

'Too late. Nana, Rosetta, Mum and Lucas … are all dead. Stay in your mansions, Benny. Including the one that was mine.'

I should have disconnected at that moment. But I wanted to punish myself for having the audacity to believe that someone like Benny — a rich, successful, handsome man — would have had the slightest interest in me — an infuriating woman with a lineage of killers, rapists, convicts, and active curses.

'What do you mean all are dead? Daphne?'

'Dead, as in not alive. Nana and Rosetta drowned in Cassowary Creek. Lucas and Mum got caught in the bushfires of Arnhem Land when they were returning after hearing about Nana and Rosetta.' I broke down. I disconnected the call and switched off my phone. I allowed myself to weep and weep until I could weep no more.

Life had taught me much. But it hadn't taught me how to live alone.

Some hours later, I switched on the phone, only to see scores of text messages and phone calls from Benny and Rosebud. The last one from Benny caught my eye: *If you don't call me back, or Rosebud by 6.30pm, I'm arranging a police chopper to get to you.*

What? Why? I quickly read Rosebud's message: *Major roads are closed because of the flooding. Please, please let me know how you are.*

I texted her first. *Sorry. I'm fine. Just fell asleep.*

I called Benny, and he answered immediately.

'Daphne! Thank God! Are you okay? I'm so sorry to hear what's happened. I got it all out of Rosebud.'

'I'm okay. But ... Benny, please don't call me again.'

'No ... Daphne, I can explain everything. I'm flying back as soon as I get a confirmed ticket. I know you need me right now. God! I need you more!'

'As you wish. But not because of me. And yes ... I'm, I'm okay. Don't need anyone right now.'

Four more bodies were buried.

Rosalyn came for the funerals. We hugged each other, cried, and left each other alone thereafter. She had Rosebud. I had no one.

Benny was back too, but I refused to see him or talk with him. I simply said that I wasn't in the right frame of mind to listen to anything he had to say. That was the only reason I could think of. Rosalyn and Rosebud also asked him to leave me alone for the time being.

I came back home alone. Too tired, I switched on the kettle, had a cup of tea and closed my eyes while still seated at the table.

From afar, memories flashed.

Kevin and I running on the driveway and hiding in the bushes as soon as I'd seen Ewa. The majestic gums on either side ... Dad throwing me high up in the air and holding me safe. I heard my own childhood laughter ... Opening all the connecting doors in the house so everyone could see and hear everyone else ... everything entangling ... I got up and went outside.

It was time for everything here to stop. Time for me to leave. Time for the fat house to stop basking.

Going back in, I swallowed extra pain killers, came outside again, climbed into the makeshift hammock between the gums past the shed and closed my eyes.

The sky was aglow. I'd never seen a fire such as this one before. Everything was alight. I heard siren sounds in the distance. I started coughing. Someone had lifted me up from the hammock and was rushing me towards an ambulance.

'Ma'am,' said an emergency services officer, 'is there anyone else inside the house?'

'No,' I told him, still feeling disoriented. 'All are dead. We buried four of them today.'

He was staring at me, and through his hard head hat and other protective gear, I saw his blue eyes open wide.

'I'm alone,' I muttered. 'There's no one else. But what happened? How?' I was now looking at the scene before me. The house was on fire. No. It was gone. Black. Raised to the ground. *Good Lord! My house!*

'Unbelievable that you could have slept through that,' one of them said. 'You're very lucky.'

Was I? Lucky? I had wanted the house to perish.

I began to feel sorry for myself. And orphaned. Unloved. And now, homeless.

I was taken to the hospital for examination.

Benny came to see me there.

'You don't even have the house now,' I said as soon as I saw him. 'It's gone!'

'Thank goodness you're okay!'

'Benny, I'm exhausted. Please, leave me. And don't come back. Ever. Never.'

'Kevin,' I whispered, 'I don't want to be alone. Take me to you. To Nana. To Mum. To Lucas. To Anna Rose. To Dad. Amen.'

3.16

I lived with Rosebud at Rose Haven for over a week. It was the last week of January 2016 when people returned to some normalcy after the holiday period. I told her I'd be leaving Brisbane and going far away.

Rosebud never asked questions and never expected anything to be told to her. She was, in a way, neither happy nor unhappy. She did what was needed to be done and stayed out of things that were not expected of her. She lived like a nun in a monastery, of which she was the abbess as well as the postulant. Just like Mum had been before Lucas had come back for her.

Living with Rosebud taught me that it was painful but possible to live alone. That over time, I'd come to know what would best suit me and that I'd be able to walk that path.

During the days I lived with her, I took long, lonely walks, at times wandering off the trodden path into a little bushland close by. One such path led to an old swamp — a pond. I'd sit there on the grass and think about my life and the shape it had taken repeatedly — observing my surroundings.

Pale-green waterlily leaves rested unmoving, each with a deep cut, some looking like cracked hearts. The unseen roots underneath mangled within themselves, putting up a calm, collaborative, concerted effort so the restful waters reflected the upturned trees, the tall reeds, the occasional bird that flew across the bright-blue sky sprinkled with grey-white clouds.

It all looked like an eerily evasive eviction of the senses. At times, a gentle breeze swept across the calm waters, distorting the upturned reflection. Or a duck would gently glide, creating a ripple of trail that soon disappeared as if it never existed. And while the duck glided and clashed in the floating leaves, a leaf would sink and rise again. I wondered what it would say … that it wasn't bothered by the duck, or nothing ever mattered. Because both the duck and the leaf were meant to be there at that time.

Up at the sky, my eyes reached as far as my sight could linger on. To find God, the ruler, the knower of all things known and unknown and those yet to be made known until he chose to let them be known. The all-important question lay unasked: 'why'. And other questions that lingered, held, like jumbled remnants of a morning dream: 'what, where, how, when'. They too died a natural death.

Such is life. Everyone sees what we wish them to see. Perfection. Happy families. Contentment. Holiday photographs. Just like the pond leaves. Tranquil outside, while the roots are all tangled beneath. Perhaps choking one another. Yet they live. And they die when they cannot live any more. New ones take their place. The world is not big enough.

With such thoughts, I'd walk back to Rosebud's house.

'Are you afraid to die?' I asked her one night as we sat in easy chairs outside on the patio, having had dinner, which was a local pizza, home delivered. She was looking up at the stars. The night was cool, and gusts of light wind blew occasionally.

'No,' she said, tucking a hair tendril behind her ear, but not looking at me. She looked tired.

'Come on. Most of us are,' I provoked. I wanted to know what she was thinking.

'Not me. I died with Raymond. He rests among the stars. When it's my turn to stop breathing, I will join him there,' she replied as though she couldn't wait to stop breathing.

I no longer felt the need to know her thoughts. While Kevin and the others were up there, Ewa was too.

Benny and I weren't in touch anymore. I had blocked his number. My world had turned over. I was truly alone.

Whoever had drafted my story in the stars was a clever manipulator. I was given life in all its glory once, but it was snatched away. Now I was empty of everything. Rosebud and Rosalyn were the only two with whom I had a link. But I had to restart my life. For as long as I had it within me.

Such thoughts continued, and I felt lethargic and wallowing in self-pity. I couldn't stay with Rosebud forever.

I took myself to Portugal.

3.17

My decision to go to Portugal was impulsive. I felt alone and felt the loss of all dignity. Who would believe my strange story? I wished to be far away from every known person. *Oh, Benny, Benny! I miss you so much. But I had to do this because of you — so you can live. The stars. The stars, Benny. It's all written. It all happens. We have no control.*

Sometimes, it was easy to sink into a pit. When you had nowhere to go, you wanted to be out. Out of everything.

I booked myself in a moderate three-star hotel in Alfama, Lisbon. The Natalia looked as non-descript from the outside as it was inside. It was located on a side street, had a small door as its entrance, which led to a tiny seating area. A narrow staircase led to the room allocated to me. It had a single bed, a table, a chair, and a lamp with a crooked lampshade. A framed picture of a waterfall hung on the wall. A small window opened to the street, and next to the window was the bathroom. It was very basic, had the bare necessities and hot water. Perfect for me in my current mood and situation.

I looked at the street, which led into a labyrinth of other cobble-stone streets that housed quaint cafés and eateries. I could easily lose myself here. After living in the vastness that was Australia, the empty spaces, the long motorways, and the straight roads that led from Brisbane to the Glass House Mountains and beyond the country roads, Alfama seemed to be closeted, contained and charming. There was so much to see and get distracted with — especially the old churches and the history. These thoughts were part of my determined efforts to stop feeling sorry for myself.

On the first day, I was content to just roam the streets, familiarising myself with the streetscape, walking into little cafés, window-shopping, stepping into majestic churches, which didn't charge entry fees. It felt good to be a tourist. Until I looked at the picture of Se Cathedral in my guidebook. Memories came back of the Se Cathedral and the Basilica in Goa.

Oh, Kevin! Are you still praying? Do you know what's happening to me?

I wiped my fresh tears with a fresh tissue. My dark night of the soul had begun afresh. But this time, I welcomed it. I continued walking the steep streets. By the time I reached back to the hotel, I was exhausted.

The second day, I wandered into an old church and sat in a corner pew, bent my head low as though I were in deep prayer. I wasn't. Outside, it was sunny and warm.

What was I doing here in Lisbon? Did being in new surroundings, far away from everything and everyone familiar reduce a human's ability to feel pain? Or did we only appreciate the old environment when we were taken out of it? My life, as it was now, didn't have any future, and there was nothing I was looking forward to. Daphne's doldrums.

It was and always will be about people, silly.

Benny shouldn't have shown me passion. But he had — and so much more.

Kevin shouldn't have become a priest. But he had — and died.

Henri should have left the Gorski twins alone. But he hadn't.

Anna Rose and Ella Rose shouldn't have befriended Henri. But they had.

Ewa should have never left Munich. But she settled in Australia.

Mum should have eloped with Lucas when she had the chance. But she hadn't.

Rosetta and Nana should not have walked towards a swollen creek. But they had.

I should have continued to dislike Benny as I had Ewa. But I didn't.

Was it fate? Or did everyone exercise free will?

In a sinister way, I hoped Ewa were alive. In living off her barbs, I'd have lived — constantly at war and alert. Not the way I was now — depressed and uninterested. What had I to live for anyway?

I wanted to see Lisbon through Benny's eyes. I missed him. I imagined all scenarios that would take place when he and I'd reconnect. Yes, much as I was hurting, I wanted to. *Just one last time.*

I'd insist we meet on neutral ground — not in his apartment or office, nor at Rose Haven. Home — I didn't have one anymore. Ah yes — at the Brisbane Botanic Gardens. Sit on the same wooden bench. In public, we couldn't get intimate. It was safer. No, I almost screamed, I wanted him to hold me … *just one more time. Just once.*

Sitting, weeping silently in a Lisbon church, I transported myself to Brisbane. I'd go to his apartment. *One last time. Because, at some point in our lives, we all want that which is denied to us.* This was that point for me. After this one last time, I'd disappear from his life.

I sighed as I gathered my bag, the tourist book and my water bottle and began to step out of the church, realising then that I had entered the church of Saint Anthony of Padua. Saint Anthony was a saint of lost things. Kevin had once said a simple prayer when I had lost Ewa's glasses while pretending to be her and had been worried, she would somehow find out that the culprit was me.

Saint Anthony, please look around; something is lost and must be found.

The glasses were found, and Kevin had said, 'Saint Anthony never fails to deliver.'

I realised I was whispering those words now. *So silly.*

'No, I've lost everything. You can't help me,' I whispered into the wind as I started walking.

It was getting warmer, and more tourists were wandering on the street. I meandered towards a little seating space on some steps and sat down. I was tired, having walked a lot the entire day — up and down the streets and the hundreds of steps everywhere. I put my head down on my knees and let my tears flow. I gave up.

'Thank you for coming here, Daphne,' said a voice close in my ear.

3.18

Hallucination. I ignored it. But someone was near me. I turned and found Benny seated next to me, looking into my reddened eyes. Shock held me still for a moment, but I noticed the film of tears in his dark ones. Or did I imagine them? He was now sporting a beard. He looked as if he hadn't slept for days. 'Who, who told you I was here?' I asked as I stood up.

'I have my ways … to know all about you,' he answered.

'Ah yes, of course. "I will get on with it. Leave it with me."' I quoted his lines back to him. *Oh my God! Where are all those lines of hatred I imagined I'd say?*

'Daphne, Rosalyn is pregnant. She asked me to help her. That's why I couldn't be with you sooner.'

I placed both my hands on my ears. I was dying inside, and he was talking about Rosalyn! 'I don't want to hear anything about you and her. But congratulations, anyway!' Then, I freaked, laughing, my feet unsteady.

'Rosalyn and I are just like Anna Rose and Ella Rose. And you are Henri. The man who slept with both sisters. No. Had sex with.'

He shook with clear rage. Grabbing my forearms, his angry eyes boring into mine, he almost shouted, 'How dare you? Your cousin is pregnant. But not by me! She's with her fiancé. An army doctor who was deployed in Afghanistan. He's back now but was untraceable for a while. She needed someone to talk with. Not her mum nor you, but a stranger who isn't entirely a stranger. That's all.' He took a deep breath, let go of my arms before continuing, 'You have no right to accuse me of such a thing, Daphne. It's deplorable, even for you.'

I sat down again. He did too. I quietened. That was my external voice. But inside of me there was a loud noise. *Daphne*, the noisy voice said, *you couldn't even get this right.*

If I could have killed someone at that time, it would have been this self of mine, which shouted each time that I was wrong, useless, and undeserving of anything good. But then, this self was taller, stronger than my other self. I murmured a soft 'sorry', feeling miserable.

His next question threw me off.

'Are you pregnant?'

'I … what? Of course not!' I exclaimed, shocked at the very thought.

'I think you are,' he said.

'Now I know you're mad,' I said as I touched my abdomen. *No. Surely not?*

'Please don't stress,' he said, 'we'll find out soon enough. And I beg you—'

'What?'

'If you are pregnant, don't abort our child.'

Our child? This is crazy, a dream. One moment, I'm considering the possibility of being pregnant. The next, I'm forced to think of an abortion? The cheek! 'You are mad! Why would I do that?'

He shrugged, and then his shoulders drooped, and he began to look everywhere except at me.

Even if I wanted to shout, at that moment, I couldn't. It was as if my voice box had clogged. This man, who had made me homeless, who made me feel confused about everything, forced me now to think about an alien subject. But again, he was the only man I had ever known. The only man who stood alive and real near me when every other person who I knew and loved laid dead. The man who had a troubled past but somehow came in search of me. *Why, Benny, why are you so good to me?* After a few moments, I uttered a guttural cry and surrendered.

Later, I'd tell him that it was his uncertainty, his tears and fears that broke me.

There on those steps that led to some more steps below, we held each other and wept, piteously, our bodies shaking, jerking, and our hands reaching out to each other to wipe tears. What could I do now? Everything was out of control.

An elderly couple came to us asking in Portuguese if we were all right and if they could be of any help. Benny thanked them, assuring all was good. The woman moved her head towards Saint Anthony's church, said something to Benny, and he nodded then replied, smiling despite his tears.

Once we calmed down a bit, I pushed myself away from him and stood up.

Before I could speak, he began with, 'First, I'm extremely sorry ... for everything. Secondly, your house was always yours. I had transferred the title deeds in your name in entirety — before it burnt down. I have the papers to prove the date.'

'I don't want it ... the estate,' I said. 'You're the one with an obsession for houses and estates. I'm leaving Brisbane.'

'Okay. Tell me where and when, and I'll move in with you,' he responded quietly.

'Benny,' I said, 'don't.'

He continued as if he hadn't heard what I said, 'And about the house fire. It was an accident. A group of young teenagers smoked and left some live cigarette butts near the vegetation. It soon lit up. Also, a petrol can was found close by. But the investigation concluded it was an accident. It was an old house and burnt easily, quickly.'

'Our insurance had expired,' I said.

'No. The claim is being processed.'

I took longer to process all that he had just told me. There was more that I had to tell him, but instead I asked him what the older woman had said to him, and why had he smiled when he replied,

'Nothing.'

I folded my arms and gave him a hard stare, uncaring of my tear-streaked face.

'Okay. She asked if Saint Anthony had found something I had lost. I said, he had. That was all.'

'Oh.'

We began to walk. He said we could break for lunch somewhere and then go to his hotel room for a chat. He opted for a small, comfortable place just opposite the Natalia.

As we were shown to our table, I said, 'That's my hotel,' pointing towards it.

'I know. Room number 224. Mine's 225.'

'You're staying there? You don't fit in. A place like The Grand or something would be more like you,' I said, my eyes wide.

'And have you disappear on me again? No. Not this time. I've been your neighbour for the past forty-eight hours. We'll talk. But let's have lunch first. They make excellent chorizos here — better than in Goa. Try some.'

3.19

It had all been Ewa's idea, he told me, after admitting that he had certainly eyed our house and had wanted to buy it long ago. Ewa had told him she wouldn't pay his fees, but he could have her own share of the house and estate transferred to his name upon her death. It was tempting.

With everything else going around, including Kevin's death, he had forgotten to remind his office assistant not to send the notice to us. When I found out, it was too late.

I believed him. It came so easily to me, and it didn't surprise me. Maybe because I always believed in him.

'How … how are Bruno and Angela?' I asked.

'They're well. I've arranged for them to live in the eastern part of the Casa and have provided them with 24/7 in-house care. The larger part of the Casa and the grounds have been leased to the government, as planned, because it's a heritage-listed building, and it'll be overseen as a tourist spot.'

'It was never about the house or land or properties, was it?' I asked as I fidgeted with my napkin.

'It was never only about hating Ewa, was it?' he asked.

Silently, we spoke to our souls. So much had happened. Would we ever be free?

'I'd like you to be my friend again,' I said. I hadn't planned to say this. 'I mean—'

'I'd like that very much. But I'd like more.' He removed the napkin from my hands and held them in his own, large ones.

I looked at our joined hands. His were strong big and dark. No black ring. Mine were smaller, unsteady. He raised them to his lips. I let him. It felt right.

We returned to our hotel and went to his room. As soon as he opened the door, he took me in his arms and kissed me frantically. I did the same. When we came up for air after a long time, my fears and uncertainties rose again. I asked him if he was sure he wanted to continue with our relationship.

He said he was but wasn't sure if I was. Then he smiled and said, 'I will get on with it. Leave it with me.'

We both laughed.

Again, I surprised myself. Benny would find a way to bring me out of my self-doubts. But that had not been my intention a few hours ago. *Just one more time. Then, I'll let him go.*

No. I had to tell him openly about my fears and convince him that we weren't meant to be. 'Benny,' I said, and then I broke down. Haltingly, I told him about my horrifying imaginations. I told him about how each person was born and died, naming each of them and drawing parallels of the Gorski lineage between the twin sisters.

'Ella Rose and Anna Rose were twins. Both had a daughter each from the same man. Each daughter gave birth to a girl. My mum had twins, and Rosebud had two children. Of those, one became a priest, the other a small criminal. Both men died in prison cells. Anna Rose killed Henri, I'm sure of that, and herself. And I strongly believe Ella Rose also killed herself on the same night.'

I told him about Ewa's curse — that the women in my family were truly cursed where their men were concerned. I told him about my own damaged, disgraced heart.

At last, with tears almost choking me, I told him it was for these reasons that I had to let him go. That I could never see myself putting him in harm's way. That I had planned to somehow prove to him that I hated him, and he'd let me go of his own accord. That I had used the notice about the house as an excuse to show him I didn't trust him, when in fact, I didn't care about the house. So sacrificial. It made me feel like a fraud.

'We can't be together. I don't want you to die because of my family curse,' I said. *I will live as Rosebud does — without you. But I do want to be with you. Just one last time.*

There was silence, and I dared not raise my eyes to look at him. This was it. He too would understand. I mean, what man would walk into such a chamber of horrors? I wasn't worth it. There were several other more apt women who would gladly step in and build their lives with him. This thought brought a familiar pain.

'I've been thinking something similar,' he said.

'You have?' I turned my face away. I felt shattered. I had to leave soon, before I humiliated myself and made it more awkward for him by asking him, *just one more time*?

'My family carries a curse too. No male member is to survive to continue the Barreto line. My three cousins died. Do you remember that old woman we met when we were caught in the rain in Goa?'

I did. She had almost twisted my wrist.

'She was talking about a curse on my family that day. My grandfather had shot hers — accidentally — and had disappeared from Goa. I think it would have been when he found Ella Rose on the train. The world is a small place. Anyway, I told her to stop talking rubbish. But she said the curse remained.'

'No.'

'Yes. So, what happens now?'

'I don't know. You … you don't tell anyone I suppose.'

'On the same basis, as you wouldn't?'

'My history is different. It's real and proven, Benny, I can't risk it with you, with us.'

'So, you and Rosalyn must remain shut in an unidentified tomb forever? Yet, she is moving on with her doctor.'

Rose Haven was sold, he said. A real estate developer had bought all houses on their street to build a shopping mall. Rosebud had moved to Melbourne.

'Are you weaker than her?' He asked.

'It's tempting. To defy that what the eyes have seen,' I said, confused, yet with a thin ray of hope.

'Can I say, "I will get on with it. Leave it with me?"'

'I'm serious, Benny,' I said, trying not to grin when I noticed him smiling.

'Okay. Remember the math school rule? Two negatives make a positive?'

'Yes, and two positives also make a positive, Benny!'

'Right. Now, let's go back a few years. Remember what a Queensland Premier said after the floods?'

'Yes. That we are to remember who we are — Queenslanders. That we are the ones they knock down, and we get up again. That we confront challenges. Or words to that effect.' I clearly remembered, and I felt so glad to tell him that. He hugged me, and I could feel the laughter in his eyes. He too was clearly remembering the earlier occasions when I hadn't remembered what he'd asked me to, and his irritation with me as a result.

Realisation dawned.

'You mean, we still can?' I asked, my eyes shining.

'Yes. We can. We should. Why take the effortless way out? Aren't we both fighters? Don't we make our own choices?'

'And what's written in the stars?'

'What stars? They do their job. Let's do ours.'

The ugly, torturous clouds were covering my beautiful moonlight again. But I promised myself I'd no longer hide anything from Benny. No more fears and secrets. Once they were voiced, they were no longer my own, and Benny knew exactly how to address them. It was then that I did some calculations in my head. And I told him of my joy, as well as my fear — it was happening again, I said. Two cousins carried a new life each.

He smiled and wept. I wept and smiled.

Benny transferred us into a special room at The Grand Hotel that same night. It reminded me of our transfer to the big suite in the hotel in Goa.

We both decided to bask in our little secret for some more time. This was not *just one more time*; this was for *all the time*.

That night, after we had settled in, had dinner, talked some more, showered, we got into the big bed. We simply held each other, smiled a lot, touched and talked more.

'Why did you think I'd abort our child?' I had to ask. He looked uncomfortable.

'A past memory. I wasn't wanted by anyone when mama and papa died. I thought …'

'Not even by Vera. Right? Yes, I had overheard your conversation that day.' He swallowed, nodded. 'So, you thought I'd not want you and therefore, our baby too?' His eyes shimmered.

'I do want you,' I said.

'In that case,' he said solemnly, 'I'm about to do something I've never done before.'

'And what's that?'

'Make love to the mother-to-be of my child.'

3.20

Next morning, after breakfast, he said he wanted to show me his mother's town — the place she grew up in between her trips to India. We drove all the way from Lisbon to Sintra.

'We must go and see a doctor first,' he said.

'No. Let's do that when we return to Brisbane.'

He agreed. 'From now on, everything will be just as you wish,' he said, smiling.

'Well, then. From now on, I want to be with you wherever you go. No travelling alone,' I said.

'I'll do the same,' he said in a serious tone.

We both laughed. Laughter freed us.

I felt wonderful. Wonderful — full of wonder!

Benny asked me to close my eyes as we began to near the place.

I could feel his excitement and indulged him. I tied my scarf across my eyes.

He laughed aloud. 'You trust me!' he screamed.

'I do. I do. I do,' I screamed right back.

At that moment, I understood his attachment and joy about houses in comparison to my own. I had loved my house. When it burnt down, my inner being was emptied of all reflections. But had any of it really mattered? The people who had lived in that big house were gone. I didn't feel that attached to it anymore.

They say you realise the worth of something after you lose it. That was true. By itself, the house was worth millions. But with no one to share, it was worthless.

Benny needed his roots, to know himself. I understood that. He too would realise someday — about the worthlessness of houses, dwellings. Until then, he needed his property portfolio. Would we be together always, like in, eternity? I wanted to believe that, but he hadn't said anything about permanency. Neither had I. What we had, for however long, was enough.

He stopped the car but asked me not to open my eyes yet. Like a blind person, I stepped out, while he held my hand and carefully helped me outside, not yet allowing me to unknot my scarf and open my eyes. We walked a few steps. I loved this moment. No one had indulged me the way Benny did. He stopped and removed my scarf, asking me to slowly open my eyes.

When I did, I was looking at a replica of Casa Barreto!

And his face! I would never forget it. Ever. It was that of a boy who had beat everyone at a race and won the coveted cup. But his eyes were looking into mine, trying to find if mine agreed with his awe. And they did. I surprised myself. I had convinced myself about my own detachment to my house, which was no more, but I couldn't deny Benny what he had looked for and found at last.

I loved this man, and I couldn't imagine my life without him.

But what was love? A floating, magnificent emotion? Sex? Being together? Hopeful expectations? Operating as a single unit? Worth fighting for? Sacrificial? It was all of that and more.

I knew that what I felt for this man, I'd never feel for another. I'd fight for him, with him. Never be able to let him go. Neither would I ever be able to hold him. I understood the pain of parting and the joy of holding. I understood sacrifice and possession. I understood surrender and passion. I wanted to jump in the well, knowing I could drown. I wanted to jump in the well, knowing I'd never drown. I just needed to jump.

Neither of us could speak. The moment was so precious, so sacred. We simply hugged each other. The sun was shining, the skies were blue with fluffy little white clouds floating, the birds were chirping, and there was a tangy, citrusy smell in the warm air. After a while, we went inside.

'So, you bought this house too?' I asked him.

'No,' he said, 'I owned it already. Mama's family had named me as the sole inheritor, unbeknown to me. That's the reason I made several trips last year settling estates. This is my family home in Portugal.'

He gave me a quick tour of the entire house, saying he was mindful of my 'condition', and I playfully punched him, reminding him that he was the reason for my condition.

He asked me if I was too tired because he wanted to show me just one more site, and we would return to our hotel after that. I said it was okay, and that I was fine. He could take me to the well, for all I cared.

But I wasn't exactly fine. I wanted to tell him what I had realised. It didn't matter whether he felt the same about me or not.

Just before we could step out of the Casa, I took his hand in mine and said, 'Benny, I need to tell you something. And I can't hide it anymore.'

'Yes?'

'I love you, Benny. Very much.' There. I'd said the words.
He was silent, trembling.

'It's okay. Don't be scared,' I said, a little worried.

His big body shook. His brown eyes welled up. Tears rolled over his proud cheeks and disappeared into his beard.

Of their own volition, my hands touched his bearded face. It felt rough, strong. It felt nice and right, as only I had the right to touch him.

He held me tightly. 'Thank you. Thank you,' he kept repeating. Then, 'I love you too. I've … ever since the day I first saw you. And you? How—?'

'How have I started loving you? I forced fear out of my being. My eyes have drained out all tears. Thank you for licking them dry,' I said, my eyes misty.

He locked the Casa, and we got into the car. I took a tissue and wiped his eyes, his face and lightly brushed my lips over his.

3.21

He smiled, took my hand in his, kissed my palm and started the ignition.

'Do you want me to close my eyes?' I asked, smiling.

'No. Not this time.'

Soon, we stopped in front of a big iron gate of what looked like a cemetery.

He was quiet but confidently led me through rows of tombstones, until we arrived at a small edifice — a chapel with an ornated cross at the top. It simply said: *The Barreto family*. There was no other inscription. The names, I saw later, were all carved behind the main wall.

This spot held the mortal remains of his parents, together with his other maternal ancestors.

'Mama's maiden name was Barreto too — Estella Esmeralda Barreto,' he said quietly.

Out of nowhere, the words sprang to my lips, 'Eternal rest grant unto them, O Lord ... may their souls rest in peace. Amen.'

'Amen,' he said, loud and clear.

'Our Catholicism, it comes back at moments such as these. Although, I'm not particularly religious,' I said.

Benny nodded. 'Neither am I. But this is what we've known.' He bent low and gently removed a piece of a blue azulejo tile that had broken and come off the wall. He brushed it lightly and slipped it in his pocket. We stood facing the edifice, heads bowed, hands joined.

After some time, Benny went down on one knee, and taking both my hands in his, he asked, 'Will you marry me, Daphne? Please?'

We explored Lisbon ... whenever we managed to get out of our suite. We were on our honeymoon before we officially married. Not Catholic at all, I said. Benny agreed. It's all circumstance-driven, he said.

After two weeks, we returned to Brisbane.

'Let's go to Somerfield,' I said to Benny.

3.22

As we neared the familiar path, I imagined some of the proud gums that had stood there. They were still covered in black; some were no more. Only charred remains of the once big fat white house remained. I closed my eyes and saw the grandiosity it had held. Once upon a time.

'We will build it again,' said Benny, believing I was upset.

'No ... we'll start afresh. No ghosts,' I said, quite seriously.

Benny looked worried. 'It can be rebuilt, exactly the way it was. I will engage specialists. Don't worry, it will be ready in no time,' he said, holding me close.

Now was the time to tell him.

'Benny,' I said, looking up into his worried eyes. 'I lit the fire.'

I had known the teenagers would be there that day again. The grass bales were close by near the shed and I had placed the petrol can there knowing the teenagers would recklessly run and one would certainly "accidentally" kick the can. They would leave their cigarette butts. The rest would happen. It had happened.

But they hadn't known I had circled the entire house including the chook pen and dripped petrol.

After that, I had lain in the hammock and fallen fast asleep.

Benny held me away from him, his worry turning into shock.

'No. I don't believe you. The investigators confirmed it was an accident. You must be upset …'

I put my hand over his mouth and stopped him midway. 'Benny. Benny, listen to me. I lit the fire.'

He shook his head. 'Why would you burn the only home you've known?'

'I didn't want it anymore. I didn't want any memories of it. But mainly, because I didn't want you to have it either, at the time. Even the tiniest part of it.'

He was processing my words. Then, he laughed. It started as a slow rumbling, his body shaking. It spread to his dark, crinkled eyes and the sound became louder. He threw back his head and his laughter echoed in the stillness of a scorched landscape. A wet sheen covered his eyes. When he slowed down, he gathered me close and said,

'Bravo.' I saw admiration in his eyes.

'Are you ashamed of me now?'

'Ashamed? Never. I love you more,' he said, before we kissed.

'And now since it's confession time — and I'm not a lawyer for nothing — I,'

'What? Tell me,' I pleaded.

'I hadn't "accidentally" happened to be at the pedestrian crossing and hit Ewa that day. It was all pre-planned. It wasn't at Ewa's funeral I saw you for the first time. It was the day you climbed the forklift and sewed the yarn on the tree. "Lovingly made and donated by the Brown family." I saw the photo frame too when Ewa had invited me for a chat here. I wanted to buy your house, yes. I also wanted you. I insisted Ewa address her letters to you alone.'

'Seriously? That's so sneaky Mr Lawyer,' I said, marvelling at his connivance. Details could be filled in later. He made a face when I called him Mr Lawyer.

He's always wanted me even when I was awkward. My heart sang. So, we all believe we've been tricked but we believe ourselves to be the greatest tricksters. In some ways, honesty must be the greatest lie.

'Now, it's your turn to say it. But from now on, also to yourself,' he said.

'Say what?' I was confused.

'I will get on with it. Leave it with me.' I laughed. 'In that case, let's rebuild our family home here. A unique fusion of Casa Barreto and *Uralbah*.' I could feel his immediate excitement.

'I will get on with it. Leave it with me,' he said.

'I only wish something from Anna Rose had survived the fire. Rosalyn has her scarves and the red bangles left for her by Ella Rose. I've nothing of Anna Rose,' I said, after we had laughed and kissed again and turned to look at the burnt remains of a grand house.

'Uh ... um. Fehroza had given me a bag for you. She said Anna Rose would have wanted you to have it.'

My eyes were shining. 'Really?'

'Really. It has pink bangles, some jewellery, hair pins, scarves and some photos.' I hugged him tight. 'And, uh ... Daphne,' he looked a bit uncertain as he pulled back.

'There was a little packet of some green powder wrapped in a newspaper, in that bag. Customs binned it at the airport. Apparently, it was a biosecurity risk.'

Epilogue

August 2016 – Brisbane, Australia

Last night, Benny and I witnessed a miracle — the birth of our twins. It is also the night I dreamt that they came into being. Estella and Bob Barreto. Perfect.

From my hospital bed in the maternity ward, I look at the night sky and ponder.

When we start afresh, we invite people passed away to be a part of us, the living. Intergenerational wounds and delights mesh with our living patterns because they are necessary to form new memories.

Is not destiny enshrined in the stars? Do we tempt destiny when we agree to defy the stars?

No, says Benny. We defy destiny. The stars are compelled to show the way. Be it through floods, bushfires, wars, love, hate, marriage, celibacy, deceptions, or sacrifices. We make our own choices and exercise our own free will.

Tonight, what I hold in my hands is no lie.

Tonight, the souls of the dearly departed — including Ewa and Henri's — rest in peace. The stars will journey along with us. The Gorski lineage may lose its steam. Mementos of rose-related paralleling peculiarities may not be seen. Because love, sacrifice, deceit and valour travel together, says Benny, and what is written in the stars, can be rewritten by us, the darers, the sanctified.

I watch our twins fast asleep. So innocent and safe. I wonder briefly what challenges they will face in life. But I also know they'll grow to be fearless and blessed humans — always saying yes to life — no matter what it brings. *Thank you, God*, I whisper.

Fearlessly, I wear Anna Rose's scarf.

I look at the huge bouquet Benny's given me. It doesn't have a single rose.

But my heart misses a beat when he removes a short-stemmed pink rose from a paper bag. He pushes the tendrils of my hair behind my ear, and carefully pins the pink rose. It is so long now — my hair. I've left it free. Just the way Benny likes to see it. I notice his strong hands, his long fingers. He wears a gold ring. He's never removed it from the moment I placed it there.

'There,' he says, admiring his effort at pinning perfection. 'It matches the roses on your scarf.'

I beam at him and then turn to look outside the window. A shooting star speeds across, and I quickly cross my fingers.

About the Author

Maffy Vaz lives in Brisbane, Australia with her husband and two adult children. A curious, compulsive reader, she's always known she'd be on the other side of a book someday. That day arrived through *Tricked into Being*, her first novel.

Ingram Content Group UK Ltd.
Milton Keynes UK
UKHW040658210423
420559UK00004B/377